DEATH ON THE APPIAN WAY

Death on the
Appian Way

KENNETH BENTON

NEW ENGLISH LIBRARY
TIMES MIRROR

FOR ERIC WHELPTON,
who encouraged me to write this story

First published in Great Britain by Chatto & Windus Ltd in 1974
© Kenneth Benton 1974

*

FIRST NEL PAPERBACK EDITION DECEMBER 1977

*

NEL Books are published by
New English Library Limited from Barnard's Inn, Holborn, London, E.C.1.
Made and printed in Great Britain by Hunt Barnard Printing Ltd., Aylesbury, Bucks.

45002733 3

Contents

PART FOUR: September 56 BC – September 52 BC

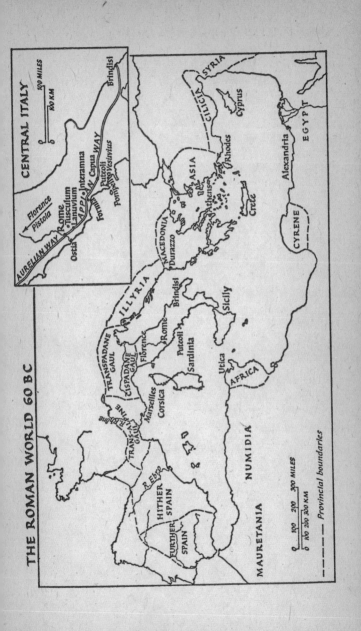

THE ROMAN WORLD 60 BC

100   200   300 MILES
0   100 200 300 KM

MAURETANIA

NUMIDIA

FURTHER SPAIN

HITHER SPAIN

R. Ebro

TRANS-ALPINE GAUL

Marseilles

Corsica

Sardinia

R. Rhone

TRANSPADANE GAUL

CISPADANE GAUL

Florence

Rome

Puteoli

Utica

AFRICA

ILLYRIA

Brindisi

Sicily

MACEDONIA

Durazzo

ASIA

Ephesus

Rhodes

Crete

CYRENE

CILICIA

SYRIA

Cyprus

Alexandria

EGYPT

------ Provincial boundaries

CENTRAL ITALY

0   100 MILES
0   50 100 KM

Florence
Pistoia

AURELIAN WAY

Ostia

Rome

Tusculum

Lanuvium

Intramna

APP. Way

Formiae

Puteoli

Pompeii

Vesuvius

W. Capua Way

Brindisi

The Background to the Story

In 63 BC, when the story begins, Rome had just gained control of the whole of the civilised world around the Mediterranean. The Republic had been built on five hundred years of enterprise, courage and discipline; now the whole structure was being undermined by the corruption bred of wealth and idleness. The men who should have been its leaders, as Cicero bitterly remarked, were interested only in keeping their fishponds stocked.

The newly acquired territories were rich, and the resulting plunder, revenues and hordes of slaves upset the traditional balance of the State. Speculators bought up huge tracts of land in Italy and used unpaid labour to make their fortunes, driving the small independent farmers – the backbone of the old Republic – into the City. The number of heads of families drawing the dole (seventy-two pounds of corn a month) rose to three hundred thousand. In Rome, out of a population of a million, ten thousand lived in reasonable comfort but a thousand were very rich indeed, and there was a sprinkling of multi-millionaires in the Kennedy-Ford-Getty class.

Tax collection in the new provinces abroad, and trade with the conquered cities, often in the hands of joint stock companies, brought in a further flood of liquid money. There was a scramble for houses, seaside villas, land and luxuries. Too much cash chasing too few commodities resulted in roaring inflation. Women began to emerge from virtuous seclusion to play the market and dabble in politics. Morality plummeted; even Brutus, the tyrannicide, regarded in his time as the pattern of honour, went clandestinely into the usury business and was most upset when he was prevented from charging forty-eight per cent on his money – four times the legal rate.

It became fashionable to be heavily in debt, as in the Regency period in England. But a man who had debtors, and squeezed hard enough, could buy their votes. Politicians and juries became targets for the highest bidder, and there was a catastrophic increase in organised violence, both as a political instrument and for protection rackets.

Three men were striving for absolute power. Pompey and Crassus, both famous generals, were men of considerable talent and distinction, with large personal following and immense wealth. Julius Caesar, just at the beginning of his official career, was up to the ears in debt and hated by all the men in high society whom he had cuckolded so flagrantly, but he was infinitely cleverer at the power game, more subtle, more far-seeing than the other two. He bided his time and played them off against each other, using as his tools political pressure groups, corrupt Tribunes, society women and gangs of thugs. He was a very skilful operator.

Cicero and some of his friends – but the trouble was that he never knew who were his friends and who had been got at – were conservatives, and still believed in the traditional system of government – oligarchy in the trappings of democracy. All they succeeded in doing was to drive Caesar, Pompey and Crassus into an alliance of convenience and later a full-scale triumvirate of absolute rulers. After that, from 56 BC onwards, the Senators and Tribunes had to toe the line. Cicero's role – he hoped – was that of a respected senior statesman who could guide the Triumvirs into paths of moderation. He failed, and civil war followed.

This description of the situation is much simplified, but may serve as a background to the story.

Some time was to elapse before the assured peace and central-heated luxury of the early Empire, but life, for a rich young man like Marcus Caelius, the narrator, was pleasant enough. Pompey's great theatre was nearing completion, plays were becoming popular, young men – to the horror of their elders – were learning to dance, there were frequent opportunities for gambling at the public games and races, and baths were still exclusive clubs where one's friends met every day to bathe and exercise, read the latest political speeches, discuss literature and show off their wittiest and most elegant conversation. The Romans, as the old regime slowly collapsed, had become great talkers.

Part One

October 63 BC – January 62 BC

1

The Forged Letters

My name is Marcus Caelius Rufus. No one knows better than I the full story of the events that led to the murder of Clodius early this year, but to tell it properly I must start at a time, eleven years ago, when Clodius and Cicero were still friends. I was nineteen, just beginning to practise as an advocate on my own account.

For three long years I had followed Cicero around like an obedient puppy, learning the old dog's tricks, and at last I was free of his tutelage. They were good tricks, and have served me well, but there were some he didn't see fit to teach his pupils – as I discovered, just in time, one October night in the year 691.* It happened at a men's dinner party in General Crassus' house on the Palatine Hill.

It was getting late. The dancing girls and a very amusing buffoon had done their turns. The Nubian slaves, in knee-length skirts of gold thread, their frizzy hair powdered with silver dust, had washed our faces and hands and sprayed us with Egyptian scent. Crassus dismissed his servants except for one cup-bearer, who was conveniently deaf and dumb, and signed to him to refill our drinking cups. It was a wine from the South, old and smooth. I knew little about wine in those days and couldn't put a name to it, but it was better than anything I could afford.

Crassus was an excellent host, and during the splendid meal and the entertainments he had kept the conversation light. But

* 63 BC

11

now he raised himself on the cushions of his couch – he had invited me, as his youngest guest, to recline at the other end of it – and looked across meditatively at the two other men, both Senators, before he spoke. It was clear that he had come to the business of the evening, and he didn't beat about the bush.

'I should be obliged if you'd give me your views, gentlemen. Is Cicero alarming us unnecessarily? Is there any truth in these reports about Catiline's plans which he allegedly receives from his secret agents?'

'One thing's obvious,' said Metellus Scipio. 'Catiline has taken his second defeat at the polls very hard, and perhaps,' he added carefully, 'as he can't be Consul he thinks there's only one way of bringing about his so-called reforms. And there's no doubt that if Catiline raised the standard of revolt many Senators would support him.'

'There are many others,' said Marcellus drily, without looking at his host, 'who wouldn't like to see him fulfil at least one of his campaign pledges.'

'You mean his threat to cancel all debts,' said Crassus sharply. 'But since he *wasn't* elected Consul there's no pledge for him to fulfil.' As the richest man in Rome, with a large part of his financial empire in usury, Crassus was more worried than he cared to show. Both he and Julius Caesar had befriended Catiline earlier but they were beginning to fear, from the tone of the popular leader's recent speeches, that he was no longer prepared to be their stooge.

Crassus continued, 'Let us speak plainly. If he *is* planning some kind of revolt, and has in mind arbitrary legislation which would be a danger to us all, it's something we should know. As you are aware, I've just returned from the country, and I can't make head or tail of these rumours. Catiline goes around the streets with an armed guard at his heels, but he avoids the baths and the Senate where we should meet him. What is he up to?'

'Clodius came to see me today,' said Metellus. 'To warn me, in his blunt way, that Cicero is well-informed about the extent of Catiline's plans and also, apparently, about the persons who are involved.' He buried his nose in his goblet. Marcellus was silent.

Crassus turned to me. 'You've been seen often enough in Catiline's company, Marcus,' he said abruptly. 'Do you know anything?'

'No, General,' I lied. 'Only what is gossip in the Forum. But surely Clodius is hardly an unprejudiced source of information?'

12

'Why?'

'If Catiline hadn't been prosecuted by Clodius for extortion last year, after his return from Africa, he could have completed his election campaign and would be Consul now, instead of Cicero.'

'That's true,' said Marcellus. 'At least, he might have been. So you think Catiline bears Clodius a grudge.' He looked up at the painted rafters of the high ceiling and stretched himself, saying casually, 'Perhaps we should, too. If Catiline had been made Consul he'd have had an outlet for his ambition and we could have kept him under control. He's a patrician, like ourselves.'

Crassus corrected him with a slight smile. 'You are an aristocrat, Marcellus, but my family is plebeian.' (So, for that matter, was mine.)

'Your family, Sir, has been famous in the service of the Republic for three hundred years, but Cicero is a knight's son, a new man. It's the first time for thirty years that we have a Consul who isn't a Senator by birth, and it's a bad precedent. We're losing control over the Assembly.'

'Cicero has shown more firmness than I expected of him,' remarked Crassus, 'but nevertheless I'm worried about how he may react to a national crisis, if that is what we must expect at any moment. I have great respect for him as an orator – as you know, Marcus,' he added, turning to me, 'for he and I both taught you your trade and many is the time I have taken you to hear him speak. But he is no politician and lacks the power of decision to act in an emergency. He should have done more soldiering in his youth. It interests me that young Clodius should be giving him so much support.'

'So is his sister,' remarked Marcellus, smiling.

'Clodia? What has she to do with Cicero?'

'She – appears to admire him very much. He often visits her house.'

Crassus stared at him, astonished. 'You mean, of course, with Terentia?'

'No, indeed,' said Marcellus, as he picked up his goblet. 'The Consul leaves his wife behind on these occasions. I believe their purpose is to discuss Clodia's literary and political education. Or so,' he added, grinning, 'Cicero may think.'

'What are you getting at, man?' asked Crassus irritably. 'I understand that the Lady Clodia is not exactly – ' he stumbled, always shy of talking about women's morals. 'I mean, she doesn't seem to me the sort of young woman who would set her cap at Cicero.' He coughed. 'She is said to be rather – well, frivolous.'

'Oh come, General, you're understating it. Her affairs are the talk of Rome. She is – '

'You forget, Marcellus,' interrupted Metellus Scipio angrily, 'that I am related to the Claudian family. There has been too much talk about Clodia. She's a very intelligent woman, is well-read and writes poetry of merit; I've read it myself with pleasure. If she should ask Cicero to divorce Terentia and marry her he would be a fortunate man, indeed. It isn't often that a member of the equestrian order – all right! I don't deny that he has been ennobled by holding the Consulship, but it's the blood in a man's veins that counts – I repeat, if a man of Cicero's origin gets the chance of marriage into the greatest family in Rome, he's fortunate, however distinguished he may be.'

I listened to my elders talking with an air of respectful attention. As I have said, I was only nineteen and Crassus had acted kindly in inviting me to this small and select dinner-party. But he also knew how close I had been to Catiline during the past few months and he'd obviously hoped that I would have news to give him. And indeed, I had – news that would have made them all leap from their silken couches.

For I had been with Catiline that very morning, in a small tavern in the Subura, and he'd told me what he wanted me to do. And I had agreed. Inside, I was trembling with excitement, but I kept my thoughts to myself, wondering only whether Crassus, whom I liked and respected, would escape the holocaust that Catiline was about to let loose on fat, rich, pleasure-loving Roman society.

And Cicero! What revenge would Catiline take on his main enemy? I felt uneasy, because although I was determined to take the post Catiline had offered and make a fortune when the revolt succeeded, Cicero had shown me much kindness. I told myself that Cicero was far too popular and respected throughout all Italy to be eliminated by even the most radical of reformers and that Catiline would need his help, but – I tried to put the matter out of my mind.

It had been a memorable dinner, not only for the exquisite dishes but for the service, which was superb. I remembered that somewhere in this great house Crassus ran a sort of sex school for his legion of slaves, so that they would learn to sleep with each other and not be tempted to seek corruptive influences outside the massive bronze doors. What a pity! One of the girls who attended us had given a look that had made me quiver.

My unlicensed thoughts were interrupted by a loud knocking, and a little later the door-keeper came in with a bundle of letter-scrolls under his arm. I looked at the water-clock. It was nearly midnight.

The old slave bowed low and placed the scrolls on the couch near Crassus' hand. With a polite excuse he picked them up. Then he started. 'But only one of these is for me. Why did you accept the others, you fool?'

'Lord,' said the old man, trembling, 'you know I cannot read, and your scribes have gone to bed.'

'But who gave them to you?'

'When I opened the little wicket in the outer gate there was a man outside with the fold of his cloak across his face. He said nothing, but pushed the letters through the hole and ran off.'

'That's strange. All right, Lucius, you may go.' Crassus broke the seal on one of the scrolls and read the contents. His face changed colour and became grim and set. He looked round at us for a moment and then passed the scroll to me, at the other end of his couch. I read it and handed it to Metellus, my mind in a whirl. It was quite a short message, and unsigned.

'To Marcus Licinius Crassus, Consular. Peace!

'I dare not give my name, but I am your friend, and what I write is true.

'Manlius is raising an army in Tuscany and will be joined by Catiline when the revolt breaks out in Rome. To pay for the rebellion Catiline has drawn up a list of persons in Rome whose lives and property will be forfeit. Your name, and those of the others to whom I send letters, are on that list.

'I urge you to have the other scrolls delivered secretly. I cannot do this myself, for my life, too, is in danger.'

I heard dimly the crackle of the papyrus as the two Senators unrolled the letter in their turn. The sweat was breaking out on my forehead. Catiline had told me that the recruiting of mercenaries in Tuscany was being carried out in the utmost secrecy. The post he had offered me was as secretary and ADC to Manlius. *And I had accepted it!*

The General was a brave man, as he had shown in battle, and I think it was the threat to his vast wealth, rather than to his life, that scared him. He picked up the other scrolls and looked at the names written on the outsides. 'All Senators,' he said quietly, 'and all rich men.' (And this from a man who was famous for his remark that no one could call himself rich

15

unless he could pay for an army out of income!)

My first thought was to leave as soon as I could, seek out Catiline and warn him of the traitor. But I remembered something that had caught my eye. The others had read the letter and it came back to me. Before handing it to Crassus I took another look at certain of the words scratched in ink on the papyrus – and just stopped in time the exclamation that rose to my lips. My heart pounded.

Crassus was saying. 'This confirms my darkest fears. The man must be put down like a mad dog.' He picked up the scrolls, his own and the others which were still sealed, and rose to his feet. 'If you gentlemen will allow me, I should like to call on Cicero at once. I think he will want to convene the Senate tomorrow morning, and if so I will support any move to grant him emergency powers. Scipio and Marcellus, you may like to accompany me. Marcus, I don't think we need you, but come if you wish.' It was like Crassus to move fast, once he had come to a decision.

I made my little speech of thanks and excused myself. It would have been interesting to see what happened when they knocked on the doors of Cicero's house after midnight, but I had more important things to do. *Not*, however, to warn Catiline – for I had changed my mind.

It was something about the 'd's' in the letter which had struck a chord in my memory. I hadn't stood for three years at the next desk to Tiro, Cicero's confidential secretary, without learning the quirks in his handwriting. He cut his reed pens at a special angle, and they always spluttered a little on the 'd's'. But for that, Tiro had disguised his hand very competently.

It was Cicero himself who had dictated those letters, and if he had that neat trick up his sleeve he might have others. Moreover, there could be no doubt that he had penetrated Catiline's headquarters with his spies.

I had my litter called, and as soon as I got back to my father's house went into my study and burned every scrap of correspondence that had any bearing on my flirtation with Catiline's cause. Poor Manlius! He would have to fight without me.

*

If those forged letters had not been delivered to Crassus I believe the history of Catiline's conspiracy would have had a very different ending, and no feud might have resulted between Clodius and Cicero, and as for Milo – But he comes into my story later on, and in any case I must get on with it.

2

Changing Sides

At that time I was still dependent on my father, who had allowed me one scribe from his counting-house to act as my secretary. This was a young Greek slave, very intelligent, named Bion. It was at dawn on the following day, while my valet was arranging the folds in my toga, that Bion came running in.

'Your friend Catiline's in trouble,' he said, fortunately in Greek, which the valet couldn't understand. I gave him a look which stopped his mouth and left him trembling.

'He is no friend of mine, Bion, and you'd do well to remember that. What has happened?'

'I meant nothing, Master,' he protested humbly, 'but they all say the Senators received a summons from Cicero in the middle of the night and are already collecting at the Temple of Jupiter for an emergency meeting. One of the messengers told me Cicero has proof that Catiline is plotting against the State.'

'Good.' I stared at him coldly. 'Then perhaps he will be warned in time, and not risk the displeasure of Marcus Tullius Cicero.' He got the message, and knew that if he dared open his mouth about what he knew of my connection with Catiline he would be in trouble. I added, in a milder tone, 'I'm interested in what happens at this meeting, Bion. You know one of the Senate scribes. Can you get me a transcript of the official record as quickly as possible after the meeting breaks up? I don't want to trust what my friends in the Senate tell me at the baths this afternoon.'

'Yes, Master.' He knew I was short of friends in the Senate, but he kept his face straight, and very wise, too. I wasn't feeling in the mood for humour.

I had struggled all night against a panicky urge to run away, or to join Manlius after all – anything rather than wait and see whether I was in danger of arrest. If Cicero knew all about Manlius, wouldn't he also know of the post I had been offered on his staff? At any moment I might expect the tread of the lictors coming to take me to gaol. But I reasoned that I was too young to be taken seriously as a threat to the State, and surely Cicero himself would hesitate before he signed a warrant for the arrest of one who had been his favourite pupil? My father was rich and respected, although he had made the fortune which qualified him for entry to the equestrian order out of the African trade, and Cicero and Crassus were his friends. In Rome a man's life is often in the hands of friends.

When Bion had gone I went into my study and worked out a plan to turn near-disaster into gain. It would all depend on what was actually being decided in the private session of the Senate, and above all on nerve and audacity.

The winter daybreak had been late in the day and the Senate, convened at dawn, only finished its short session at about ten o'clock. I was biting my nails with impatience when Bion came back at half past eleven. He had a stack of waxed tablets under his arm, and I set to work.

It was obvious that Cicero's ruse had had spectacular success. He had begun by telling the House that Crassus had a statement to make. The General explained how he had received the letters and read out the one which had been addressed to him. Then Cicero, with his sure sense of the dramatic, called on the other Senators concerned, one by one, to break the seals on their scrolls and read out what the mysterious well-wisher had written. (According to Bion's friend some of them could scarcely hold the paper for fear of being incriminated!) But, as Cicero well knew, each letter merely contained the same warning – you're on Catiline's list, so leave Rome if you want to keep a whole skin – and went on to reveal further details of the conspiracy.

All this 'new information' dovetailed in beautifully with what Cicero's alleged spies had already reported, and which he had previously retailed to lethargic meetings of the Senate. They had taken the earlier reports with a grain of salt, because they thought Cicero was exaggerating. But now, in theatrical detail, it seemed there was confirmation from an independent source. The old fox!

When all the letters had been read Cicero produced his masterstroke. He informed the House that Manlius was to raise the standard of revolt in seven days' time, according to reports just received from his agents. Three days later, on November 1st, the rebels would launch a surprise attack on the town of Palestrina. Meanwhile, he added, the plans for revolt and massacre in the City were being completed.

According to the official report that Bion had copied there was pandemonium in the Senate, and when order was restored Cicero spoke again, to say simply that he was at the disposal of the Republic. The Senate would know what course to advise.

18

Before anyone else could speak Crassus was on his feet. He proposed, in brief military terms, that the Consuls should be given full powers to deal with the emergency. The *Senatus consultum ultimum*, only introduced in times of the gravest emergency, was passed without delay, and the House broke up.

Bion's eyes were shining with excitement. 'Now we shall see,' he cried, 'what Cicero can do with absolute power.'

I reflected that what he said was true. It was well known that Cicero had bribed his Co-Consul, Antonius Hybrida, to allow him a free hand in the central government, in return for which Antonius was to have the lucrative province of Macedonia to loot the following year, as Governor. It was just as well, since Antonius was suspected of being heavily involved in Catiline's plot. So Cicero, in effect, was sole Consul. It was time, I felt, that I offered him my services.

Cicero had always taught me that a defence advocate was not necessarily concerned with truth; his task was to defend his client. I remembered him saying, 'If, Marcus, you decide – in your client's interest, mind – to tell a lie, make it a lie of generous proportions, something that will make your hearers catch their breath in surprise. A *transcendental* lie always stands a chance of being believed.' In this instance, I reflected, my client was Marcus Caelius Rufus.

I was given an appointment late in the day, and when I arrived at Cicero's house on the Oppian Hill the last of the recruiting officers he had commissioned for the emergency levy of troops came clattering down the steps, vaulted into the saddle and was off at a canter.

The great man received me in his library, politely, but without his accustomed warmth, and I guessed the worst. More ominous still, Clodius was with him. I knew I should be lucky to get away from this interview a free man.

Clodius was thirty then, but looked younger. He had an attractive face, in a slightly effeminate way, but his mouth was cruel and his dark eyes stared at me with an expression of contemptuous disdain. I had never met him before, but I know his face and his reputation. The Claudian family, which during the past five hundred years has produced some of our greatest men, occasionally throws up a man or woman whose only purpose is to rebel against all convention and restraint. Clodius was a good example.

He had chosen to vulgarise his name from Claudius because he wanted, I suppose, to show his contempt for his family traditions and at the same time proclaim a sense of one-ness with the people. Sent to serve in the war against Mithradates he stirred up a mutiny; determined to be a popular leader he caused riots in the streets. But at the same time he was a patrician at heart, with all the aristocrat's disregard for convention, and his whoring in high society was done with a complete lack of discretion. His sister Clodia, who had also changed her name, to please him, was said to be one of his mistresses. It was she who had been mentioned at Crassus' dinner-party the night before. At that time I had never even seen her; later, as this story will show, I was to know her all too well.

As I made my salutation Clodius turned to Cicero. 'Another little bird,' he said, 'trying to escape our net.' Before he finished speaking my stylus was in my hand. There wasn't the lightest chance that I should have to use it. I knew how much Cicero disliked violence in his presence.

'I do not know you, Sir,' I said stiffly, 'but I am a knight, and I don't use this only for writing letters.'

'I will not have brawling,' said Cicero sternly. 'Marcus, this is Publius Clodius Pulcher.'

'I beg your pardon,' I said to Clodius. 'If I had realised that I was in the presence of so distinguished an orator I would not have been so hasty. I read your prosecution of Catiline with great respect. Nevertheless, I must ask you to withdraw your words.'

'By all means,' he replied, sneering, 'if you will explain to us why you called on Catiline yesterday morning.'

'To ask him for an appointment in Manlius' command,' I said calmly.

Cicero stared at me, shocked and unhappy. 'Have you gone mad, Marcus?'

'Let this young cock-sparrow explain,' invited Clodius.

'He offered me the post of secretary and attendant on Manlius, which I accepted.' I let them puzzle it over before I added casually, 'Of course, I hadn't the slightest intention of joining Manlius.'

'Why not?' asked Clodius, smiling slightly.

I turned to him impatiently. 'I am not unintelligent, Senator. With Cicero as Consul there was never the remotest chance that Catiline would succeed in his desperate scheme, and that was quite clear to me yesterday, even before the Consul was voted his emergency powers. His reports to the Senate had convinced me beyond any doubt that he had penetrated the rebel organisation effectively, and that he could crush the conspiracy any time he wished. You forget, Sir, that I had the honour of serving Marcus Tullius Cicero for several years, and knew better than anyone what courage and determination he would display in a national crisis.'

It was, I thought, the right kind of flattery for Cicero, and I was disconcerted when I saw him smile. 'Then why, Marcus,' he said gently, 'did you put your neck in the strangler's noose by accepting a commission from Catiline?'

'It's enough,' said Clodius grimly, 'that he did put it there, and the noose will be drawn, Caelius, make no mistake about that.'

'Let him explain,' said Cicero, still with that slight smile at the corners of his mouth.

I managed a wriggle of embarrassment, looking at my feet. 'It was because of Sempronia,' I said in a low voice.

On occasions like this an orator's elaborate training is useful. I counted three seconds while they were still dumb with surprise, and then followed up fast. 'You gentlemen are aware, of course, that this cultured and talented lady, the wife of a Consular, is one of Catiline's most devoted and active supporters. You will also know – since it is the talk of Rome – that she is in debt and that her great charms are on offer to anyone who can pay a fee which – alas! – is beyond the means of a struggling advocate. But she has recently let it be known that she will offer her favours free to those who accept to serve as officers in Catiline's forces. And it is said,' I added, with my eyes still on the ground, 'that she is greatly skilled.'

It was Cicero, who held my life in his hands, whom I was trying to convince, but his handsome face was inscrutable. Clodius, whose feelings always dictated his opinions, believed me completely. He burst into a roar of laughter that left him gasping for breath, and slapped me on the back.

'This is a story for the crowd at the baths,' he said, wiping his eyes. 'It'll hurt Catiline more than all your levies, Consul.'

I shuddered. The bodies of men carved up by Catiline's thugs were not pretty to look at. But I had one more card to play. 'The Lady Sempronia,' I added casually, 'congratulated me on my appointment. She thought Lentulus would be pleased, because he would need good lawyers when it came to the proscriptions.'

It was of course Catiline, not Sempronia (whom I'd never met), who had told me this. It was in fact the one bit of inside information he had given me. Lentulus was a praetor, one of Cicero's chief magistrates, and Catiline had said he would be in charge of the confiscation and disposal of the property of the men to be proscribed, and I could help him. I thought the fact that Lentulus was so heavily involved with the rebel leader might be new to them, and from the look they exchanged I knew I had guessed right.

Cicero said sharply, '*Did* she tell you that, Marcus?'

I was aggrieved. 'But yes, Master. She said Lentulus had to keep his head down, for fear of your anger, but that he was Catiline's most trusted leader in the city.'

'Tell us about Sempronia,' said Clodius, still laughing. 'Is it true that she – ?'

But Cicero was in no mood for salacious stories of the lady's prowess. 'We have work to do, Publius,' he said sternly, 'and I think Marcus Caelius' services may be useful.' His bleak eye raked me from head to toe. 'For the time being let us keep this story of his foolish behaviour a secret.'

Clodius laughed. 'All right, if you wish. He certainly seems to have talents. But remember, Caelius,' he added, seizing me by the shoulder, 'if you betray us as you did Catiline I will personally attend to you.'

I was feeling more confident now and threw off his hand. 'The Consul knows,' I said coldly, 'that my loyalty is and always has been to him and to the State he serves so nobly. My youthful lusts may have made me imprudent, but never disloyal.'

'Well spoken, cock-sparrow, but don't forget that it's better to have me as a friend than as an enemy.' (They were words that Cicero, as well as I, would have done well to remember.) Clodius swaggered out of the room, and in the silence that followed I heard his high patrician voice calling to the guard.

*

Cicero went over to his big walnut work-table and sat down. He didn't invite me to be seated. 'The transcendental lie, Marcus,' he said, with a thin smile. 'It works, doesn't it?'

Wisely, I said nothing.

'If you really wish to serve the country in this time of crisis – ' he paused – 'and restore yourself to my favour, it will be on these terms. You will leave your father's house and take up residence here until this business is settled. You will continue to be watched, as you have been for several weeks past. And there will be a great deal of work for you to do.'

'I am not afraid of hard work.'

'That, at least, is true. It will take many weeks, I fear.'

Now that I was out of danger my spirits were rising. 'But, Master,' I protested, 'since the Senate has given you all the power you need you could arrest Catiline, Lentulus and even Caesar on suspicion. If you did that many men would at once desert and testify against them, and there'd be no difficulty in getting convictions.'

I was genuinely puzzled. At the moment all the ballot balls lay in Cicero's urn. Pompey was still in Asia and too far away to interfere; Caesar had been elected Head Priest and was putting up a show of decorous behaviour and playing his usual game of wait-and-see; and the Senate was scared out of its wits. All Cicero had to do was to lead, be ruthless and bloody in his actions, and Rome would have let him have his way and raise no objection if he made a fortune out of the proscriptions. So why was he hesitating?

Then I realised. Although Cicero is one of the most learned, astute and altogether remarkable men of this age the game of power politics is something he has never understood – even now when, politically, he has been neutered.

He smiled ruefully. 'You are too young, Marcus, to understand the great responsibility attaching to a man in my position. It is the *people* of Rome who in the last resort must take the decisions, and it is my task to guide them rightly. At present they are under the spell of Catiline's rosy promises; they see any change as good. They must be convinced by overwhelming evidence. And Caesar,' he added, almost to himself, 'is watching for me to make a mistake.'

That was it. He would have to crush the conspiracy step by step, with guile and secret intrigues, never making a move unless he felt sure the Senate and the Assembly were behind him. In a flash of premonition I could see that it would end badly for him, and although I should have held my tongue – well, he had spared my life, and I was not ungrateful.

'Sir, you are a great statesman and I am very young and inexperienced in politics. But in the situation we have in Rome today I have an advantage over you.'

He was amused. 'A complete lack of principles, Marcus?'

'At least the principle of democratic government isn't one of them. This is no longer the Rome of responsible leadership in the Senate and responsible decisions in the Assembly. Votes go to the man who stages the most lavish games and can bribe or intimidate the voters. Rome has suddenly become rich, and it's turned everybody's head. We all want to get rich quickly and don't mind how we do it. What we desperately need is a strong hand to restore order, suppress corruption and re-distribute the wealth our conquests have brought us. It can't be done by democratic means, but only by force. If *you* use force now, however bloodily you may act, there will be less bloodshed in the end and you will have saved the Republic from chaos.' I was quite carried away by my own sincerity, but when I saw the broad smile on his face I knew it was no good.

'I've heard you argue on these lines before, Marcus. Tell me, did you really think that once Catiline had, as you call it, redistributed the country's wealth he would restore power to the Assembly?'

'Yes, Sir.'

'You're wrong. He's a bandit and a murderer, and he would have clung to absolute power. Even if *I* did what you say – and I admit it's a tempting thought – I should only be the first of a line of dictators. Violence breeds violence; never forget that. Enough of this. You accept my terms?'

'I am at your service, Master.'

'I know your gifts, boy, and will make good use of them. Go home now and tell your father I need you here, and return with your books and baggage. Tiro,' he added pointedly, 'will accompany you. I will see Terentia and arrange for your accommodation.' He smiled suddenly, with that mischievous charm I knew so well. 'It's lucky, Marcus, that I didn't show Clodius this.' He picked up a tablet from his desk and handed it to me. It was a short list of men's names, but mine wasn't among them. I looked up at him, puzzled. How could this incriminate me?

'It is a list of the gentlemen who called on Sempronia during the past day and night,' exclaimed Cicero gently, and my heart turned over in my chest.

When I could speak I said, 'It was Catiline, Sir, who told me about Lentulus. That at least was true. He only mentioned Lentulus' name because he said I should help him later on, with the proscriptions.'

'I realised that, Marcus. Now go.'

3

Fulvia the Spy

Cicero's great house on the Oppian was buzzing with activity during the week that followed. He was lucky in having two generals waiting outside the gates of Rome for permission to enter and hold their triumphs; they were given orders to march as soon as they could reassemble enough troops – Marcius Rex to Tuscany to hold Manlius in check, and Metellus Creticus to Apulia, where slaves were already rising in revolt. Two praetors were also given commands: Q. Metellus Celer (who afterwards married Clodia) took over three legions stationed in Picenum, to stop Manlius from escaping into Gaul, and Q. Pompeius Rufus went to quash another slave revolt in Capua. More troops were brought into Rome to keep order and Cicero recruited a special bodyguard of young men like myself from the equestrian order.

But my job was intelligence, and it took me from dawn every day until late at night. The quantity of secret reports about the conspiracy was impressive. Luckily the sky was overcast during that week, and slaves could bring a closed litter through the pitch-black streets at night, deposit its occupant at the postern door and disappear round the corner without attracting attention. Every morning I had to attend on Cicero with a précis of the reports and then complete our records of the chief conspirators, their meeting-places, movements and plans. I helped to de-brief many of the spies – slaves and freedmen mostly – but there was one whose identity was at first kept from me. It was a woman, and she was always seen by Cicero himself, a tall woman with a thin black veil over her head. She had a way of walking that struck a chord in my memory, and I was curious about her. But Cicero sent me out of the library when she came in. Only Tiro remained with him, to take down the report in his special shorthand.

Her reports were the best. She gave details of every meeting of the chief conspirators within a few hours of its taking place. The overall plan was not clear. It had been intended that Manlius would put himself at the head of his troops on October 27th and march south, by-passing Rome, to attack the fortified hill-town of Palestrina by night on November 1st. In the mean-

25

time, on the 28th, the conspirators in Rome would raise fires at specified points in the City and provoke riots, under cover of which Catiline would slip out of Rome and join Manlius.

But of course Catiline had been warned by Cicero's disclosures in the Senate, and instructed Manlius to stay in Tuscany. He raised his standard, as foretold, on the 27th at Fiesole, and the war-veterans whom Sulla had settled in Tuscany flocked to join him. So did many of the debt-ridden aristocracy. The rebel army soon became too strong for Marcius Rex to engage, and for a time there was stalemate. The outbreak of revolt in Rome was postponed, but Catiline was still to be seen everywhere with his armed guard – in defiance of the law, which forbids the carrying of arms within the City – and Cicero was losing ground by his failure to arrest the conspirators. Almost half the Senate was still sitting on the fence, waiting to see which way to jump down.

On November 5th I was working with Cicero in the library, when Tiro came in. It was late at night. 'She is here,' he said to Cicero. 'It's urgent news.'

The Consul glanced at Tiro's face. The man was dropping with fatigue. 'Go to bed, Tiro,' he said kindly. 'Marcus can stay.'

A woman came in, hesitated for a moment when she saw me, and then dropped her veil. I gasped.

There was no longer any mystery about her reports. She was Fulvia, the mistress of a disgraced Senator named Quintus Curius, one of Catiline's lieutenants, and I had met her several times in Catiline's company. She was an attractive woman, and I had made more than one tentative pass at her, but although she had allowed my hands to stray that was as far as I'd ever got. Like Sempronia, she was an aristocrat with no morals and no money, and her favours were expensive. So, I learned afterwards, was her information. Cicero was paying her well, and through her, Curius, who attended all the main meetings of the conspirators.

'Greetings, Marcus,' she said demurely, and turned to Cicero. 'They will all meet tomorrow night at the house of Porcius Laeca in the Street of the Scythemakers. Catiline is to give them his final instructions before he leaves Rome.'

Cicero rubbed his hands. 'Curius must tell you every name, every disposition. Make him come to your house immediately after the meeting, so that I can have your report before dawn. You can come here at any time of the night.'

She hesitated. 'My slaves are getting curious about my

26

nocturnal expeditions, and I'm afraid of being followed. It would be better if you sent someone.' Her eyes turned towards me, calculatingly. 'Marcus, for example.'

'Hm.' I met his doubtful glance with a look of grave dedication to the job. 'All right. Marcus can see Curius himself, which might be better.'

She was affronted. 'You haven't complained before, Consul, about any inaccuracy in my reports.'

'Of course not, dear lady,' he said hurriedly. 'But Marcus knows exactly what I want and he can cross-examine Curius if necessary.'

She stood up. 'Very well, then. At three o'clock tomorrow night.' She extended her hand in a languid, aristocratic gesture, and Cicero kissed it with unsuspected gallantry.

Bion woke me at half past two on the following night. Cicero had allowed me to go to the baths in the afternoon, because I told him I needed exercise and massage. Which was true. It was also true that I had lived a celibate life for a fortnight and I had hopes of getting Fulvia to take pity on me, if I could get her alone.

I had a dagger under my toga and walked the short distance through the dark streets to her house. But I met no one and when I knocked on the side door a slave let me in without a word. He led me through the atreum and pushed open a door. Then he disappeared, taking his torch with him.

She was alone, lying on her couch in a transparent silk shift, with a taper by her side. There was little I couldn't see.

'Give me some wine, Marcus, and take some yourself. Curius isn't here; he's had to go home to his wife, who's sick.'

I poured wine from the silver jug that stood on a table nearby. As I offered her the cup I let my hand run down her bare arm, and she shivered, looking up at me.

'You're a handsome boy, Marcus. I suppose you know that?'

'Yes.' I let my toga slip from my shoulders.

'You may come and sit here, but business first.'

'Business first.'

After that there was no problem, no problem at all.

*

The meeting of the Senate the following afternoon didn't work out as Cicero had expected, because Catiline was sitting in his usual seat, blandly ignoring the cries of disapproval from some of the Senators. This upset the Consul, who had planned to lead up slowly and dramatically to his disclosures of the information I had brought back from Fulvia. (That, and a scented scrap of silk!)

As it was, according to Clodius, who told me the story afterwards, Cicero lost his temper and there was a long slanging match, with Catiline holding his own remarkably well. He dared Cicero to put the question of his expulsion to the vote, and Cicero backed down. Catiline said all he wanted was justice and a fair distribution of wealth, and added that it was unthinkable that he, an aristocrat from a family renowned in the history of the Republic, could really plot against its very existence. He asked what the Senate could expect from a man like Cicero, who had come from the country and was only a lodger in Rome. It was good invective, but in the end Cicero won by the sheer force of his indignation, and the eloquence which all the Romans love.

Catiline left Rome that night, as indeed Fulvia had told me he would. The silver eagle of Marius, which had been handed down to him, had already been sent ahead to Manlius' camp. He let it be known that he was going into voluntary exile in Marseilles, but in fact he went no further than Fiesole, where he joined Manlius.

Although Cicero, in another speech, invited the rest of the conspirators to leave Rome, without fear of arrest, they remained in the City, and the danger was far from over.

So it went on throughout the rest of November, with no meeting of the opposing forces in the North, and the conspirators becoming bolder and more careless in Rome. In the end they delivered themselves into Cicero's hands with such damning proof of treason that even he had to act.

A delegation of Gauls from the other side of the Rhône were in Rome, with a long list of grievances, and the conspirators got into contact with them and offered great rewards in the future if they would stir up trouble in the North and provide Catiline with the cavalry he needed if he was to defeat Marcius and Metellus Celer in battle. But having received these proposals the Gauls cannily decided to ask advice, and invite greater rewards, before they accepted them. They went to see their tribal 'patron', Q. Fabius Sanga, who told them to play for time. Meanwhile, Sanga called on Cicero and gave him the whole story. I was with the Consul at the time, and we planned the next move carefully.

The envoys agreed to act the part of stool-pigeons, and did so with Gallic guile and panache. They told the conspirators that they would recommend to their leaders in Gaul the provision of cavalry, but only provided they received signed letters from the conspirators in Rome. On our instructions, they also offered to take letters to deliver to Catiline on their way north. They swore allegiance to him, but by Roman gods (not Allobrox, their tribal god), so that in their view the oath was not binding.

We prepared an ambush by the Mulvian Bridge. I went with the two praetors who were in charge of our picked force, and we lay hidden in a farm on the near side of the bridge, over which the Via Flaminia crosses the Tiber. The old paved road ran straight and narrow between the farmyard on one side and the farmer's house on the other. It was a clear night, with a rising moon.

My task was to block the road. For over two hours I stood waiting in the farmyard mud beside a big wain, to which four mules had been harnessed. I was shivering in spite of the thick cloak I had put on over two tunics, and the smell from the midden was overpowering. There was a low call from a look-out, and I could just hear in the distance the jingle of mounted men and the sound of horses' hoofs. I waited until the leading horsemen were between the two walls and then gave a cut to the leading mules and ran forward with them into the middle of the road. They tried to go into the farm gateway, but I halted them in time and the road was blocked from side to side. Four of our mounted men swept out from behind the farm and cut off any possibility of retreat, and the rest scrambled over the farm-yard wall and attacked. One of the conspirators, whose task it was to lead the envoys to Catiline's camp, drew his sword, but was quickly overpowered; the Gallic guard, as arranged, sur-rendered without a fight. The envoys themselves were escorted back to Rome with full honours. So was a leather satchel full of scrolls.

Next morning Cicero called a meeting of the Senate. During the night Lentulus and four of the other leaders had been arrested, and the rest had fled. The five prisoners were brought into the House and the proceedings became in effect the trial of these men.

Cicero staged the same dramatic trick he had played after Crassus' dinner-party. Again, the captured scrolls were still sealed when he had them opened and read out to the assembled Senators.

It was spectacular evidence of treachery, and the conspirator who had been accompanying the envoys broke down and made a full confession. The prisoners were interrogated, and all but

Lentulus confessed. He, being a magistrate and theoretically inviolable, at first denied everything, and it was only Cicero's deadly invective that made him at last give in. He even resigned his office, and thus signed his own death warrant. By late afternoon all the accused had been found guilty, and being men of rank were lodged with certain Senators for safe keeping, pending final judgement. Five of their colleagues, who had gone into hiding, were condemned *in absentia*.

A great crowd had gathered in the Forum, waiting to hear what had happened in the Temple of Concord, where the Senate had met. Cicero went straight to the Rostra when the House broke up and harangued the people for over an hour. He excited them with a blood-curdling account of the rebel plans for wholesale massacre and fire-raising in the City, and received great shouts of acclaim for what he had done. As was his custom, he didn't forget to give himself full credit for what had happened.

But he still wasn't satisfied, and when I saw him whispering to Tiro before he went to the Rostra I wondered what other trick he had up his capacious sleeve. Not content with all the earthly evidence he had collected against Lentulus and the others, Cicero wanted a sign from heaven. And he got it.

4

The Sacred Flame

In his speech to the crowd in the Forum Cicero had spent some time extolling the influence of the gods on human affairs and talking of soothsayers, portents and the all-seeing eye of the new statue of Jupiter that looked down on them as they listened to his words.

It wasn't that he believed in these things – in fact he has written a book de-bunking them – but many educated people still have faith in them, especially women, and women's influence on their menfolk is something no advocate can ever afford to forget.

That day, December 3rd, was the great festival of the Good Goddess, celebrated by women alone, and as usual there were sacrifices and secret mysteries in the house of the chief magistrate. So it was Terentia, as the Consul's wife, who was in

30

charge of the ceremonies, and no man might enter Cicero's house until the Vestal Virgins had left and the house had been de-consecrated.

It is of some significance – let me say no more – that one of the Vestal Virgins who was officiating in the house was Fabia, who years previously had been tried on a charge of adultery with Catiline. He had been discovered in her room, and that was enough for the Head Priest. If she had been found guilty she would have been entombed alive, and it is not unlikely that she harboured a grudge against Catiline for putting her in such danger. But she came of a patrician family and was well defended, so she was acquitted. Now Fabia was Terentia's half-sister.

The mysteries, which included ritual dances and conjurations as well as sacrifices, are not wholly solemn, because it is the custom for the women to drink wine pretending it is milk, and some of the capers that follow appear to have secular motivations. Clodia once told me that she used to return from these ceremonies black and blue from the playful pinching of some of the older matrons. On this occasion, however, towards the end of the day, something most remarkable happened.

Because of the Feast Cicero, although he was dead tired after his long day, couldn't go home when he left the Forum, and took me with him to dine at the house of his brother Quintus. Afterwards, some of his friends, including Clodius, gathered round and urged him to exact the death-penalty for the conspirators. They argued, reasonably, that Lentulus and the others could not be kept in prison indefinitely and that in any case the only possible sentence for their crimes was death or banishment. But in exile they could be troublesome, whereas if they were executed there was a good chance that such a show of firmness would make the whole conspiracy fall apart. It was pointed out that the emergency decree gave Cicero the power of summary execution.

So it did, but it was still a dangerous thing for Cicero, a 'new man', to execute persons of high rank without giving them the chance of appeal to the people, which is the right of every Roman citizen who receives a sentence of death. Cicero knew this, but appeals would mean great delay and give a chance for Catiline to march on Rome with his ever-growing army. So he was wavering, or at least putting up a show of it, when the door burst open and Terentia appeared.

She is a big woman, with a commanding presence, and her eyes were blazing. 'The Good Goddess,' she declared in ringing

31

tones, 'has given the Consul a sign that he must not flinch from his manifest duty to destroy all traitors without mercy.'

There was a polite, but sceptical, silence, while Terentia looked round at us challengingly.

'My wife,' said Cicero sternly, 'would not have disturbed our deliberations without good cause. Tell us, dear Terentia, about this sign from heaven.'

She had collapsed on to a couch, and was having a little difficulty in getting her eyes to focus, but her voice was steady enough.

'The priestesses,' she said 'had completed the final sacrifices and I and the other ladies were preparing the house for deconsecration. The fire on the altar had burned right down and all that remained were a few pieces of sacred bark, half-charred and dead. Suddenly – ' Terentia stretched out an arm that would have done credit to a butcher's wife – 'a great flame sprang up from the altar, a blue and golden flame pointing to the sky. We were terrified, but Fabia and the other Vestals told us not to be afraid, since this was a good omen for the master of my house. It meant that success would attend him if he completed the great task to which he had set his hand.'

'And the ladies,' said Clodius with a faint smile, 'the other ladies who were with you – did they all hear what the Vestals said?'

'Of course,' she said contemptuously. 'By tomorrow morning all Rome will have heard of this divine revelation.'

There was a general sigh of satisfaction. Cicero rose from his couch and took Terentia's hand. 'We are all grateful to you, dear lady, for telling us so promptly of this important omen. I have no doubt now where my duty lies.'

As we went out I felt Clodius' hand on my arm. 'Strong milk they must drink at these ceremonies! I've never seen that formidable matron half-pickled before.'

'Nonsense!' I whispered. 'It was religious ecstasy.'

He made a rude noise. 'I wonder,' he continued, 'who the pyrotechnist was.'

I didn't reply. I had a clear memory of how Tiro used to delight Cicero's small daughter Tullia with his skill in producing flames of different colours. He used sulphur, I think, and iron filings and – yes, naphtha from Egypt. I suppose if you take a piece of thick oak bark and drill a hole in it, then fill it with naphtha and block up the hole. . . . But someone would have to put it on the fire just at the right time.

*

The following day Caesar came under attack, and it is interesting to compare his tactics with those of Cicero. If Cicero could make good use of women's influence, so could Caesar, but his method of acquiring it was more direct. He succeeded in seducing almost every influential woman in high society and they continued to approve of him even after he had dropped them. In addition, although crippled with debts, he had managed to get himself made Pontifex Maximus and thus contrived a very special control over the superstitious people of Rome. At the time of which I am writing he appeared to have turned over a new leaf in his private life and his public appearances were dignified and decorous.

But when attacked his feline claws came out like lightning, and this is what happened the day after the so-called trial in the Senate. First a professional informer named Vettius laid an accusation against Caesar before one of the magistrates, declaring that the Head Priest had come to a written agreement with Catiline. Then Cicero's spy Curius, who had already been voted a rich reward for his services, made a similar charge in the Senate. No one knew better than Cicero the latent danger in Caesar's scheming mind, and he probably put Curius up to it.

It was a mistake. If Caesar had been arrested his friends in the Senate might have forsaken him, but once he stood up to defend himself, and as always spoke brilliantly, persuasively, holding up Curius and Vettius to ridicule, they rallied to his support. Cicero found himself in the wretched position of having to apologise for Curius and actually agreeing that his reward should be cancelled. Meanwhile, Vettius was attacked by a hired gang in the Forum and thrown into prison badly wounded. The magistrate who had accepted Vettius' charge against Caesar was also imprisoned, because he should not have accepted any complaint against the Pontifex Maximus. Cicero was badly shaken, but when some of my friends in his bodyguard offered to rid him of Caesar once and for all he refused.

Caesar again appeared in the Senate on December 5th, at the meeting which was to determine the fate of the condemned conspirators. When it was his turn to speak he recommended, not death, but permanent imprisonment, which he said would be a greater punishment. It was a long and able speech, impressively delivered.

Cicero's contribution was equally long, but it can be summarised even more briefly: he made no recommendation either way. Then Cato, the arch conservative, spoke, and in a violent diatribe swung the House towards summary execution, without benefit of appeal. The vote was taken and Cato's proposal was accepted. Cicero sent orders for the prisoners to be prepared.

But Caesar had not finished. He insisted that their property should not be confiscated, and thus went on record as having done what he could for their families. Cicero gave in. He wanted the whole thing finished before nightfall, in case Caesar took some unforeseen action during the hours of darkness.

The Senate meeting had taken place in the Temple of Concord, opposite the State prison. As soon as the House rose Cicero went to fetch Lentulus and lead him in a procession along the Via Sacra and across the Forum. A large crowd collected. Executions in Rome are rare, and carried out in a peculiarly horrible manner.

In one of the rooms of the ancient prison there is what used to be a well, twelve feet deep, and the prisoners are lowered down to the dark and noisome room beneath, where the stranglers await them. This happened to Lentulus, brought to the place by Cicero, and to the other four conspirators, who had been attended by magistrates befitting their ranks.

It was dark when Cicero's cortege, with his twelve lictors bearing the Fasces, left the prison and marched down the steps into the crowded Forum. To the expectant people he called out one word, 'Vixerunt,' and turned wearily away. 'They have lived.' To mention death was ill-omened; the past tense was sufficient.

In spite of the nagging fear that had worried him since Caesar's calm, eloquent speech, the clamour in Cicero's praise, the waving torches and the horde of friends and clients convinced him that he had been right.

But the fear returned later, and he had to bolster up his courage by repeating over and over again, until it became a joke in the Senate, that he, Cicero, had saved the Republic. It was of course true, but it would have been equally true if he had accepted Caesar's proposal and condemned the prisoners to close imprisonment for life and the sequestration of their property, and it would have spared Cicero the disaster that befell him later. For he knew, as I did, that in spite of his emergency powers he had broken the law. Every Roman has the right of appeal against a sentence of death, and to deny that right to any citizen is serious enough. To deny it to a patrician is ten times more dangerous.

For the time being, however, everyone acclaimed his firm action, which effectively broke the back of the conspiracy. The Senate gave him the title of Father of his Country and statues were built in his honour. He was still the most powerful man in Rome for that last month of his term as Consul.

5

The Battle of Pistoia

There was to be a dramatic end to Cicero's Consulship, but I only heard about it later. From the middle of December to the tenth of January I was away from Rome.

The army which was assembled to defeat Catiline had been sent north with Cicero's Co-Consul in command. It had to be Antonius Hybrida, but it was an awkward appointment, because as I have mentioned he was a friend of Catiline's and could not be relied on. However, his Chief of Staff was a first-class officer of thirty years experience and a staunch conservative, and Cicero also had an agent of his own, Sestius, on the General's personal staff.

Some of Sestius' secret reports had been disquieting, and Cicero decided to send me north as Antonius' attendant, with orders to help Sestius in his spying. In fact, as I discovered later, Antonius' apparent inability to force Catiline into battle was not his fault, because the rebel leader and his lieutenant were excellent campaigners and had used the goat tracks of the Appenines to avoid contact with either Metellus Celer, on the east, or Antonius, near Florence. They had raised twelve thousand men and were just preparing to move against Antonius when the news of the collapse of the conspiracy in Rome hit them. Shortly afterwards Cicero sent me on my way.

By this time I had no intention of changing sides again, and Cicero's faith in me was justified. I wasn't particularly proud of the way I had deserted Catiline, I wanted a chance to get away from Rome. There was nothing to keep me, since Fulvia had turned against Cicero when he tamely agreed to cancel Curius' reward, and I got the full blast of her anger. Any further visits to her bed, she told me with a most unwomanly oath, I could pay for in gold, at market prices.

As I rode up the Via Flaminia with my escort of twenty swordsmen we began to meet deserters from Catiline's forces, and I interrogated them and sent the reports back to Rome by messenger. It was obvious that he was losing men fast, but not his trained Sullan veterans, and although the deserters were sure that he would capitulate I didn't believe them. I knew Catiline. He had been a butcher of men, with any number of crimes to his name, but he was an aristocrat of conviction and great courage, and he would not surrender.

I had been with Antonius for two days when a soldier from Metellus' army in Picenum came into the camp. He was nearly dead with fatigue and could scarcely speak, but he handed me a scroll and I took it to the commander's tent.

Antonius was a self-indulgent man, and believed in taking his comforts with him on campaign. The big tent was carpeted with fur rugs and stinking hot from the braziers, and the women he had lying around made the atmosphere worse. He was half-drunk, and signed to me to read the letter.

Metellus wrote that he had intercepted some deserters who had told him that Catiline was planning to break out to the North and try to get into Gaul on the other side of the Appenines. Metellus had decided to move northwards at once, taking the deserters with him. He had promised to crucify them if their story proved false, and from their reactions was convinced that they were telling the truth. He would try to intercept Catiline as he came out of the mountains.

Antonius was in no condition to decide anything, so I got hold of Sestius, who was a friend of mine, and we went together to show the letter to Petreius, the Chief of Staff. He was an impressive officer and quite unafraid of Antonius. We were on the move before dawn.

Metellus Celer lived up to his name, and when the remaining hard core of Catiline's veterans came down towards the plains of Gaul he was waiting for them with his three legions. Catiline knew he had no chance against that army. He decided to give Antonius a run for his money and went back into the Appenines, with Metellus pressing behind.

We passed through Fiesole, where Manlius had first raised his standard, and reached Pistoia, and there, with the snowy mountains in front of us, we made our camp. The road went forward through a narrow valley into the mountains from which we knew Catiline must debouch.

Everyone knows what a military camp looks like, but this was my first experience of watching one being created, and it gave me a new impression of trained Roman soldiers in action. I had only seen them on guard in Rome, or marching in a triumph with long trains of loot in the rear, and I'd seen the fun they had afterwards in the streets and taverns. Antonius had two legions under his command, but only half of them, at most, were experienced men and the other six thousand were for the greater part raw recruits. It was the regular soldiers who laid out the camp, while the others dug the surrounding ditch and the latrines and erected the tents. Everything was done according to the book and unbelievably fast – the great tent of the General, with his aides on both sides, facing the broad *via principalis*, and the side roads separating the quarters of the cavalry, foot-soldiers and auxiliaries. I couldn't see as much as I should have liked, since my first job was to get the cantankerous Antonius bedded down, which wasn't easy. Then I had to attend on Petreius and take down his orders, and accompany him on a tour of inspection. He had already sent mounted parties into the country, foraging, and patrols to scour the foothills on either side. A strong fast scouting section was despatched up the road leading into the mountains. They returned the following day to report Catiline's advance guard approaching twenty miles away.

My mother's girls had woven me a fleecy woollen cloak, which I wore against the bitter cold and slept in at night. My father had given me a coat of chain-mail and a helmet, of which I was rather proud, but I kept these in my baggage, secretly hoping it wouldn't be necessary to wear them.

On the third day I awoke to hear a great stir in the camp and went out into the clear, frosty air. A mile or more away, where the road first came into view round a shoulder of rock, there was a thin mist, the steam from the sweating bodies of men and horses who had marched all night.

Catiline must have gambled on finding our legions unprepared, and had hoped to break through. When he saw it was too late he pitched camp at the head of the valley, well protected on both sides, and let his men rest. As darkness came we could see their fires and hear faintly the sound of shouted war-songs. Antonius held a conference of his senior officers; I was at his side with a pile of tablets to take down his orders.

'They will be gone by morning,' he said hopefully, but Petreius shook his grey head.

'The scouts reported that there are only four thousand now,' he said, 'but they're all his veterans, the men who learned to fight under Sulla. If he retreats he'll only run into Metellus, whose legions are better trained than ours. So he will fight here. In fact,' he added with a grim smile, 'he might even attack us tomorrow morning, when his men have fed and slept and can

37

give a good account of themselves. Which they will. Don't let us imagine that because we are three times as strong in numbers it is going to be a walk-over. I know those men, and I know Catiline.'

'But they may still try to get past us in the night?'

'No, General, he will let his men sleep. But of course I have forward patrols who will inform me at the first sign of breaking camp.' He went to the tent door and pointed to the sky. 'The moon is rising already. Catiline wouldn't have a chance of getting past us unseen, and on the plain our cavalry would break his ranks in pieces. I think he'll attack us in the morning.'

Antonius shivered and drew his fur cloak around him. 'Very well, Petreius. Make your dispositions at dawn.'

*

I slept well, to my surprise, and woke up just as the sun was rising over the mountains. Petreius was in full armour, coming out of the General's tent. There was an amused smile on his face. He saw me, and said blandly, 'The General has been overtaken by a severe attack of gout, and has made over the command to me. Call Sestius.'

When we were both waiting for him to speak he looked us over thoughtfully. 'I shall be speaking to the officers in a few minutes, but neither of you need attend. I want you both for special duties. You aren't much of a soldier, Sestius, and I gather, Caelius, that you've had no military training at all. But I've seen you control a horse quite passably. Can you in fact use a sword?'

'I have trained on the Campus Martius, General.' I gave him his temporary title, but Petreius was immune to flattery.

'Stabbing a bag of corn swung from the branch of a tree is one thing; killing men is another.'

'I shall do my best, Sir,' I said firmly, wondering what on earth he had in mind. Was he going to put me in the ranks?

'Indeed you will, Caelius. I will have no gentleman setting a bad example to my men. You will remain by my side, wherever I am, and act as runner. Haven't you any armour?'

'Yes, Sir.'

'Well, put it on. Now, Sestius,' he said more kindly, turning to the older man, 'I want you to stay with Antonius from now on. Keep him well supplied with wine. It will be good for his gout. If the enemy should break through and reach the camp you will defend him with your life. Now understand this.' He held out the tablet on which Antonius had scrawled some sentences, appointing Petreius Acting General and commander in battle. 'If Antonius should change his mind and wish to interfere with my dispositions, you will accept his orders but on no account give them to me. You may get lost in trying to find me. Is that understood?'

'Yes, General,' said poor Sestius, looking very worried.

Petreius turned to me. 'I knew your father, Caelius. I count on you not to disappoint him.' He had never mentioned my father before.

I saluted and went outside his tent and told the officers to enter. Then I walked to where I could see Catiline's camp breaking up, and mounted units moving towards us, the sun flashing on breastplates and shields. I was as frightened as when I first spoke in a law-court, and that is saying a lot. But not more than that – not paralysed. Petreius had deliberately stung my pride, and it's astonishing how much pride can do to calm quivering limbs.

I got out my chain-mail smock and tried it on. It was like standing in a cold shower, and I hastily took it off again and pulled on another tunic under it. Then I went to the horse lines and found my charger, a mare with a lot of spirit. As Petreius had so grudgingly remarked, I did know something about horses.

One of the officers told me what Petreius had said to them. A scout had reported that Catiline was drawing up his troops on level ground and appeared to have had his horses sent to the rear, so that all his men would fight together, and on foot. Petreius intended to launch his best legionaries against the centre of Catiline's line. His auxiliary cavalry squadrons would be on the wings and the raw levies behind. Petreius himself would remain at the head of the praetorian guard and use them where he thought best. It sounded simple, and I admit I had hopes that the much smaller army of Catiline would be destroyed before Petreius and his picked guard – with me among them – were brought into battle.

I don't remember much of what followed, except in little patches of things seen and heard. There was the quiet voice of Petreius talking to his troops and calling his veterans by name, just as Catiline was doing two hundred yards away, with the silver eagle of Marius flashing by his side. Then the jingle of armed men moving forward, and horses neighing with excitement; the whicker-whicker of darts passing overhead and the horrible thud as one hit the man beside me. I was concentrating on keeping my horse's head alongside the flank of Petreius' white charger.

The front line legionaries halted and threw their javelins. They fell like a gleaming spray and our men were running forward before they landed in Catiline's ranks. It was incredible that his men could withstand that fierce impact of a superior force, but they did. Those Sullan veterans had broken their oath to the State and knew what to expect if they were captured. They took the assault on their long shields and stood firm and then, a wide wall of bronze and leather and flashing swords, they began to move forward, forcing our line back.

It must have taken longer than that, but all I can remember is Petreius cursing and shouting to the leader of the guard, and then he raised his sword and uttered a howl like a wolf and charged.

I had never imagined that it could be like this. All I could see was that white rump in front of me, bumping and swivelling. I caught glimpses of the praetorian guard forming around us, and we were in the middle of a packed, chaotic mass of fighting men. A dozen yards ahead I caught sight, for a moment, of Catiline's standard-bearer on a black horse, holding the silver eagle high above the tossing sea of men fighting on foot.

Someone slashed at my leg and hit the mare, who reared with a scream and bounded forward, past the General, trampling and lashing out at the men below. I turned her, still screaming and kicking, and found Petreius surrounded by three men, one of whom had caught his rein and was trying to get the point of his sword into the charger's throat. I pushed my sword into him, somewhere, and he dropped the rein and fell. By this time the other two were dead.

Petreius shouted something and the praetorians formed a compact mass around us and we charged back through the line, stumbling and bucking over the men on the ground. The recruits were in the front line now and we went through them and halted. But only for Petreius to see what was happening on the wings.

Catiline's right was commanded by Manlius, and he had thrust through between our ground-troops and cavalry and was coming across the rear. So we charged again, and again all I saw was that great white rump that never stopped moving. By now I was too excited to be afraid, and I slashed and parried and thrust like a madman. My helmet caught two blows that nearly knocked me out, and if it had not been for my father's chain-mail I should have been dead several times over. How the mare escaped serious damage I shall never know; she was the heroine of my private battle.

We fought until Manlius was killed, and his men began to waver. By this time our cavalry had re-formed and they completed the slaughter. We got back to the centre. The veterans and the levies were slowly overpowering the men who had fought so well in Catiline's van. Sheer weight of numbers bore them down, and as our troops moved forward they despatched the dying. Catiline was killed, too, in advance of his guard and surrounded by a ring of dead men. I saw someone pick up the silver eagle and bring it to Petreius.

He held it in his hands for a moment, then passed it to me. 'It is over, Caelius,' he said. 'You did better than I expected, and are your father's son. Take the standard and show it to the men, and tell the centurions to let them break ranks.'

I cantered through the field from one side to the other, holding the silver eagle high, and heard the growing roar of cheering as the men shouted the news to each other. Then they scattered hurriedly to start killing the wounded and stripping the dead. One of the praetorians brought a scarf and tied up my arm, which was bleeding from a deep cut. My body felt as if it had been trampled on. I rejoined Petreius and we rode back to our camp.

Petreius' slaves had borrowed Antonius' great leather bath and filled it with near-boiling water, but by the time I had seen to my mare and waited my turn the water was dark pink. However, it did its task and when I climbed out I found Petreius looking me over. The slashes that had struck my iron shirt had only left bruises, but where I had stopped the point of a gladius the mail had broken the skin underneath, and my body was a glorious mess. Petreius grunted, mildly impressed, but all he said was, 'You've got a good mare, Caelius. Is she all right?'

'The cuts have been bandaged, Sir, and there's no great harm done. She fell asleep half-way through her feed.' He smiled and called the doctor to attend to me.

That night we all got drunk, and after Antonius was carried off Petreius and the others tried to get me to boast about my prowess in the fight. I was the youngest officer and they wanted to have fun with me, but I saw that coming and said it had all been a great white blur.

Everyone laughed, as men do in their cups, but Petreius was puzzled. 'Why white?' he asked me.

'Your horse's arse, Sir. I never saw anything else.'

He was delighted at that and clapped me on the back, but he still wanted to pull my leg, and said he gambled I was a great one with the women. So I let myself go and told a lot of lies, and borrowed a lute to sing them love-songs. The story of my bragging got around, of course, and when we were marching south there was one of the legionaries' songs that went something like this:

'Cocky Caelius needs no sword,
He has another weapon . . .'

and you can imagine the rest. Quite flattering, in a way.

Still, it was a pleasant evening, and helped us to forget those other brave men who had sung their defiant war-songs as the sun rose, and were now lying in the bitter wind, naked and dead.

6

The End of Cicero's Year

Clodius met us in Florence. He had come to see his cousin, Quintus Metellus Celer, the praetor who had blocked Catiline's escape into Cisalpine Gaul and was now beginning his term as Governor of that province. Antonius, who after the victory at Pistoia had recovered very quickly from his attack of gout, had asked Metellus to join him for consultations, and he had caught us up.

By this time Clodius and I were on good terms. We were at dinner with the two Generals when I heard him say casually to Metellus Celer, 'Your brother is playing a dangerous game, Quintus. He's been lucky not to have been knifed.'

I pricked up my ears. Metellus Nepos was Pompey's man. He had been his legate and had just been elected Tribune for the year we were entering.

'What's he been doing?' asked Metellus.

'It was on the last day of the year, and Cicero went to the Rostra to make his final speech as Consul, and you can imagine what that would have been like. Although he's my friend I'm getting bored with his constant references to his own courage and cleverness. But as it turned out he didn't get a chance of delivering his speech.'

'Why?' asked Antonius anxiously.

'Because cousin Metellus Nepos and Bestia had already been

elected tribunes and they sat down on their benches in front of the Rostra and forbade Cicero to speak. Metellus said that a man who had sent Roman citizens to death without a hearing should not have the right to a hearing himself.'

I groaned. I had feared something of the sort, but not such a bitter blow in the hour of Cicero's final triumph. He hadn't deserved that.

'You mean,' said Antonius incredulously, 'that they actually stopped Cicero's mouth.' He guffawed. 'That's no mean task.'

But Nepos and Bestia had acted within their rights as tribunes. If Cicero had defied them they could in theory have hailed him off to prison.

'No, they didn't,' said Clodius, laughing. 'He played a neat trick on them. He said that as retiring Consul he had to swear his oath of loyalty, so they let him speak. Up gets Cicero on the Rostra, waving his arms, and shouts, "I swear by the gods that I have saved my country," and the crowd cheers him like mad. The tribunes had to run for their lives.'

'But Nepos was right,' said Metellus Celer. 'To condemn to death a praetor, and a member of the Cornelian clan, without a proper trial, was an act of arrogance in a new man.'

'Sir,' I said, greatly daring, 'Lentulus had already resigned his magistracy when he was condemned. It was surely an admission of his guilt.' Nobody answered.

'But who put Nepos up to it?' asked Antonius.

'My brother,' said Celer stiffly, 'doesn't have to act as a front for anyone.'

'Oh nonsense, Quintus,' said Clodius scornfully. 'It was Pompey. He wanted to cut Cicero down to size. You don't suppose his vanity could stand that speech of Cicero's a fortnight ago, when he told the Senate they were fortunate to have him and Pompey, to protect them at home and abroad? It must have made Pompey furious. But anyway, the attempt failed. The crowds shout for Cicero louder than ever.'

'He has not heard the last of this matter,' prophesied Celer, and events much later, after Celer's mysterious death, proved him right.

Later that evening Clodius and his cousin got into a corner and I heard one of them mention Clodia's name. At the time I paid no attention, except to note that Clodius lost his temper and went off in great dudgeon.

7

Clodia

When we entered Rome there was no triumph, first because however bloody-minded we Romans are supposed to be we don't
accord a triumph to a general who kills his own countrymen,
and second, because you have to chalk up five thousand killed,
and although I don't think there could have been any survivors
of Catiline's army the dead were not as numerous as that. In
any case, Antonius couldn't have afforded it. He was bankrupt,
and itching to get away to his pro-consular command and start
milking the Macedonians. So he was on his best behaviour and
among other things spoke about me to Cicero in terms of high
praise. Of Petreius, of course, he would only say that his own
precise instructions for the conduct of the battle had been
carried out efficiently. I never forgot that bit of churlishness, for
I admired Petreius, and years later, as I will recount, had
occasion to let Antonius feel the scourge of my best oratory.

My own triumph was very pleasant. My father had tears in
his eyes as he went over the chain-mail, pointing out proudly to
my mother the places where the links had been strained or
broken.

'I fought with Petreius in the Marian wars,' he told me, 'and
wrote to him when I knew you were joining Antonius. My old
colleague tells me that he took you into the thick of the battle,
so that you could show me what you were worth, and you
fought well.'

So that explained my odd assignment as a 'runner'. It seemed
a curious way of doing a favour for an old friend, and from my
mother's dark looks it was clear she thought the same. But she
never misses an opportunity.

'Now that Marcus has made such a name for himself,' she
said, 'he will need a bigger allowance.' And I got it.

My study had been re-decorated, with a design of Greek
temples on the white-washed walls, and Bion had brought all
my books back from Cicero's house and arranged them on
new shelves. I sat down at my desk for a spell, reading letters,
and then wandered restlessly out of doors and through the
noisy, smelly streets. It was good to be back in Rome, which
had never seemed so much the centre of the world nor, I

thought, so full of opportunities for a man like me.

Cicero gave a great dinner that night for Antonius and his staff, and greeted me with warmth and affection. He was full of his plans to create a merger of the moderates in the patrician and equestrian orders, representing the best and wisest men in the State, and of course it was understood that he would be its leader. He was generous enough – and I mean this sincerely – to offer me the chance of leaving my career as an advocate for the time being and helping him full-time in his great plan, but I hedged.

Although I had barely passed my twentieth birthday I knew the basic facts of political life in Rome better than Cicero. In some ways, although my father would not agree, I had used the time after I left Cicero's tutelage to good purpose. In those eighteen months I had been a great frequenter of the baths and had attended many parties where my elders spoke loosely and too much. Cicero's grandiose scheme might have worked if there were enough men of responsibility and independent mind, but there were not. Most of the Senators and half the knights were not their own masters; they had about as much sense of duty to the community as a flock of sheep. The new wealth had brought an orgy of over-spending, then inflation on a scale we had never seen before, and finally debts, corruption and organised violence. I have said this before, and may sound like a moralist – which I am not! – or a man writing with the wisdom of hindsight, but I repeat; it was clear to me then that Cicero's plan – or any plan that foresaw a democratic solution to our problems – was a poppy-dream. Otherwise I would have jumped at the chance he offered me.

No. I wanted to stay his friend, but on my own terms, and my first task was to make my name as an orator.

*

I met Clodius at the baths the following afternoon. Although his family was excessively rich he never seemed to have any money, but my pockets were full and we had a night on the town. We had left the girls and were drinking in a tavern in the early hours of the morning when he began to mutter to himself. He had been knocking it back unwatered, and by the jugful, and I asked him what was the matter.

'It's Clodia,' he said. 'She wants to marry Cicero. She says it's time she settled down.'

'But *Cicero*? Would it work?'

'What a stupid thing to say! She wouldn't want to have babies by him, if that's what you mean.'

'And anyway, what about Terentia?'

'Oh, that could be arranged. She doesn't know, of course, but it wouldn't matter if she did. Cicero's rich enough now to pay back her dowry.'

'I doubt it. She brought him a large fortune; it's what gave him his start. And he's made very little out of his Consulship.'

He looked at me, astounded. 'You don't mean that?'

'But I do. And he's going to buy Crassus' house on the Palatine, so he'll be in debt up to the eyes.'

'That'll please Appius,' he said sombrely. Appius Claudius was his eldest brother, and the head of the family since their father's death. 'Appius won't give her a proper dowry if she marries Cicero.'

'Why? Does he want her to marry someone else?'

He looked down at the table-top, sloppy with spilt wine. 'He wants to give her to that dry stick Metellus Celer, and keep it in the family. As if we hadn't sufficient connections with the Caecilii Metelli already!'

'So you don't approve of that idea, either?'

He stared at me. 'Of course I don't,' he shouted. 'I don't want her to marry *anybody*.' He wept into his wine.

*

The following day I went to the baths at noon, as soon as they opened, and sweated the wine out of me. Afterwards I swam twenty lengths of the pool and was being pummelled by my masseur when Clodius threw himself down on the next slab, looking the worse for wear. Besides his massage men he had a swarm of slaves around him. A cup-bearer, a barber, a depilator, men to see to his finger and toe-nails and others to oil him and scrape him as soon as the massage was over. He was an impatient man and liked to have everything done to him at once. It was a joke in our baths that when Clodius was being groomed he was like a steak on a butcher's counter, with no one to whisk away the flies.

He rolled a bloodshot eye at me. 'Don't go till I'm ready. Clodia wants to see you.' A patrician's order, brooking no refusal. I had a new toga, and my mother's white cloak had been to the fuller's, so I would be presentable. Clodius had litters waiting, and we soon reached Clodia's house on the Palatine, in the same street as Crassus' great mansion, where this story started.

But while Crassus' house had a row of money-spinning luxury shops on each side, Clodia's showed blank walls on the side-alleys, with no sign of the riot of affluence inside. And while Crassus' slaves were courteous and quiet-spoken, drilled to the last detail of obsequious attentiveness, hers chattered like a cage of monkeys, and at first sight looked thoroughly spoiled. It was only afterwards that I learned how devotedly they served Clodia and would react to her changing moods with immediate subservience. They had braziers burning everywhere, and the air was warm and scented.

The girls took our cloaks and led us through the first court into the peristylium at the rear. It was already dark, and the chandeliers under the arches shone on the oranges gleaming in the dark foliage in the centre of the court. It was a charming and well-planned little garden, with winter flowers everywhere and marble statues of nymphs and fauns, and water trickling in stone channels.

Clodius left me on a bench under the colonnade and went to the back of the court, where the entrance to the exhedra was closed by damask curtains. He pushed his way between them, leaving a space through which I could see something of the room beyond. It was brightly lit, with fur rugs on the floor and gold couches, and I could see a cage of yellow birds hanging from one of the painted beams.

I heard a high voice cry, 'Oh good, brother, you've come just in time to help me choose. Which shall I buy, this one? ... Or this?'

'I can't see them properly with all those clothes,' he grumbled. There was a sound of giggling from the slaves and a pause, and then she said softly – her clear voice could always be heard, even in a crowded room – 'Is this how you like me?'

I saw her come across the gap in the curtains, a slight figure of a woman with fair curls arranged on top of her head and ringlets falling down to her naked shoulders. She held her dress together at the waist, and the light gleamed on her small breasts and the great red jewel hanging between them. Then someone rushed to draw the curtains together.

Later a Syrian merchant came out, backwards, bowing and calling thanks in execrable Greek. He turned and passed me without a glance, stuffing a bag of coins into his satchel as he went. A smirking slave-girl came and summoned me.

By this time I was not a little annoyed at being kept waiting while Clodia haggled with a jeweller's tout and flirted with her own brother, so I held my head high as I went into the exhedra, and perhaps struck a bit of an attitude. Anyway, her great dark eyes widened and she turned to Clodius with a dramatic gesture. 'Behold!' she breathed, 'Telemachus, like a young god, entering the court of Menelaus!'

She was making fun of me, but I took up her classical allusion – rather neatly, I think. 'To find Helen,' I said with a bow, 'busy as usual with her domestic duties.'

She was lying half-reclined on a couch, the red jewel flashing on the folds of her robe, and idly fingering an emerald necklace. She laughed, and gave me her hand to kiss. 'You won that throw, Caelius. Come and sit here.' As I sat down on the end of her couch the little bare feet withdrew slowly, until they were hidden by her dress. Clodius was sitting on the other side of the room, scowling.

She was many years older than I, but her skin was quite unlined and smooth and clear as ivory, dominated by those extraordinary eyes under the wide-curving brows. I couldn't take my eyes off her face.

'Tell me about your campaign, Caelius.'

I told her, being careful not to boast; I didn't want to give her another chance of using her quick wit. She never lowered her gaze, as women are supposed to do, but watched me thoughtfully, with a slight smile. Then she switched to the subject of Cicero, which I had guessed was the reason for my visit, and we first talked about his published works. She knew them well and particularly admired his poems, rather to my surprise.

'I like him,' she decided, 'more as a man than as a politician. He can be so witty and amusing when he wishes. But in Rome you can't be a great man without a great deal of money, and it was unwise of him to give up Macedonia to that oaf Antonius and half Gaul to my cousin Metellus Celer. With a province to govern this year he could have made himself rich.'

'Cicero thought it was his duty to stay in Rome at this time.'

'And buy Crassus' house?'

'Yes, that has been arranged.'

'It will set him back a million denarii,' she said thoughtfully. 'That's what the old miser wants for it. So Cicero must have made *some* money out of his Consulship.'

'That is not for me to know, Lady Clodia. But I don't think he did.'

'I think you know a lot, Caelius.' She extended her hand, and I realised the audience was at an end. I stood up, and held her hand for a moment before I kissed it.

Her eyes were on my face. 'You must call and see me again,'

she said, and suddenly gave an impish smile. 'I've heard so much about you, especially the song the soldiers sang in your honour.'

I glanced angrily at Clodius, and saw his grin, and to my horror found myself blushing. I went out hot with annoyance, vowing I would never call on her.

Three months afterwards she was married to Metellus Celer, and the families insisted on using the ancient patrician rite, *confarreatio*, which is almost impossible to dissolve. Except, of course, by death.

4

Part Two

December 62 BC – March 58 BC

8

Clodius and the Good Goddess

During the first few years that followed his term as Consul Cicero floated on a cloud of self-satisfaction. He continued to remind the Senate, the Assembly and his friends how well he had merited the title of 'Father of his Country'. It may seem strange that a man as astute as Cicero, so little prone – in his own thoughts – to false pride, could have acted so stupidly, because of course he alienated Pompey and many of his well-wishers; but as I have already mentioned he had a nagging fear always at the back of his mind. The shades of the conspirators he had executed haunted him, and when he boasted how right he had been to have them strangled it was because he knew in his heart he had been wrong, and that one day they might have their revenge. And so they did, and it was Clodius, Cicero's friend, who was their instrument.

I was seeing a good deal of Clodius, and one day when he was more broke than usual he bet me a large sum that he would not only attend the mysteries of the Good Goddess, but take the opportunity of sharing a bed with Pompeia, Caesar's current wife. For this year the ceremonies were to be held in the house of Caesar, the Head Priest. Pompeia was a pretty, rather simple girl, and Clodius had made some headway with her already and thought that if he could get into her bedroom she would fall into his arms.

So in December, on the day of the feast, Clodius came to our house and Bion and I shaved off the wispy beard he wore and dressed him up as a lute-girl. Padded out, and with his toe-nails painted under the long stola, he made quite a good-looking girl, and I began to be afraid for my stake. I needn't have been, for he was too careless to organise things properly.

I took him in a closed litter to the postern gate of Caesar's house and made sure that he went in with the other musicians and servants who were crowding into the doorway. Then I hurried to the baths and bribed the gate-keeper to say, if anyone should ask, that I had arrived much earlier. Two hours afterwards Clodius turned up, chuckling with triumph, and demanded the money.

'What d'you mean?' I asked. 'You were only in the house for half an hour.'

'How do you know?'

'Because I sent Bion to watch the postern, and that's what he told me.'

'You *spied* on me,' he shouted, quite outraged.

'Of course I did. It's a lot of money.'

He was just going on to say something scathing about the lower orders and their penny-pinching when he bethought himself, and looked wary. 'What else did Bion say?'

'He said you were thrown out by a crowd of spitting women, with no lute and only your tunic on, and that had been torn.' I looked at him smiling. 'Come on, now. It must have been a laugh. What happened? You're not going to convince me that you had time to lay Pompeia.' He was going to bluff it out, so I said quickly. 'It's obvious that if they'd found you in her room you wouldn't have got off so lightly. Fornication on consecrated premises? They'd have torn you to pieces.'

'All right then.' He gave a guffaw of laughter. 'I'll tell you. I'd bribed Abra, one of Pompeia's dressing-girls, to meet me inside the door. But she wasn't there, and I wandered around for a bit, watching the dancing – and some of those society girls, stripped to the buff, are *good* – and then a whole group of women came up and asked me to play my lute, so that they could dance, too. Well, it was no good, because I can't play the thing, so I said I had to see Abra first. But my voice gave me away.'

We both roared with laughter. 'What happened then?'

'They tore my dress off and found what they were looking for, and then – I tell you, I thought they were going to castrate me, and ran like mad, up a stair leading to the maids' bedrooms above the atreum. There by good luck I found Abra, and she took me into her room. But then the real trouble started. I heard Aurelia's voice, and she was in a flaming rage.'

I knew Aurelia by repute. She was Caesar's mother, a matron of the stern old school of Roman women, who had moral values and believed in the gods. She, of course, and not Pompeia, was the mistress of the house and in charge of the ceremonies, so she would be held responsible for any desecration of the rites. 'Go on,' I urged him.

'Aurelia organised a room-to-room search,' said Clodius, still laughing, 'but I waited behind the door curtain and when they came in I sprang out and down the stair and was out of the postern before they knew what was happening.'

I stared at him. 'But they'll guess Abra knows about you, and beat her until she squeals.'

He shrugged his shoulders. 'Well, I'm sorry for the poor girl,' he said casually, 'but she's probably used to it, with Aurelia in charge of the house. And anyway, if she'd met me as I arranged nothing would have happened, except me and little Pompeia, in bed.'

He was sometimes extraordinarily thick-headed. 'But don't you see, she'll give them your name and tell them you planned to lay Pompeia, and there'll be hell to pay.'

He called to his slaves to undress him. 'They'll hush it up. You don't think Caesar's going to bring a charge against a member of my family, do you? He's been suspended by the Senate once. D'you think we couldn't stop him from taking up his command next year, if we really wanted? And that's all he's got to keep his creditors at bay.'

He wasn't so stupid, after all. He went on to argue that as he had got into the house and stayed some time without discovery I should pay half the stake. But as he had to admit that he hadn't even seen Pompeia we called off the wager.

*

Clodius was right, as far as Caesar was concerned. He stated publicly that he was satisfied that Pompeia had not committed adultery with Clodius and brought no charge against him. Nevertheless, he divorced his wife at once, saying that Caesar's wife must be above even the suspicion of immorality. This solemn statement, from one who had cuckolded half the men in upper-class society, was the joke of the year, and it was only some time afterwards that I realised what a shrewd move that subtle man had made.

Julius Caesar had been elected Head Priest, or Chief Pontiff or Pontifex Maximus – call it what you will – on the strength of the flamboyant games he had staged when he was curule aedile, and a lot of bribery. He was only thirty-seven when he was appointed, and it is an office for life, bringing a large house and a good deal of immunity from personal attack, as he had shown when he was accused of conspiring with Catiline. He knew what he was about, even if he was nearly ruined by the expenses of the election, following the games.

He divorced Pompeia for the effect it would have with the common people, who as I have said still hold to the old beliefs and are extremely superstitious. Caesar knew how much he would need their support for his long-range plans, and when he said, in effect, 'Whatever you may think of me as a man, I am your Head Priest, and I will not allow any suspicion of unworthy behaviour in my household,' he was saying what they expected of his office. He regained a lot of the popularity he had lost in the Catiline débâcle.

But while they were applauding this dignified attitude in the head of their religion the crowd in the Forum began to ask itself why no one was prosecuting Clodius for desecrating the feast of the Good Goddess, and the women were particularly vociferous. None of the priests or magistrates wanted the silly prank to be given the publicity of an open hearing, but the pressure of public opinion was such that they gave in, and Clodius was charged with sacrilege and – in a technical sense, since this was the crime of having disturbed Vestal Virgins in the discharge of their duties – incest.

Clodius was furious, because by his curious and unorthodox talents as a popular leader he had begun to form a following among the plebs, and the trial would set him back. He never thought for a moment that he could be condemned.

The court was to meet in a few days' time when I chanced to be discussing the case with Cicero and his wife, who had invited me to dinner. I kept quiet about the part I had played myself.

Cicero said, 'That young man doesn't deserve to be let off; it was very unwise of him to go into that house when he did. But of course he'll be acquitted. The only witnesses they can bring against him will be slaves and women, and if he has good counsel they'll make mincemeat of the evidence.'

'Besides,' I said casually, 'he has a cast-iron alibi. A friend of his, Cassinius Schola, will swear that Clodius was at Interamna that day, and it's ninety miles away.'

'He can't do that,' remarked Cicero, picking an orange from the bowl. 'Clodius was in Rome. He came to see me that morning. Schola must have made a mistake.'

'Are you sure of this, Marcus?' asked Terentia, looking at me with a searching eye.

'Quite sure, Madam. Clodius told me.'

'Then he is forging evidence,' she said to Cicero. 'Are you going to allow him to make a mockery of a court of law?'

'It would not be the first time, my dear,' said Cicero, smiling, 'that justice has been seen to miscarry. In fact, I may admit on occasion to have produced such a fog of uncertainty in the court that my client's obvious guilt has been invisible.' He glanced across at me with his mischievous grin.

But Terentia would not let him off the hook. 'As the leader of the Roman bar you cannot connive at such false witness. Oratory is one thing, the deliberate suppression of evidence another.'

'I am not suppressing evidence, since I have not been called as a witness.' (A nice piece of disingenuous pleading, that was!)

'Then you will be.' The indomitable woman rose to her feet. 'I will see that the prosecution is informed.'

Now both Cicero and I were thoroughly alarmed. 'Terentia, my dear, I forbid you to do any such thing. I have no quarrel with Clodius, who as you know is my friend.'

'Like his precious sister,' she retorted, with biting scorn.

'Clodia is now a married woman. I cannot understand why you see any objection to my continuing friendship with her. I am delighted to find young women these days with such an intelligent grasp of our literature and history.'

Terentia snorted, and tried a new tack. 'Where,' she asked, 'will the "Father of his Country" be hiding when Cassinius Schola perjures himself in the witness-box? You will make a point of going to the villa, I suppose, for fear that someone might ask you to speak for the people and push the liar's words down his throat.' She really does talk like that when she's aroused, and the reason why she was making such a fuss wasn't far to seek. She went on, 'My sister Fabia tells me Pompeia is heart-broken, because she is quite innocent, and devoted to Julius. She scarcely knows Clodius and has never given him the slightest encouragement. But this is typical – the innocent woman is condemned to shame and hardship, but as for the guilty man, all his friends gather round to protect him from the punishment he so justly deserves.' She swept out.

Cicero looked at me with a hint of a smile, but he was worried. 'Terentia's motivations sometimes puzzle me,' he said, 'but you must remember that besides being a supporter of women's rights and having an illogical prejudice against the Claudian family she is also a devout woman, and I cannot stop her from revealing what she has just heard. She will think it her duty. I don't want to offend Clodius, still less his – er – family, so get hold of him and tell him to change his alibi. It's a bad one, in any case. There must be hundreds of people who know he wasn't at Interamna.'

When I found Clodius he paid not the slightest attention, but raged against Cicero. 'So this man I helped to triumph over Catiline plots to cut my throat,' he cried. 'Let him try!' He looked up at me suddenly. 'And I suppose you will testify against me, too? It's only what I can expect from the – '

I was angry now. 'Don't be a fool, Clodius,' I said sharply. 'I should only implicate myself if I told what I knew.'

'Then go into the witness-box after Scola and say you were with me at Interamna. You know the town well enough,' he added scornfully. 'I'm told you were born there.' For a patrician, even to be born outside Rome is something disgraceful.

'If I did that I would be giving the lie to Cicero. Be reasonable man. It's sound advice he's giving you. You've got good counsel; they'll find another alibi for you.'

It was no good. He called me a false friend, unwilling to do the slightest thing to help him, and we parted on bad terms.

On the first day of the hearing Cassinius Schola gave his evidence. Then a people's tribune stood up and shouted that Cicero could disprove the testimony. He was called to appear in court, and on the second day a great crowd of people were present to hear Cicero speak.

I don't know what he had intended to do. Obviously, he was annoyed with Clodius for not taking the sensible advice he had offered him. Probably Terentia had been getting at him as well. But whatever he had thought of saying, everything else went out of his mind when he heard the roars of the crowd. It's also true that he had had no opportunity during the past month to tell the Roman people, once again, how much they owed to him.

As it proved afterwards, it was the most unwise speech he ever delivered, but brilliant and devastating. He reminded the court who he was and what he had done for the Republic, and asked whom they chose to believe, him or Cassinius Schola, the friend and lackey of Clodius. Then there was a lot about the scandalous state of public and private morals, the corruption of youth, the arrogance of the aristocracy and finally the horrible nature of the crime Clodius had committed. He ended with a picture of the gods looking down and pondering their revenge on a society which could allow such things to happen. The jurors were beginning to look up apprehensively at the sky.

When he sat down the whole jury rose to their feet and applauded, and when he left the court the crowds followed him, cheering.

There was a gap of a day before the final meeting of the court, when the counsel for both sides would make their speeches and the verdict taken. During this time Crassus got busy.

Why Crassus? He was no particular friend, at that time, of Clodius, and in fact was still on excellent terms with Cicero. It may be that he and Julius Caesar, who was heavily in his debt, had already come to an arrangement by which any further attempt by Cicero to show himself a popular leader would be checked. Pompey, too, was back in Rome, and he'd already shown his irritation at Cicero's claims to be Number One in the people's affections.

Whatever the reasons, it was Crassus who went to work on the jurors, some sixty in number. Every one of them was interviewed at Crassus' house and offered bribes; more than half accepted. They had already been intimidated by the roars of anger from the Claudians after Cicero's speech, and the court had provided guards to protect them. Whatever each man needed, he got; cash down, bills counter-signed, legal advice or in special cases introductions to ladies of fashion or youths of noble family. (In his private life Crassus was a model of propriety!)

The final speeches of the counsel for defence and prosecution mattered little. Clodius was acquitted without a stain on his character, by a vote of thirty-one to twenty-five. As some wit pointed out, the guards provided by the court were some use after all; they prevented the jurors' pockets from being picked on the way home.

Cicero was shattered. His famous oratory had been shown to be quite useless against well-organised corruption. The whole framework of the judicial system, in which he still believed in spite of the tricks he played with it, was proved to be rotten to the core. For days after the trial he would not go out. But he wasn't considering how he could come to terms with an established state of affairs; he was plotting how to take his revenge by the only means he knew – and not on Crassus, but Clodius, who he thought was more vulnerable. He could not have made a worse mistake.

Thus began the great feud which is the subject of my story.

57

9

The Water-Party

During that year 692 which followed Cicero's Consulship and ended with the Feast – or should I say farce – of the Good Goddess I had had a few cases to plead, mostly on Cicero's recommendation, and had made many friends.

We were a group of young men, including some patricians, like Dolabella, who saw no future in the traditional steady climb to fame through the magistracies, but aimed to enjoy ourselves while there was still time. Catiline had failed, it was true, but surely when Pompey – Pompey the Great, as he had been allowed to call himself – returned from his spectacular conquests in Asia, with his vast army and fleets laden with slaves and booty, he would make short work of Caesar, Crassus and the Senate and set himself up as Dictator. It had happened before in recent history and the gods knew that if some semblance of ordered government was to be restored an authoritarian hand was needed. Our time would come then, we thought.

In fact, of course, Pompey did nothing of the sort and upset all our calculations. When he landed in December all he tamely asked for was a triumph the following year, farms for his veterans and the ratification of the excellent dispositions he had made for the settlement of Asia. But in the meantime it was a year of parties and amusing escapades in the streets after dark, and endless discussions of ways of getting rich quickly. The roaring inflation made a nonsense of salaries and the normal expectations of well-born young men.

But it cost my father, who would have been reckoned by earlier standards a very rich man, more than he could afford, and in the end he struck.

His trade with Africa was increasing, but not enough, and he was getting too old to travel with any comfort. So he proposed I should get myself posted for two years to Africa, leaving my law career for the time being, and look after the foreign end of the family business on the side. Although it was not a bargain I could boast of to my few aristocratic friends I saw it was sensible and agreed.

Strings were pulled, and I was appointed as attendant on the praetor, Quintus Pompeius Rufus, who governed Africa from his palace in Utica, on the Bay of Tunis.

Africa is of course a very small province, and peaceful, so I couldn't expect to return to Rome with a string of campaigns to my credit and trains of loot, but it is rich, and most of my family's trade in ivory, manufactured goods, spices and slaves is shipped from Utica. I was to sail in the spring.

So while Cicero was plotting his revenge on Clodius, I was very busy making preparations and spending a good deal of time in our offices and warehouses at Puteoli, where the ships from Africa discharge their cargoes. It was there, by chance, that I met Clodius.

I was standing on the quay watching one of our charter ships coming into harbour when eight slaves came trotting up, carrying a litter. I heard a shouted command and they halted near me. Clodius stepped out, dressed for the country in a tunic, like me. To my surprise he came up and greeted me as an old friend.

'What on earth are you doing down here?' he asked. 'I thought you never strayed from Rome.'

'My father has bought the cargo of slaves in that ship,' I said, pointing. 'I thought I'd take first pick.' This wasn't strictly true, since the whole lot were bespoke for clients in Rome, but it sounded better than to say I was learning how the trade was handled. Luckily, he didn't stay to see what happened.

'I won't compete,' he said, wrinkling his nose. 'I can't stand the stink before they've been washed and anyway, I'm broke again. I've come to see the boats Clodia's hired for her water-party.'

My heart missed a beat. 'The Lady Clodia?' I spoke without thinking.

'The Lady Clodia,' he mimicked. 'She's left her dull husband in Gaul for the winter and I'm staying with her in the villa at Baiae. Come and see us. We're bored.'

I was not sure that I wanted to see Clodia again, but it was a tempting invitation, all the same. I looked over the blue, sunlit water at the group of palaces and villas across the broad bay. I had never been there. It was a reservation of the aristocracy, and members of the lower orders and even Knights (First Class) like my father and myself were, to say the least, discouraged.

'What does she want with a water-party, in March?'

'Oh, it's an idea of hers – poetry by moonlight, and all that. It's tomorrow night. Come and see, if you like. I want you to tell us the latest gossip from Rome and how old Cicero squirmed when I got out of his clutches.'

'He didn't want to testify against you,' I said. 'I hope you realise that.'

'Nonsense! The old blabbermouth exulted in it. But we slapped the proud "Father of his Country" down. He won't give us trouble again.'

Next morning I spent some time in the strong-room of the ivory warehouse, looking at the carved figurines which had come from Utica. I found what I wanted.

*

The evening was perfect, warm and windless, and I was rowed across the bay by twenty men in our house livery and landed at the private jetty beneath the house. The caryatids supporting the porch were flushed with the last gleam of the setting sun. As I climbed the steps the sound of a lute came from the painted colonnade flanking the porch, and the echo of a light laugh.

Other people were arriving, and I saw at once that I was wrongly dressed in the formal clothes of a Roman gentleman, but the slaves quickly took away my toga and put a laurel wreath on my head. The atreum was half-full of guests, some of whom I knew – intellectuals and poets like Cinna and Licinius, and of course young Dolabella, who was at every party in high society. I couldn't see Clodius, so I asked to be taken to his sister, bringing one slave with me to carry my small parcel.

There was the same air of careless luxury that I had seen in her town house, rich hangings trailing on the delicate mosaics of the floors and slaves everywhere, with the same look of slightly insolent complicity.

We crossed the peristylium with its flowering shrubs and fountains and passed through a small door into a colonnade. It gave on to a garden where water plashed and roses were trained around columns and statues.

The image of Clodia I carried in my mind, since our meeting a year ago, was disturbing. This time I was wary, and determined to make my entry seem casual. I took the parcel from the slave and dismissed him.

She was sitting on a bench with a fair-complexioned young man, about my own age. For a moment she didn't move, and her great eyes stared past me gravely, as if she were thinking of something else. Then she held out her hand and said, 'Welcome to my house, Caelius! This is Gaius Cutullus from Verona, the poet.'

I had never heard of him, and it was curious to find a provincial in this society, but I recalled that Verona was in her husband's province of Cisalpine Gaul, and assumed she had met him there. He had an interesting face, constantly changing, a sign of a restless mind. It was the beginning of a friendship that was to be sometimes gay, and sometimes very bitter.

Clodia made polite conversation about Rome, and I told her Cicero was unhappy that he had fallen foul of her family. She shrugged her shoulders. 'He should know better than to make powerful enemies. He couldn't have expected the Claudians to take that speech lying down. But he'll get over it, and I've told Clodius to make amends, some time.'

(She never called her brother Publius, which was his *praenomen*. I think that when they had both changed their names, in defiance of the family, these remained a token of the deep current of incestuous love that ran beneath their lives and welled up from time to time like a boiling spring.)

'Cicero would be sad,' I said, probing, 'if he felt he had lost your friendship, too.'

She made an impatient gesture and turned to Catullus, who was fidgeting with a little scroll, and held out her hand. He drew back.

'Let me keep your verses, Lady Clodia,' he pleaded. 'I want to read them tonight, with the others, so that everyone shall know Rome has a Sappho of her own.'

'No,' she said, smiling at him. 'Not with yours and Cinna's. You mustn't think me as immodest as that.'

He said eagerly, 'They are beautiful, as beautiful as she who wrote them. Let me speak them as they deserve.'

'No, Catullus. But you may come another time – I'll tell you when – and read them to me alone.' His eyes shone and he hurried away, walking on air. She put the scroll beside her on the bench.

'May I not read your poems?' I asked jealously.

'Perhaps. When I know you better.' Then she frowned at me, but with a half-smile on her lips. 'Now,' she said, 'tell me why you never came to see me last year. When I'd *asked* you,' she added in a tone of surprise. Perhaps nobody had ever disobeyed a command to attend on her before.

'So that you could play with me again, like one of your lapdogs?'

'So that I could play with you, perhaps,' she said serenely.

We were silent for a long moment, looking at each other. I heard again the sound of water, trickling in a fountain among the ferns. The air stirred, bringing the scent of flowers. It was one of those silences that would-be lovers know, when many things are left unsaid. I slowly unwrapped the ivory statue of Pan and put it into her hands. She held it high and laughed with delight.

'But he's beautiful,' she cried. 'Greek, and very old. Where did he come from?'

'From Utica. Where I'm being posted at the end of the month.'

'You must make the most of your time, then,' she said, and leaned forward and kissed me lightly on the mouth – no more than a soft touch, but very sweet. 'That's for thanks. Now I must go.'

*

The dinner began late, at six o'clock, and went on, with the entertainments, for several hours. She had Clodius and the poets at her table and I was far away, at the other end of the dining hall. Afterwards, when the moon had risen high, we put on our cloaks and went out on to the porch.

It was an enchanting night. Across the bay the temples in Puteoli and the villas along the shore gleamed white under the moon, and beyond were the dark mountains that hid Naples. Tied up at the jetty were four boats, large and flat-bottomed, and they had been decked in to make platforms at the stern, covered with rugs and cushions, on which the guests could lie, men and girls together. There were musicians in the well of each boat and rowers up near the bows.

The master of ceremonies, a freedman in a Greek robe, ushered Clodia and her brother into the largest boat, which was ringed with lanterns, and they took their places with the poets around them.

The rest of us chose our places in the other boats and the slaves covered us with rugs. For a time we drifted about on the bay, while the musicians played their pieces and wine was served from pitchers cooled with ice from the mountains.

With good food and wine inside me, and my hands touching an attractive girl, I was content, but still intrigued – half attracted and half repelled – by Clodia.

Then the lanterns at the bows of her barge were hoisted high and the rowers brought us nearer, so that we could hear the voices of the poets. Cinna and Licinius read their poems first, and we applauded. They had chosen light lyrics, well suited to the evening's mood. I saw Catullus get to his feet, obviously nervous, and the lights wavered on his eager face and on the scrolls he held in his hand.

I had never heard his poetry before, and was captivated by it. The use of metre was uncommon, and there were words from his province that were strange to a Roman, but his touch was sure, and as he recited his shyness left him. My girl pushed my hand away and we both turned to listen. When he had finished we called for more, and so did everyone else.

He hesitated, and then picked up a lute and began to sing, not looking at Clodia, but across the bay at the distant lights. His voice was clear, but possessed with passion that trembled like a plucked string. As he sang even the slaves turned from their oars and listened. I remember some of it:

> 'I see you, Lesbia, and my voice fades
> Strangled in my throat.
> My tongue lies stricken, fire
> Writhes through my limbs.
> My ears are deafened by their throbbing
> And darkness
> Blindfolds my eyes.'

When he had sung there was a long silence, and he turned and looked at Clodia, who sat with her lips parted and her eyes on his face.

I broke the spell. Tearing off my cloak and tunic I dived from the platform into the sea and swam across to the barge, hauled myself out and swung over the side. My loin-cloth had half-unwound, and there was a roar of laughter as I held it together with one hand and embraced Catullus with a dripping arm.

'Hail to Orpheus!' I cried. 'All Rome must hear your songs.' Everybody shouted for him, and the applause made him laugh excitedly and wave his lute.

'Perhaps Caelius will sing for us now,' suggested Clodia, acidly.

I made a modest gesture of dissent, but her brother seized the lute from Catullus and thrust it into my hands. 'Yes, let's hear him. Silence for Caelius the Clown.'

I have a good voice, and this trick – which Clodius knew – of clowning, and I sang them several bawdy songs, with mime and suitable gestures. In the end even Clodia was amused.

*

A few days later, crossing the Forum in Puteoli, I met Catullus, looking pleased with himself. He told me he was staying at Clodia's villa.

'I have a pavilion at the end of the garden,' he said, 'where I can work quite alone. It has its own bath and water-closet.' How like a provincial, I thought, to mention such details! He went on, 'Clodia comes every afternoon and I read her what I've written, and we discuss it. She is my Muse,' he added, starry-eyed.

'And your mistress, too, I suppose,' I said tartly.

He was horrified. 'But no! I would never – Do you imagine that is the only relationship between a man and a woman?'

'It's not unusual.'

'You're just as Clodia described you, I'm afraid. And I had hoped we could be friends.'

I put my arm round his shoulder. 'I hope we *are* friends. But what did Clodia say?' (She had at least spoken about me.)

'She said it was a pity, you were so intelligent and the most promising of the young advocates, but like all orators you were only concerned in acting a part. She thinks you have no depth or feeling,' he explained kindly.

'But why should she assume such a thing? She scarcely knows me.'

'She's angry that you broke up the poetry readings.'

'But I didn't. I only swam across to your boat because I couldn't wait to embrace you, after hearing your song. And it was she who asked me to sing,' I added indignantly.

'I know,' said Catullus warmly, seizing my hand. 'I told her so, but she shook her head. We mustn't let her think so badly of you, Caelius. Come to the villa and explain how it was.'

'From what you say I doubt if she'd receive me,' I remarked ruefully. 'It's a pity, because I'd like to hear more of your poems. That last song – it reminded me of the verses Sappho wrote for the Lesbian girl,' and I quoted the Greek to him.

He was delighted. 'But of course. I used the same form and metre, and that's why I addressed the poem to 'Lesbia', when I meant – We must discuss the Greek poets together. Come back with me now, I've got a boat waiting.'

'I've work to do this morning. But in the afternoon, perhaps?' I suggested craftily.

He hesitated, and then, 'Why not? Come early, at three o'clock, and I'll show you what I'm writing. And when Clodia comes – well, that'll be your chance, d'you see? She'll find us talking poetry and the classics and she'll soon realise that she misunderstood you completely.'

I thanked him earnestly for his excellent suggestion. Poor Catullus! His spontaneous generosity made him both well loved and easily exploited.

*

The afternoon was warm, and we were sitting on the steps of the little pavilion, hidden from the main villa by the trees, when Clodia arrived, preceded by slaves carrying a day-bed, a basket of scrolls in monogrammed leather covers, a parasol, fly-whisks, feathery fans, and wine in a bowl of crushed ice. There must have been eight slaves, at least, and four were needed to minister to her while we talked. She greeted me coolly, but made no mention of my behaviour at her water-party, and we were soon listening to Catullus, reading his new long poem on the marriage of Peleus and Thetis.

I am very fond of poetry, although I can't write it or even read it aloud with any effectiveness. Catullus recited his poems as beautifully as they were written, and the time passed quickly. I was more than content to listen, my eyes on her face, and watch the changing expressions that passed like shadow-patterns on a sunlit pool. (It always fascinated me to find new depths in her, as well as the sudden shallows.)

She didn't speak to me or even look at me very much, but I sensed that she was aware of my thoughts, and when I left I knew that I would meet her again. But how? Had she, or had she not, made an assignation with me?

It was something she'd said. In his poem Catullus describes the plight of Ariadne when she awakens on the weed-strewn beach of Naxos and finds her lover Theseus has forsaken her. She runs wailing into the surf, calling after the boat, already far out at sea, and finally begs the gods to wreak vengeance on this man whose promises, like all men's promises, are playthings of the wind.

It is a moving passage, and when it came to an end and Catullus looked up at us, avid for praise, Clodia said, 'There's a beach beyond the point, where the storms drive the seaweed far up the sand and it dries in piles of silver thread, that shine under the moon. I sometimes go there at night, alone, and now I shall imagine I am Ariadne, and cry for my lover.'

Catullus' eyes shone with excitement. 'Take me there tonight, and I will speak the lines.'

She shook her head. 'Not tonight. Perhaps another time, before the moon wanes.' Then she told him to continue reading,

65

and as his eyes went down to the scroll hers held mine, for a brief moment only, but one that gave me hope.

*

The beach was easy to identify, and for three nights I lay under the moon on a soft dry pile of seaweed, waiting. On the third night she came.

I had told myself that she wouldn't, that she was playing with me again, or that if she did come it would be in her regal style, with a dozen rowers and attendants, and Catullus with his lute. The sand was still warm after the hot day, and stretched away empty between the silver line of the seaweed and the crisp white of the breaking waves.

She came running along the sand, barefoot, in a filmy tunic, and when I stood up in my long white cloak she laughed and called 'Theseus!'

I ran to meet her and held out my arms, half-choked with desire. But when I tried to kiss her she put a finger on the end of my nose and held me away for a moment. 'This one night,' she said, and then I felt her lips. She reached up to unlatch my cloak, and I spread it on the sand.

'Ariadne,' I whispered, 'let all her clothes fall to the ground. It says so in the poem.'

So she did, and I felt her body trembling and fragile, like a captive bird, and made love to her, there on the spread cloak, between the two lines of silver and with the rush and crash of the sea in our ears.

10

Africa

A week later I left Puteoli to spend at home the last few days before my departure. I did not see Clodia again, although I had begged her to meet me on the beach once more. As we walked hand in hand along the shore she said that now I would not forget her, and that was enough.

My father was pleased with my grasp of his business, and arranged that I should draw a handsome commission on any new trade I could develop. This suited me very well, because I felt sure that in the African hinterland there would be new things to amuse the Romans.

Although Carthage, twenty miles from Utica, had been utterly destroyed eighty years before, it had after all been a city of half a million people, and enough had survived the slaughter to keep alive the trade with the interior, where there were gold and silver mines and fine craftsmen to work the metals. Utica had developed this trade and also its own industries. My suggestion, which my father agreed to in the end, was that since the hordes of slaves brought back by Pompey were causing a glut in the market we should discontinue our own occasional shipments and use the space for manufactured goods. Provided, of course, I could discover new lines.

He also agreed that we should ship small consignments of gold bars, if I could buy them direct from the smelters, so that we could form a stock of bullion in the cellars of our house in Rome. The silver coinage was becoming badly debased, and we expected that the time would soon come when gold coins would be minted, for the first time, as a regular form of currency.

By the time I set sail, in early April, my father and I were on better terms than we had been for years, and we both shed tears on parting. My mother, of course, was inconsolable. Although Pompey had chased the pirates from the seas a sea voyage was still an uncertain affair, and she spent much time praying for good winds.

It was a sound ship that I boarded at Puteoli, about two hundred tons, with a Syrian captain and crew. My crates of scrolls and personal baggage were lowered into the hold with a cargo of goods for bargaining, chiefly jars of strong sweet wine (which keeps well) and bales of cheap cloth. I had Bion with me as my personal slave. We had a good run down the coast to the Straits of Messina, cruised along the north coast of Sicily to Palermo, where I spent a few days with our agents, and then across the channel to Utica, on the Bay of Tunis.

Quintus Pompeius, the Governor, was a tough and blunt man, the adopted son of a famous soldier. Although on the make, of course, like all provincial governors, he was nevertheless a person of culture and wit, with a good-sized library which he put at my disposal. On the first night after my arrival, while we were sitting over our wine, he stated his attitude to his job with admirable clarity.

'This is a small province, Caelius, and not like Sicily or Macedonia where the pickings are so great you can fill a fleet of ships in six months. If I tried to do that here I'd run into a trial for extortion as soon as I returned to Rome, and I can't afford the risk. You know what happened to Verres; all his powerful friends and his bribes couldn't save him from exile when your friend Cicero got to work on the case. I don't intend to be exiled. I came here a poor man and I want to go home rich enough to buy a large estate and settle down to a pleasant life in the country. No standing for the Consulship for me; it costs too much. I'm opting out of the official career.'

'So,' he continued, filling our cups, 'I'm going to avoid a charge of extortion by keeping on good terms with the locals. They're proud of having a free city that's a thousand years old, and they're proud of their record of friendship with Rome, and the moment I go too far they'll be scratching out letters to their patrons and I shall get a hot reception. But the point is, they're traders, always have been, and what they want is peace and order, so that they can go, on making themselves rich. That's fair enough. I tax them, on my own account, too, but never more than they can afford, and the taxes are spread across the board. You'll see. Your father, whom I've known for years, says you've got a good head for figures, and according to Cicero you can use your tongue and your pen. I admit most of Cicero's letter was about the smart things he's been saying in the House to Clodius, but he seems to have a good opinion of your abilities. I can use them.'

I said I wasn't afraid of hard work, and he nodded and went on, 'Now there are one or two points I want you to remember, because if you don't you'll be in big trouble. I've no objection to your helping to develop your father's business. It's all taxed, so I stand to gain. But if you fall foul of the Africans or the Colonials by slave raids on other people's territory, or by cheating them too flagrantly, I'll send you home. Is that understood?'

'We have in mind to cut down on slaves, Sir, and work up new lines by barter.'

'I'm glad to hear about the slaves. Nothing upsets the people more than to see men in irons going through the port. Now another thing. You're a young man and will go whoring around like the rest. But not in my household. Not with my daughters, nor my wife – not that it's likely! – nor the girls. Nor the daughters of our local friends; they're touchy, being easterners, most of them. The standard of women's morals here is old-fashioned, as it used to be in Rome. Understood?'

'Yes, Sir.'

'If you want a girl, go and buy one in the market. They're cheap and docile, and some are real good-lookers.' He glanced at me speculatively. 'And so are some of the boys.'

'Girls for me, Sir.'

'Good. Mind you, the locals have their own ideas about that. You're a good-looking young fellow, and they'll be round you at the baths like bees at a honey-pot. They love a white skin, being darkish themselves. If they get too fresh, just give them a good crack in the crotch – to hurt, but *smiling*. That's the diplomatic way of telling them where they get off, without hard feelings. And remember, diplomacy is a big part of your job here.'

*

I was puzzled by what Pompeius had said about Cicero. When I had dined at his house before my departure he never mentioned Clodius, and I hoped he had already forgotten his humiliation, but a letter that came shortly after I arrived showed that he had not.

'I told Clodius,' he wrote, 'in front of the whole Senate, that justice had only held its hand at his trial so that it could condemn him later to the death-chamber.'

This, I thought, was going a bit far. Clodius' acquittal must have turned to bile in Cicero's stomach. What good could it do to harp on that theme, dead months ago? And his talk of justice was nonsense. As he'd said himself, before the trial, 'Justice is often seen to miscarry,' or something like that. But of course he wasn't used to defeat in a court of law – even if he had only been a witness – and it gnawed at his vitals, especially the wholesale bribery of the jury.

'Clodius,' he went on, 'replied that it was quite simple, the jury had not believed my evidence. What impertinence! I snapped back, "On the contrary, at least twenty-five of them gave me credit. The other thirty-one gave *you* none; they insisted on getting their cash in advance." You can imagine, my dear Marcus, how the Senators roared with laughter at my quip, and I can tell you that Clodius was silenced, utterly discomfited. How that miserable man must hate me!'

I wondered whether Cicero had any idea what he was doing by this stupid game. Didn't he realise that Clodius would resent ridicule from a 'new man' more deeply than a blow in the face? And that the people would see the joke aimed not just at Clodius, or the Claudians, but at the aristocracy as a whole? The very persons whose support Cicero needed most.

There was much to keep me occupied during those first weeks, but before the next fast ship left for Puteoli I wrote him

69

a letter, paying him the kind of compliments he expected from one of his former pupils, telling him all my news and finishing with a carefully drafted paragraph:

'I was delighted to hear, my dear Master, how neatly and amusingly you turned the tables on Publius Clodius in the Senate. I am sure that now you have paid off that old score you will show the magnanimity for which you are so rightly praised, and not let Crassus and the Claudian family feel more of your displeasure – for of course they were all equally guilty of that shocking piece of corruption.'

I knew Cicero would always listen to advice from any source, even one of his pupils. Whether he'd act on it was another matter.

*

As Pompeius had suggested, I bought a girl or two, and kept one of them with me during the whole of my posting – a charming, affectionate creature, true Phoenician by the look of her, who shared my bed and bath and entertained me and my friends with her pranks. Like all Romans abroad I felt nostalgia for the gossip at the Senian Baths, the wit of my own age group, the parties, the spectacles and the almost sensual thrill of listening to the speeches of great orators like Cicero and Hortensius. In Utica most of the men I met professionally were a good deal older than I, and less interested in politics and philosophy than in making money. (All my friends in Rome were equally obsessed with money, but not with *earning* it by any regular job; it was bad form to talk about such a thing. Ideally, you either inherited the stuff, or borrowed it, or won it on a gamble.)

Nevertheless, my life was pleasant enough. I was a member of an excellent bath club, with a well-equipped gymnasium, and every villa had its swimming pool or its private beach. I rented a small house in the hills and gave house-parties which got me a reputation for providing amusing entertainments, and there was plenty of riding and hunting.

My official work kept me busy, what with writing speeches for Pompeius to deliver, arranging dinner-parties and receptions and accompanying him on tours of the province, and so on. In the end he wouldn't trust anyone else to keep his personal accounts for him. By and large, I served him well, and he was not ungrateful. Whenever our ships were due to arrive or leave he let me off duty, and I had time to keep a close eye on the family business, and foster a scheme of my own.

I hadn't mentioned it to my father, in case I should be proved wrong, and it took most of the first year to work up, but in the end my plan paid off very nicely. It was a completely new line, because my father had never bothered much about works of art, except the little ivory figurines which came our way occasionally.

There was a part of Roman society that I knew better than he did, the new-rich knights – tax farmers and bankers and moneylenders. At auctions in the Vicus Tuscus I had seen them buying up anything of Greek or Egyptian manufacture which would give their new houses an air of culture, and at fancy prices. The great advantage of the auction, to these people, was that everyone knew how much they had paid. The snob thing to do was to buy some ancient piece of statuary, however mutilated, and exhibit it on a magnificent pedestal in your atreum, with a certificate attached to show that it came from the court of either King Minos or Agamemnon. Then your friends, who knew you had paid fifty thousand sesterces for it, would feel you must be a connoisseur.

When our forefathers reduced Carthage to rubble and drove a plough over the site the place was thoroughly sacked and the legionaries removed all the valuables they could find. But, I reasoned, they were looking for gold and jewellery and figurines, perhaps small marble statues which could be easily carried away. Anything else would be left, and broken up when the roof fell in. In a rich city of half a million inhabitants there must be thousands of sculptures still lying under the ground, and as the Carthaginians were never great artists in their own right, but excellent craftsmen, the statues would be copies of Greek or Egyptian models, and very well made. In fact, I thought, they might even pass for Greek or Egyptian.

I rode over to the site and had a look around. Where the city of Carthage itself had stood there was little to be done; I could still see the forms of immense pieces of masonry under the thin grass and sand but it was obvious that only excavation on a vast scale would be of any use. In the suburbs, however, where an attempt had been made in the time of Gracchus to found a colony, there were ruined villas only half-covered by the wild growth of trees and shrubs, and many of these were no doubt built on the foundations of Carthaginian houses.

There was a man called Titus, who farmed some land nearby, the descendant of a Roman legionary, and I found him intelligent and interested in my idea. He had made a floor for his terrace of crushed marble from bits of statues he had cleared

71

from land now under the plough, and showed me a barn full of other bits and pieces which he intended to break up. I chose an orator with no head and only one leg, a handsome bust of a woman with the head badly defaced, the torso of a hermaphrodite and three pieces of a fine frieze of slaves bearing gifts to some king, probably Egyptian – and paid cash for the lot. Titus' eyes glistened, and he at once offered to set a gang of slaves to work on the remains of two old buildings on his land. I told him, of course, that I wasn't interested in anything connected with the Carthaginian gods Baal-Hammon and Eshmoun, or the gruesome goddess Tanit into whose red-hot womb living babies were thrown in sacrifice. The cult was still very much alive, and the local people might well object. In three months he had assembled enough statues for a first shipment.

My father's incredulous reaction to a cargo of this kind was tempered by a long letter I sent him at the same time, begging him to put one or two pieces on show, with ridiculously high price tags, and refuse absolutely to say where they had come from. They sold within a week. I had been careful to choose statues of apparently Greek or Egyptian origin, to judge from the subject or the clothes, and most buyers concluded that they had come from Alexandria, where the export of antiques is heavily taxed.

This trade grew most satisfactorily, and I made Titus a rich man by local standards. He handed over the management of his farm to a freedman and went around the country buying statues, friezes, small painted columns, fountains and almost everything marble he could lay his hands on. Most of it was worth sending to Puteoli. At the other end, my father opened a special shop for the antiques. He never gave a certificate of origin, partly to salve his conscience and partly for the good practical reason that he thus avoided any possible charge of fraudulent practice. My commission he allowed to accumulate at interest in the bank, refusing steadfastly to let me have any of it before I returned to Rome.

However, I was able to make some money on the side by defending or prosecuting in the civil courts. Although in Rome I should not have been allowed a fee but only to impose an 'obligation' on my client, in Utica there was no such nonsense. 'Obligations' were at once liquidated in cash or expensive presents. So I didn't do so badly.

I must return to my story. I have made this digression to explain how it was that when I returned to Rome my purse was full, for the first time in my life, and also why and how I came into possession of something which was to be very important in my life. It happened as follows.

I was dining with Titus one night in a tavern in Utica when he said, 'I've seen something that'd make your mouth water, friend Caelius. The pity of it is you can't take it away.'

'You mean the owner won't part with it?'

He laughed and banged his fist on the table. 'That's a good one! He'd part with it all right, or I think he would – but you couldn't move it. It's a mosaic pavement.'

'What's the good of that?' I cried in disgust.

'I know. That's what I meant. But you might like to see it, all the same.' He looked across at me, thinking. 'It's the sort of thing that might interest you a lot – small, but special, and with a history attached to it. The owner is the descendant of one of the Carthaginian shophets, like our Consuls in Rome. He's not well off, and I bought a lot of stuff from him on my last trip and we got drunk together and he showed me this thing, which he usually keeps hidden. The next morning he could have cut his tongue out.'

I was intrigued, and began to think how a mosaic could be broken up and transported. But the cost would be a hundred times as great as the price I could conceivably pay, if you counted the business of detaching the mosaic from its base, and all the difficulties of reassembly.

A month later we were looking at it. I'd had to bully and cajole the old man for hours before he took Titus and me into a ruined bath-house near his villa, unlocked a heavy door and showed us into a room lit by a breach in the domed roof. The middle of the floor was covered an inch deep in silver sand, but there was a broom standing against the wall, and he took it and swept the sand away from one corner of the mosaic.

'My ancestor, the Lord Shophet, had it made for him, section by section, in Alexandria by one of the great masters, whose name I forget. He was a great lover of the art, and when the end of the city was near he had another mosaic laid on top, so that no one would ever find the Alexandrian one. So when they stormed the villa they didn't discover it.'

It was unlike anything I'd ever seen. The colours glowed like fire, each tiny piece made of gold or silver leaf, or slices of lapis lazuli or green or red porphyry, bonded on to the glass cube and covered with a transparent flux. Between the cubes were thin walls of a white material, which I afterwards found to be ivory, and this set off the colour and brightness. The effect was of a jewelled plaque, not a mosaic at all.

I seized the broom and swept away more of the sand. It was a hunting scene, a lion surrounded by a ring of men with shields, who were driving him into a net. His eyes flashed red fire. In the background were trees and papyrus reeds, and birds flying away in fright. I was trembling with excitement, but I controlled myself and asked him casually if the design was complete.

'There's not a tessera missing,' he declared indignantly, 'nor a crack. My grandfather said there were sixteen sections, each sent separately from Alexandria in a wooden frame, but I've never been able to see where they were joined. The base must be very solid.'

I shook my head regretfully. 'That's the trouble,' I explained. 'How could I lift the mosaic from its bed? It's usually six inches of cement on top of nine inches of hardcore, which was probably mixed with mortar and has gone hard. It would be too big a risk to try and break up the mosaic and take it away piecemeal. Still, I suppose if the price is low I might try.'

He said nothing, but began to brush back the sand, covering up every last trace of that glowing picture. We went back to his house, where we were to spend the night, as it was up in the foothills of the mountains, far away from the site of Carthage. It was only after dinner that he came back to the possibility of a sale.

By this time I had discovered that the old man had lost contact with his children, who had emigrated to Rome, and was dreaming of making a last expedition to see them before he died. He'd never been to Rome, and was curious, so I filled him up with descriptions of its splendours. Still, he was obviously uncertain of the reception he might get from his married sons and scared of being robbed by the Romans – we always have such a bad reputation abroad! – and when I urged him to make the visit he shook his head. Then I had an inspiration.

'I'd be glad,' I said, 'to give you passage on one of our ships and provide a coach to take you from Puteoli to Rome. And also, if I take the mosaic, you could stay if you wish at my father's house, so that you could watch my attempts to put the pieces together.'

'Your father would invite me?' he asked sharply.

'Indeed yes. He would be delighted to meet you.' Which was true, since he was a well-read and dignified old man and my father would have enjoyed talking to him. He loved to reminisce about his early trips to Africa.

So it was arranged. I bought the pavement from him for a

fairly modest sum, with permission to destroy the rest of the bath-house so as to be able to get at the foundations, and had the deal ratified by the local magistrate. Then I got to work.

The foundations were formidable, nearly two feet deep and very hard underneath, but the top layer, under the tesserae, was a lime mortar, which was soft enough to saw. I had papyrus glued over the whole surface, and then three layers of linen. The site was cleared and a trench dug along each side, deep and wide enough for men to stand and work at the layer under the mosaic. Long saws were made specially, with very fine teeth, and as the men sawed an inch below the tesserae, very slowly and carefully, the cloth, with the mosaic and its cement backing sticking to it, was rolled round a drum of oak planks, which I'd had made for the purpose. When finished it was a cylinder four feet thick and I had it covered with more linen, sewn together, and lifted into a box of thick planks of cedar of Lebanon, lined with dry grass.

The old man thought at first, quite rightly, that he had been misled about the difficulties, but I smoothed him down with tales of what we would do to entertain him in Rome and in the end he was as keen as I to have the job done properly, stepping down creakily into the trenches every few minutes to see that the angle of the saw was dead horizontal, and swearing in Punic at the slaves. When, ten days later, the task was complete and the box was driven away in a wagon hauled by four mules, with Titus and me riding beside it, he was weeping, but cheerful.

It was placed in our warehouse at the port of Utica. I had no intention of sending it on in advance of my return, for I had plans for that mosaic. It was for Clodia.

And so I return to my story.

11

News from Rome

I had never before found any difficulty in banishing a woman from my mind, but Clodia was different. It wasn't that I was deeply in love with her at that time, but intrigued, attracted, consumed with a burning wish to be taken seriously by her.

When I had held her in my arms, that night on the beach at Baiae, we had been equals in love, but I wondered whether she spared me more than a passing thought the following day. I didn't forget that she had made me wait like a love-sick boy until the whim took her from her bed to run down on to the sand and find me, waiting.

Behind every deal I made in Africa was this thought, that when I returned to Rome there would be no more playing at love; I would come as a man of consequence to compete with any other man, and bearing rich gifts. I wanted above all to hear her laugh with delight, as she had when I unwrapped the ivory Pan. I had never forgotten that laugh, or the careless kiss that followed it.

It was still difficult to get news of her, except from Catullus, who was her devoted slave – and perhaps more; it was difficult to discover from his letters. He seemed to have taken an extreme dislike to her husband Metellus Celer, who during my first year abroad was busy with his election campaign. He was duly elected Consul for the following year.

Julius Caesar had got away to Spain one jump ahead of his creditors, and went far beyond his instructions. Nobody had expected him to prove a good soldier, but when he decided of his own accord to carry the frontier of the Republic to the western coast he did it with exemplary efficiency, and incidentally re-stocked his treasure-chests.

As Dolabella put it, the impossible was about to happen. When Rome saw Caesar again he would be in a state of solvency.

Dolabella, who in spite of being the most irresponsible and frivolous of my Roman friends – and that is saying a good deal – is a faithful letter-writer, also told me in detail, and very amusingly, about Pompey's triumph in September. It was a remarkable affair, with elephants being slaughtered in the arena by the dozen and an impressive display of captives and loot, but when it was over Pompey made no attempt to make capital out of his popularity. He still only wanted the ratification of his edicts for the settlement of the East and land on which to settle his veterans.

Next year, 694, the Senators, who ought to have been delighted that Pompey was acting so reasonably, put every difficulty in the way of his fair demands. According to a letter from Cicero this was chiefly because Clodia's husband, now Consul, was annoyed with Pompey because he had divorced his wife Mucia, Metellus' half-sister. The divorce was well grounded, because while Pompey was away in the East Caesar had occupied his bed, but Metellus took it as a slight on the grand family of Caecilii Metelli and persisted in opposing a bill to grant land to the veterans. In the end the tribune who had introduced the bill exercised his right and threw the Consul into prison. It took all Pompey's authority to get him out again.

Cicero wrote to me quite frequently. Referring to that first letter of mine, in which I had ventured to suggest he should stop needling the Claudians, 'My dear Marcus,' he wrote, 'I have always regarded you as a shrewd observer of the political scene, in spite of your youth, and your thinly-disguised but well-meant strictures on my handling of the quarrel with Clodius were acceptable. But I cannot compromise with tyranny, nor be silent when I see injustice. In this time of pressure-groups and corruption there must be one man, at least, who will have the moral stamina to speak, to guide and if necessary, chastise.'

He was doing his best to make friends with Pompey, and in his letters harped so much on the great man's devotion to him that I began to wonder. The other thing still on his mind was Clodius, and as well as describing the amusing remarks he had made for his discomfiture he showed signs, at last, of a realisation that he was playing with fire. In particular, he kept referring to Clodius' plan to have himself adopted by a plebeian family so that he could be elected People's Tribune. Metellus Celer was supporting his brother-in-law and Cicero could not understand why.

I could. Admittedly, the idea of what Clodius might do with a tribune's special powers was frightening, particularly as he was reported to be recruiting more toughs to help in moulding public opinion, but Cicero always underestimated the centripetal force that holds together the few remaining aristocratic families, and although Metellus Celer had little use for Clodius he was not only his brother-in-law but his cousin.

Clodius, incidentally had been doing a stint as quaestor in Sicily, and apparently in an attempt at conciliation with Cicero asked him how he could get free seats in the arena for his Sicilian clients. He grumbled that Clodia, who as the Consul's wife had any number of seats at her disposal, would only offer him standing room. Cicero couldn't resist that chance. 'Don't ask your sister for standing room,' he said kindly. 'After all, you can always lie with her.' And of course went round telling everybody how clever he'd been.

I was interested in that small indication that Clodia and her brother were not on the best of terms. It might, I thought, be connected with the fact that Clodius – whether to spite his sister for marrying Metellus, or for some other reason – had got married. It wasn't a success.

Caesar returned from Spain in June and sent messages to the Senate, asking for a triumph and also permission to stand election for Consul by proxy. The point is that if a triumph were granted it would be many months before Caesar could enter Rome, during which time the Consular election would take place. So if he had a triumph he could only appear on the hustings by proxy. The Senate, still failing to realise that Caesar was not a man to be trifled with, refused. Upon which, he moved fast. He withdrew his application for a triumph, entered Rome, stood for Consul without any help from the Senate, and won hands down.

He then made conciliatory gestures towards the other two strong men, Pompey and Crassus. He offered Pompey his daughter Julia in marriage and promised to pass the decrees Pompey wanted for the welfare of his veterans. Oddly enough, Pompey fell in love with Julia and she with him, and for a long time he gave Caesar his full support.

As for Crassus, Caesar offered him a Consulship and a juicy province to follow. Crassus accepted the proposal with alacrity, and by the time I returned to Rome, at the end of the year, the stage was set for trouble. The Senate, still wearing blinkers, was faced with an unofficial coalition of Caesar, Pompey and Crassus, with their followings; three men who could call any tune they liked, as long as they stayed together.

12

Rome

My father and mother came to Puteoli to meet me and there were great celebrations. They had both made plans for me. My father said, 'You have shown more business sense than I ever credited you with, Marcus. Why don't you give up your legal career and work with me? You'll make far more money and I shall be glad of your help. You'd have a share of the profits in your own name and by the time you're of age to stand for the magistracies – if that's what you still want to do – you'll have all the money you'll need. Give me five years. Then you'll be twenty-seven and can campaign for quaestor with a full purse. Better still, work with me until I retire and then take over the business.'

'But you always wanted me to be an orator, Sir, and finish up in the Senate.' We were sitting in the porch of our house at Puteoli, from which there is a fine view of the bay and the shipping. He loved to watch the ships entering and leaving the busy port, which owed part of its prosperity to his enterprise and hard work. My mother sat next to him, working on an embroidery frame, and he turned to her affectionately and laid his gnarled old hand on her arm.

'It was always one of our dreams,' he said, smiling, 'that you would become a Senator, and raise our family to a higher order, but times have changed. Listen, my son. I hear a lot of gossip in the baths and my club in Rome, and I can tell you that Senators have become either the dogs'-bodies of the oligarchy or men who stay at home whenever there's a decision to be made and heads are counted. Even Cicero agrees that half of them are only interested now in keeping their fish-ponds stocked with lampreys. There's no sense of responsibility left.'

'Then responsible men are needed more than ever.'

'I suppose so. But what power will they have, when it's the gang-leaders and the Generals who make politics? Your friend Clodius is one of the worst.'

'I hear he's trying to get adopted as a pleb.'

'It's disgusting,' said my father, who always had an old-fashioned respect for the aristocracy. 'What would his ancestors think of a Claudian who gives up his red shoes to lead a gang of rowdies?'

'He's doing it to be tribune, and I suppose he wants to introduce some of the reforms he was always talking about.'

'Nonsense! From what I hear he's become nothing more than a stooge of Caesar's. Think carefully about my offer, Marcus.' He changed the subject. 'What's all this I hear about a wooden chest you've forbidden the men to open?'

'I meant to tell you about that, Father. It's an old mosaic pavement which I'd like to keep for myself. I want to see if it's possible to put down intact.'

He stared at me. 'You could have chosen something more valuable for yourself, and one that wouldn't have taken up so much expensive room. Is it worth anything?'

'It's about two hundred years old, a hunting scene, and very beautiful.' I told him how I'd had it lifted from its bed and transported. He chuckled to himself and slapped me on the back.

'There you are,' he said. 'No one else would have thought of rolling up a pavement like a scroll. All right, you can have it. When d'you want it to go to auction? We can't display it in one of the shops.'

'I'd like to keep it for the time being.' I thought it best not to mention the visit of the African owner of the mosaic at this stage. The main thing was that I could now call it my own.

My mother's plans for me were quite simple. She said it was time I got married and gave her a grandson, and had prepared a list of girls, all reputed to be well-educated, healthy and still virgins, from whom I could take my pick. She would do the rest and was sure she could get a large dowry.

I temporised, telling both my parents that I needed time to think over what they had said and would in any case have a great deal to do in Rome, including the preparation of a case which would make my name known again, both in society and in the legal world. Antonius Hybrida, under whom I had served in the Etruscan campaign, was due to return to Rome after looting and misgoverning Macedonia for two years, and I was not the only man sharpening a knife for him.

I spent the last two days of the year staying with Cicero in his villa at Tusculum. He was delighted with a piece of statuary, almost intact, which I had brought him from Utica, and even Terentia was mollified by the gold brooch I gave her. They made me very welcome, and Cicero read out to the guests at a dinner-party a letter Pompeius had written about my work. The following day, when he was showing me his garden, I told him my father wanted me to give up my legal career, at least for the time being. He was horrified.

'We need you, Marcus,' he said earnestly. 'You have a great gift for oratory and I can put many good cases in your way. We *must* control any excesses that may develop in these troublous times by prompt action in the courts. I can handle affairs in the Senate, but in the courts I need prosecutors who can be relied on. Fortunately Pompey' – he looked at me impressively – 'who is my firm friend, is a force for moderation, but I fear Caesar and Crassus may go too far.'

'Can you rely on Pompey, Sir? I thought he'd thrown in his lot with Caesar.'

'It may appear so, but he assures me that he will keep Caesar under control. Did you also know that Caesar had invited me to use my influence in support of the legislation he intends to bring in as soon as he takes office?'

'There is a rumour about that.'

He laughed harshly. 'Does he think he can stop the mouth of Cicero with bribes? I told him I was only his friend as long as he respected the Constitution.'

'He is an impatient man.'

'Then we must let him feel the reins. I've already blocked his plan to get Clodius plebeianised.'

'That's new to me,' I said. 'The last I heard was that it would go through.'

He chuckled. 'I persuaded Metellus Celer that it was essential that the whole ridiculous proposal should be ratified by the Comitia Curiata. Adoptions into the plebeian gens, as you well know, cannot in law be determined by the Head Priest acting on his own. Metellus was worried, because at first he had supported Clodius' application, but he's an honest man and he had to agree. Whatever,' he added with a smile, 'his wife, that Juno of the Palatine, may say about it.'

'So Clodia wants her brother to be a plebeian?'

'Who can tell? Her salon has become a hot-bed of intrigue this last year. She has almost as many clients in her atreum as I have.'

'But surely the Comitia will ratify the adoption, if Caesar as both Consul and Head Priest tells them to?'

He looked at me sadly, shaking his head. 'There is some sense of responsibility left, Marcus, and the Comitia Curiata is composed of solid men who will do their duty. They won't give their sanction to a low trick aimed at arming a man like Clodius with all the powers of a People's Tribune.' He smiled. 'Besides, although I did not agree to all the bribery involved, Caesar's Co-Consul, Bibulus, will exercise his veto when Cato and some of my other friends in the Senate tell him to.'

'Bibulus is a weak man.'

'Yes, he is. But he knows he was only elected Consul to keep a check of Caesar, and that he has our backing. It's only this year of Caesar's Consulate that worries me. For next year we've voted him a province where he won't be able to use his new-found military genius by any stretch of the imagination.'

*

Cicero's illusions about means of controlling Caesar's ambitions received a rude shock in January, when the new Consul began to introduce his legislation.

His first bill was a fulfilment of his promise to Pompey. He proposed to provide land for the veterans of the Asian wars. Cato opposed the decree and had it relegated to the Comitia, where it was to be vetoed by three tribunes. But the Comitia met in the Forum, not in one of the temples where the Senate was usually convened, and where entrance could be controlled. Caesar had taken the precaution of organising gangs of Pompey's veterans, who chased the tribunes off the platform and prevented Cato from speaking. When Bibulus, the Co-Consul, tried to restore order a basket of dirt was emptied over his head and his lictors manhandled.

However, Bibulus had the courage to call at once a special meeting of the Senate in his own house and spoke firmly against Caesar's bill, declaring it unconstitutional. Metellus Celer also spoke against it, but then the three strong men, Caesar, Pompey and Crassus, rose and intimidated the House to such an extent that they tamely gave in, and a land commission was set up to execute the provisions of the new law.

I have mentioned this one bill and its passage because it illustrates both the strength and ruthlessness of the so-called triumvirs and the stupidity of the Senate leaders. The bill in itself was reasonable; the Senate was opposing not the bill, but Caesar. Much of his subsequent legislation was good, but good or bad he allowed no opposition. If organised violence was needed to enforce a point, it was available.

I saw little of Clodius, who undertook a mission abroad at this time, nor his sister. My plan required that I should make my name known again before I met her.

Antonius Hybrida was back in Rome, and the case for misgovernment was brought against him, to be tried in public. I and two other advocates were chosen to prosecute. It was a beautifully documented case and his guilt was so evident that even the enormous bribes he could afford out of his ill-gotten gains would be unlikely to get him acquitted – provided the Triumvirs did not take his side. And they didn't intervene; no one had a good word to say for Antonius.

Except Cicero. He couldn't have chosen a worse case to defend or a worse time to do it, but he was faithful to the old concept of honour, which did not allow one to let a former colleague go undefended. He and Antonius had been Co-Consuls at the time of the Catilinarian plot, and however much he despised Antonius he could not desert him at his trial.

He begged me to drop the case, but I was adamant, and this led to a partial estrangement that lasted three years. It was too good a chance for me to miss. I *knew* Antonius, I could talk about his failings from personal experience, and this is always of the greatest value to an advocate. I had persuaded my colleagues to let me speak last and had prepared my speech very carefully. I delivered it without notes.

I began quietly, telling the court that I'd had the unusual honour of having attended Antonius on the eve of a crucial battle, so that I could testify to his valour. He told us, I said, that he would personally lead his troops against Catiline's seasoned veterans and rout them to a man. But when morning came – how unfortunate! Antonius explained that he had a slight touch of gout, and would not be able to take the field. But was it gout? No one could doubt the General's courage, because he had taken not one but several women into his tent that night – and I described them one by one, in colourful terms – and perhaps it had been too much for even his iron constitution. Whatever the cause, I explained with a straight face, I could testify that when the sun rose Antonius could scarcely stand. (I paused while the laughter died down.)

Then I went on, with a change of style and tone in Cicero's manner, to tell what really happened at the battle of Pistoia, giving unstinted praise to Petreius and his legionaries and modestly passing over my own share of the fight – while still making it clear that I was in the thick of it from start to finish. I put in a piece here about the outstanding virtues of the Roman soldier, demonstrated recently in our campaigns in the East and Spain, when the Republic had been fortunate in having such brilliant commanders in the field. (This, of course, was a bouquet for Pompey and Caesar, and there were cheers from their clients and debtors.)

So to Antonius' pro-Consulate in Macedonia. I said my colleagues had brought out in their speeches the factual evidence of his misgovernment, the harsh suppression of liberties in a friendly province, the weight of unfair taxation which filled his pockets, the bribery and extortions, the falsification of his returns to the Treasury. But Antonius hadn't been content with his plunder. He had dared, without the authority of the Senate, to invade the territory of neighbouring tribes, intent on stripping them of their wealth. And what had happened? He had been ignominiously defeated, and his camp overrun by the enemy.

I pictured Antonius in his banqueting tent, drunk, with the women trying to tell him the enemy was attacking the camp. They shout in his ear, but he thinks they are asking him to make love to them again and – always the gallant gentleman –

attempts to oblige them, with signal lack of success. Asleep in their arms, they carry him away, while his centurions form their legionaries in ranks to fight a desperate retreat.

It was a good piece of vituperation, and has been much quoted. When I sat down I knew I had done what I'd set out to do. No one was going to take me too lightly in future.

Cicero spoke for the defence. He paid me sad compliments on my speech and did what he could to save his client. He is incapable of making a bad speech, but it fell flat, and Antonius was convicted and later stripped of his possessions and condemned to death. The sentence was, as usual, commuted to one of exile.

It was when I was celebrating my triumph that night, with a crowd of friends and well-wishers, that someone brought the news that Clodia's husband, Metellus Celer, was dead.

13

The Death of Metellus

There was a grand patrician funeral, and I caught glimpses of Clodius, wearing a *lugubrium* like the other mourners but not looking in the least as if he had anything to mourn, and Cicero, also in black, weeping for a man who had never been a close friend but who had fought for the same traditional usages and, like Cicero, had lost. Clodia's slight figure was hidden under the black veils of mourning. The procession passed slowly down the Via Sacra and out through the gate on the Appian Way. The coffin was to be held in the family shrine until the tomb was ready for it.

After a decent interval I put on my own mourning robe and called on Clodia. She sent her slaves away and made me sit down. We looked at each other like two gladiators in the arena, wary of the first move. She had defied convention and was wearing make-up and her fair hair dressed, and even the shapeless black gown looked elegant.

'I only met Quintus Metellus once,' I said, after the ritual condolences. 'Was he as good to you as you deserved?'

'Keep your sarcasm for the courts, Marcus. He was a good husband, according to his lights. But stupid, with me.'

'Perhaps he ought to have beaten you.'

'He did, once. And then apologised, so it didn't work.'

'That's one mistake I would never make.'

She laughed gaily. 'Oh Marcus, you're presuming a little, aren't you?'

'Presumption is part of an orator's stock in trade.'

'You made a good speech against that lout Hybrida. I liked the way you neatly insinuated compliments to Caesar and Pompey. Very diplomatic. Unlike poor Cicero.'

'He did all he could.'

'Of course he did,' she said impatiently. 'But it was that silly remark he made about leaders who don't carry the mandate of the people and pass laws without proper sanction. Why did he have to stick his neck out?'

I was startled, because that passage had escaped me. Cicero had made several digressions during his speech and my mind had wandered. I was too busy, I suppose, thinking how good mine had been. 'Yes,' I said, 'that was unwise.' I thought for a moment. 'Was *that* why Caesar at once began the moves to get Clodius adopted?'

'But of course,' she said. 'Caesar's afraid of Cicero's influence, and he couldn't let even that remark go unpunished.'

'But what's Clodius' adoption got to do with punishing Cicero?'

'You'll see, and so will Cicero, although I've warned him to keep out of the way.'

'So you've talked to him recently?'

'Yes. He came to offer condolences and stayed on talking politics, but looking very stern and suspicious. I'm sure he thinks I poisoned Quintus,' she added calmly. 'But I didn't. In fact I did all I could for him as soon as he got those awful pains, and stayed by him till the end, and it was very unpleasant,' she added, wrinkling her little nose, 'because he couldn't stop vomiting.'

'A lot of people in the Forum are saying you poisoned him, Claudia.'

'What can you expect? It's quite true, I think, that he *was* poisoned, but when the cooks were tortured they gave nothing away.' She looked down, and said slowly, 'Perhaps they were more afraid of the man who did it than of the rack.'

'And you think it was Clodius?'

She was very serious now. 'I don't know, Marcus. I scarcely recognise him these days. He's unhappy with his wife, of course, and obsessed with this foolish feud with Cicero. But I

85

know adoption into the plebs is part of his plan, and Quintus stood in his way. And he was always jealous of him, naturally.'

'More than of your other lovers?' I asked, bitterly.

'Yes, Marcus. More.' She frowned. 'And if we meet again you'd better remember that I will not have jealousy. It's ugly, and I don't like ugly things.'

'I'm not jealous. Besides, if you take me as a lover there won't *be* any others, so the question won't arise.'

That made her laugh, as I'd hoped, and then she looked at me rather sadly. 'We shall see, Marcus. Come back soon. I never thought I could be lonely, but I am now. The family disapproves and everyone else either suspects me of murder or fawns on me. I was really glad to see Cicero, because at least he had no ulterior motive. He's a kind man and I admire him.'

'So do I, but he won't have much time for me now. You said you warned him to be careful. Did he pay any attention?'

'No. He did his "Father of the Country" act, and I was just an ignorant woman interfering with politics. He'll never learn sense.' She looked up at me. 'I wonder if you will. You can do very well for yourself, if you toady to Caesar, like the rest.'

'I know that. But I don't toady to people.'

'You will, when the time comes, and I shan't blame you. Caesar is a most persuasive man.'

I stopped myself from asking if she'd been the subject of his persuasive powers; she'd said she couldn't stand jealousy. But I put another idea into her head. 'Of course it's Caesar who stands to gain most from Metellus' death.'

She looked startled, and I explained. 'You know he made the Senate reverse last year's decision about his next posting, and they've had to give him Southern Gaul?'

'Of course I know that.'

'Well, what he wants now, apparently, is Transalpine Gaul as well.' This was the province which Quintus Metellus would have governed if he had not died. He was preparing to leave at the time of his sudden death.

She stared at me. 'Who told you that?'

'Dolabella. He had it from Vatinius, who is preparing the decree. Caesar will have both Gallic provinces next year and Illyria, with all the troops he needs and full powers to campaign and found new colonies. He'll conquer the rest of Western Europe before he's finished.'

'So that's what he meant,' she whispered, looking at the floor. 'Caesar?'

'No, Quintus. He told me Caesar had tried to get him to ex-

86

change his province for Cilicia, but he'd refused. He said he'd put at least that bridle on the man's ambitions.' She shivered. 'I suppose it could have been Caesar who killed him, not Clodius.'

'Possibly. But it's not something I would speculate about in public.'

'No. Stay alive, Marcus.' She gave me a pale smile. 'I need friends.'

'Just friends.'

'I've got to be careful, or the family won't help me to get back what I owned before my marriage. The Caecilii Metelli are already quarrelling with Appius about the will.' She put her hand on my arm. 'Go now, Marcus. You've been with me quite long enough for the spies to start scribbling their reports.'

'I'll come back,' I said. 'On a warm night, when there's a full moon.'

'Is it only two years? You look much older. You were so young, Marcus, and appealing.' She looked at me sadly as I rose and took her hand. 'We were alone then, with just the sea and the sand and no one else at all. In Rome it's different; you're never alone, and nothing is simple.'

'We'll be alone again,' I said soberly. If I hadn't left then I should have made a fool of myself, and I'd sworn never to do that again.

*

Caesar got Pompey to assure the Comitia Curiata that the adoption of Clodius was perfectly in order, and the ceremony took place without any further opposition from the Senate. Cicero retired in disgust to his villa at Anzio, to write a book about geography.

Clodius came up to me in the Senian Baths and greeted me cordially, and we dined together afterwards. 'That was smart,' he said, 'the way you defeated Cicero at the trial of Antonius. I knew you wouldn't be able to stand his arrogance for long. You were wise, too, because Cicero's on the downward slope at last. Wait till you see how I'll chasten him next year, when I'm Tribune.'

'You're sure you'll get elected?'

'Of course I am. Crassus and Caesar will back me up. What's more, I'm getting together a band of fellows trained to break up political meetings quickly and efficiently. The layabouts I used to employ were too dumb to act except as a body, but these men are taught to operate in two's and three's, just quietly roughing up the people we don't like on their way to the platform. The training has to be done in secret, of course, because of the law against political clubs, but next year I'll get that changed, too.'

'But what's your object – I mean, ultimately?'

'Power, of course. I'm not going to tell you my plans in detail, but I'll say this. In these days a People's Tribune who can get the people to follow him has more power than any Senator, or any general, for that matter. D'you know how many families qualify for the cheap corn ration, here in Rome?'

'No idea.'

'Three hundred thousand. Just think of it. Three hundred thousand heads of families without work, living on the State to a large extent. Thousands of them are lusty lads from the country who've been squeezed out by the slave farms, able-bodied men with nothing to lose. All that's needed is to organise them, and then we can dictate to the Senate, the Assembly, the College of Priests and the Triumvirs. I tell you, Marcus, by this time next year you'll be begging me for a job, so why not join me now? You've got a tongue, man, and that's more use to me than any number of swords. There's a lot of organisation to be done, too, and I'm not too good at that. I'm too impatient.'

'Thanks, Clodius, but it's not for me. I'm just re-starting my career, as you know.'

'Oh well, you'll change your mind. What are you aiming at, the Senate?'

'Yes, of course, in half a dozen years' time.'

'But that's just what I'm telling you. Long before you get your purple stripe the House will be no more than a cypher.'

'It's practically that already, but it won't necessarily stay that way. Next year Caesar will be in Gaul.'

He gave a sinister sort of laugh. 'That's right. General Caesar will be in Gaul, and Clodius the Tribune in Rome.'

I asked him if he was going to spend the summer in Baiae, but he shook his head. 'No, I'll be campaigning. Anyway, I wouldn't repeat my experience of last summer. I don't want to spend my time in Clodia's villa watching her moon around with that love-lorn fool Catullus.'

'He's getting quite a reputation as a poet. Everybody's talking about his recitations.'

'It's his reputation as Clodia's lover that makes me sick. Whenever Quintus Metellus went out of the door Catullus came in through the window. But she's dropped him now, and good riddance.'

'With Metellus out of the way he'll be able to come in at the door.'

'He'll be scared of her, I think. She's a dangerous woman, Marcus. I know she took a fancy to you before you went to Africa, but keep out of her way.' He looked at me sideways. 'She poisoned Quintus, you know.'

'So I've heard people say. But did she?'

'Who else?' he said, sniggering.

14

Clodia's Garden

Dolabella invited me to spend a few days at his family villa in the Alban Hills. He said, 'Calvus will be there, and Catullus and Helvius Cinna and several others you'll know. We all meet quite often now to discuss literature, pull the politicians to pieces, write epigrams about them and poems to each other and so on. And of course we get the girls in and have fun. Do join us; everyone wants to see you and hear about Africa.' There were several other people around us in the tavern and he lowered his voice conspiratorially. 'It's the only way you can let off steam, these days.'

His parents were away at Gaeta for the summer and we had the house to ourselves. It was a pleasant place, spread over the top of a hill, with a view across the plain towards Rome and a garden with shady pergolas where we ate when it wasn't too hot. Down the hillside by the slave quarters, were stables for twenty riding horses, and some of us rode through the vine-yards and olive-groves every morning before going to the baths. They were interesting men, all young, and the conversation was effervescent and stimulating. I enjoyed myself, and tried again to write poetry, but without much success. To get my own back for the jeers of Calvus and – what was worse – the kind encouragement of Catullus, I exercised my wit against the efforts of the other amateurs. I've always been better as a critic than as a creator.

But one part of the evening's entertainment was hard to bear, and that was when Catullus recited poems about his 'Lesbia'. Everyone knew that this was Clodia, and he seemed to think he was still her lover. Perhaps, I thought, Clodius was wrong in saying she's dropped him. To judge from his verses you would have thought she scarcely allowed him out of her sight. It was all 'Lesbia, let us live and love', and 'Lesbia, give me another hundred thousand kisses', and it made me sick. He had even introduced a new word for 'kiss', taken from his cold province in the North, and every poet in Rome was now scribbling *'basia'* instead of 'oscula'. When Catullus wasn't raving about Clodia his poems were acceptable, because he had a superlative sense of rhythm and the use of words, and I must admit everyone else was enchanted with them. (Jealousy, I told myself; she said jealousy was ugly. Well so it was. Once I had ousted Catullus and every other rival from her bed I could think of them as friends.)

He had greeted me with delight, telling the others that it was I who had encouraged him when he first came south, and that he'd gone to hear me prosecute Hybrida and wept tears of delight when, as he said, I had humbled the tyrant. It was orators like Calvus and me, he cried, who could make Caesar feel the righteous scorn of the men he oppressed. Calvus, who was an ambitious politician as well as a poet, caught my eye and smiled warily. Neither of us wanted a dagger in the back.

Catullus sought me out alone and told me the story of his love for Clodia, how for a long time she would only let him hold her hand but that in the end, overcome by passion, she had yielded to him, and had told him afterwards that if only she hadn't been married already he could have been her husband. So – and this explained Clodius' words – as soon as Catullus heard of the Pro-Consul's death he had thought fit to keep away until it would be proper to approach Clodia as a suitor for her hand in marriage. He had explained his action in a letter smuggled in to her by the slave-girl who had acted as an intermediary previously.

I asked if she'd replied, and he said no. But he knew that during this period when she couldn't be seen in public she spent much of the day in her garden on the bank of the Tiber.

'So I took a boat,' explained Catullus, 'and rowed past, and there she was, reading in a summer-house above the bank, with her maids around her. It was in the evening, and the columns of the porch were glowing like mellow gold, and throwing long mauve shadows on the grass. I rested my oars and sang to her, and she let the scroll fall in her lap and raised her hand, sadly, to greet me. She could do no more, in decency, before her slaves, but I knew she was burning for my caresses.'

I listened to this, and much more, with mixed feelings, and that evening, when the others were laughing at some of the scurrilous epigrams Catullus had written about Caesar and his lovers of both sexes – and very funny they were, I'll admit, funny and filthy – I was plotting. I knew the garden well from the water. It had smooth lawns sloping down to the steep bank above the river. Besides the summer-house you could catch a glimpse, between the tall cypresses and groves of myrtle, of a pavilion lying back from the stream among the trees. It looked quite large.

The following week I went to call on Clodia, carrying a scroll in my hand to suggest a business visit. I was shown through the peristylium to the exhedra, where I had first met her. She was alone, and looking bored.

'Gossip, Marcus,' she cried gaily. 'Tell me all the gossip. I've seen no one under fifty since you were here before.'

'The main item of news at the baths is that you've got your property in your own hands again.'

'Yes. Herrenius has arranged it.'

'Then you can behave as you like?'

'Not yet. Appius insists that I mustn't go to Baiae this season, and stay house-bound for another month. It's too ridiculous, but that's my family for you. If I don't agree he can make trouble, because I still haven't got the deeds back. Appius is making Herrenius hold on to them until I've done what he wants.'

'But it's much too hot for you to sleep in the middle of town through the summer. Isn't there anywhere else where you can be more comfortable at night?'

She looked at me mockingly. 'You're very solicitous, my friend. What's in your ingenious mind?' She pulled me towards a couch and we sat down. I turned and took her gently into my arms and kissed her, and suddenly her cool arms were round my neck. 'It's been too long,' she whispered.

'Can you trust your personal slaves?'

'I think so. It's the door-keeper who reports back to Appius.'

'Then say it's too hot here at night and take a few maids with you and sleep in your pavilion near the Tiber. And I'll come.'

'Oh Marcus, it's no good. The door-keeper will be sent to guard the gate into the garden.'

'Let him. I'll get in from the river bank.'

Her eyes sparkled. 'I'll have to bribe the guards who patrol the garden at night. When will you come?'

'Tonight, as soon as it's dark.' I picked up the scroll.

'Yes, yes, you must go now.' Her face was flushed and radiant, and I kissed her hand and went away.

*

There was no moon when I landed under the river bank and dismissed the boatman, who took my money and promised to be back at dawn. I climbed up the steep slope and heard the snarl of an angry dog, and then a man's voice calming it. By the time I stood on the lawn near the summer-house the guard was moving away, and did not turn round. I made my way between the dark shapes of the trees towards the colonnade of the pavilion, and saw something white shimmering under the arches. It was a girl, who came and took my hand and led me without speaking through the open door and into a court filled with the scent of lemon blossom and the sound of dripping water. On the other side was a heavy door, which she opened quietly and then stood back. Inside were dim lights, a couch – and Clodia.

*

During those first two weeks we were insatiable. We moaned with despair when we parted in the grey light of dawn, and every night when I had scrambled up the bank she was under the trees, and we ran silent and avid to the pavilion. She was beautiful and tender, passionate and kind, all that a man could ever wish, and I was in love for the first time in my life and almost lost in an enchanted labyrinth.

But not quite. I knew the flimsy net of desire wouldn't hold Clodia for long; a time would come when she would break through the mesh and exult in her freedom, and that thought made me groan aloud and clench my teeth. I had to find other bonds to hold her.

I had planned my conquest in Utica, sweating under the African sun, and now I sent to Puteoli for the cedar chest that contained the mosaic. When it arrived I hired a bigger boat, brought tackle, bribed the guards to haul the box up the bank and into the pavilion, and made Clodia wait in another room for nearly an hour until I had the thing rolled out of the chest, unstitched and spread out on the floor of her bedroom, with lamps all round it. I distributed silver to the guards, made them carry away the chest and finally told one of Clodia's maids to bring hot water and cloths. Then I went to call her. She was tapping her foot, and looked at me coldly. 'I'm not used to being kept waiting, Marcus,' she said, frowning.

Without a word I took her by the hand and led her into the other room. She stared in bewilderment at the linen covering on the mosaic.

'But what is it? I can't see. Take the cloth away.'

'This is something we're going to do ourselves.' I dipped a rag in the water and began to soak the linen in one corner and peel it back.

'The girls can do that in the morning. I want you, in that bed.'

'Not until I've finished,' I said calmly, 'and if you're not going to help me it'll take twice as long.'

She didn't stir. 'You're making very free with my bedroom,' she said tartly, and added contemptuously, 'I suppose it's a mosaic.' But I could sense that she was curious.

'Look.' I had stripped back the three cloth coverings from the corner and was soaking the papyrus, which was more difficult to detach. But the water made it translucent, and the colours underneath began to gleam through. She gave a cry and knelt beside it with her hair falling over her face and watched, fascinated, as the papyrus came away and the tesserae appeared, streaked with the remains of the glue but glowing like jewels.

She threw her arms round my neck and bit my ear. Then she ran to the crock of water, dipped a cloth and was just about to slop it down on the mosaic when I snatched it out of her hand. 'If you do that,' I said severely, 'you'll soak the base and the tesserae will break away. If you want to help, use a little water at a time, and just clean off the surface of the stones. Keep rinsing the cloth. I'll strip off the linen.'

She had of course never done anything like this in her life, and I had to wring out the cloths for her, but she applied herself to the task, murmuring with delight as the gold and silver and the brilliant colours of the stones shone clear. After half an hour she sat back on her heels and looked up at me appealingly. 'I don't want to rush this. It's unbelievably beautiful, Marcus, and I want the fun of seeing it appear a little at a time. Let's leave it for tonight.'

'You'll tell the maids to finish it, and I told you, this is something we must do ourselves.'

'I swear by the gods I won't let them touch it.'

'You don't believe in them anyway. Swear by our love.'

So she did, with her mouth on my mouth, and I scooped her up and carried her to the bed.

*

It took us three nights before we had uncovered and polished the whole pavement, and when day broke I stood looking down at the mosaic, while Clodia watched. It was true, what she had said. The thing was even more beautiful than I had remembered. In the grey light the colours shone as if they had a life of their own, and the scene of the lion and its hunters was perfect in every detail. I could see no flaw. Moving it was going to be another problem, but I had a plan for that, too.

At the back of my mind – although it seemed more in the pit of my stomach – was the knowledge that if I auctioned the mosaic it would bring in a magnificent sum, enough to buy a house. The businessman in me couldn't forget that fact, while the lover argued speciously that I was only losing what I'd spent, which wasn't a great sum – although I still had to keep my promise and get the old descendant of the shophet to Rome. The truth remained that I could have sold the mosaic and hadn't, because I'd wanted to give Clodia something that no one else could give. Something she could never look at without thinking of me.

Clodia could always read my thoughts. She rose from the bed, and twitching a blanket round her naked body came across to the mosaic and bent down to stroke it, purring like a little cat. Then she straightened up and said, 'You don't have to buy me, Marcus.'

'I'm not trying to – ?'

'Oh yes, you are. But there's no need. I'll pay you for it, and be just as grateful. You know I'm rich.'

'No,' I cried in anguish, 'it's yours. Whatever happens, even if you send me away tomorrow, I shan't want it back or accept money for it.' I was almost in tears, horrified that I had been tempted to renege on a gesture that meant so much to me.

She put her arms round me and held me close. 'All right, then,' she said, laughing. 'I'm content to be bought.'

I kissed her and said eagerly, 'I've thought what you can do with it.'

She stroked my hair. 'Tell me.'

'Have it set into the wall of your bedroom in the house on the Palatine.'

'Too many people would see it.'

I pushed her away angrily.

'Men?' she said, laughing. 'My dear Marcus, I receive half the women in society in my bedroom in normal times. No, I want it here in the garden. I'm going to build a little house around it, among the trees, with a marble dome and columns and a fountain to keep the surface covered with a thin film of running water, so that the colours will never be dull. I've made a sketch, and I'll show you tonight. It'll be hidden among the cypresses and no one shall see it, except you and me.'

I was going to protest, because I'd wanted it to be near her bed, as a perpetual reminder. But no, my gesture had to be absolute, so I said her idea was better.

We swore we'd love each other, and no one else, and I went down through the garden with my heart singing in triumph. But what were those words of Catullus? That lovers' promises were playthings of the wind?

15

Summer in Rome

During that month when Clodia was confined to her house and the garden by the Tiber, my parents were as usual spending the summer in our house at Interamna, where I was born, but my father came to Rome on business and was at once told by the slaves that I hadn't slept in my bed for weeks. He gave me a penetrating look from under his bushy eyebrows and smiled.

'If you were spending all your nights in debauchery you wouldn't look as healthy as you do. What is it? Have you got a nice quiet girl somewhere?'

'Very quiet, so far.'

'Well, I won't interfere, but try to put in more appearances at home when your mother comes back in the autumn, or she'll get worried. She's set on getting you married, and once it's known that you've got a steady mistress it doesn't help. Now what about my offer of a partnership in the business? You mustn't keep putting me off, you know.'

'Cicero feels very strongly that I shouldn't give up my career as an orator at this time, Father.'

He chuckled. 'I think he regretted that advice when you opposed him at Hybrida's trial. You said you'd make your name in that case and so you have. All my friends in Interamna heard of it and congratulated me, and I'm very proud of you, son. But all the same, I should be sorry to see you lose Cicero's friendship. He's been a good friend to me, not least when he took on your tutelage in oratory, and don't imagine his career is finished because he's out of favour with Caesar. We may both be glad of his patronage as time goes on.'

'I'll do my best to please him when he gets back from Anzio. But as regards the business, Father, I really am keen to go on with my career and not lose the ground I have gained. Perhaps I could relieve you at least of your trips to Puteoli?' Clodia would be spending next spring and summer in Baiae, so there was an ulterior motive to my suggestion.

My father considered. 'I confess I'm beginning to find the journey fatiguing, and I'd be glad to think you were keeping an eye on the work at the port.' He looked up. 'You'd be near your aristocratic friends.'

'There are a lot of influential people who spend the summer in Baiae, and I need good contacts for my legal work.'

'Yes, I suppose you do. But be careful, Marcus. Patricians are useful as patrons, and I've done a lot of work for them and made good profits, but I would hesitate to call any one of them my friend. Keep your relations on a business basis and show the respect due to their blood, and you won't go far wrong. Try to get on terms of intimacy with them and you're in trouble. Remember they will never hesitate to double-cross a member of a lower order. They think it's their right.'

We were sitting in the big office that opened off the atreum in our house, and I looked across the table at his lined, well-loved face. 'They're not all like that, Father.'

'Most are. Just don't trust them. Your best clients will always be men of our class, or those whose families have been ennobled by holding the Consulship.'

He always gave me sound advice, and almost always I disregarded it.

*

That night when I met Clodia she had a surprise for me. Her ideas always had to be put into execution at once, and we had no sooner agreed on the design of the building which was to house the mosaic than she'd summoned the best architect in Rome and told him what she wanted. But first, she had to be sure that the design was good, and she showed me a charming model, a foot high, of a small temple, circular and surrounded by a colonnade. The dome could be lifted off to show the inside, which would be just big enough to allow two people, hand in hand, to walk round the mosaic. Thin panels of alabaster allowed light to filter through. On the floor was a picture of the mosaic covered with a sheet of mica to imitate the water flowing over its face from the wounds of a stag shot by a marble Diana. I was delighted, but Clodia, who had a critical eye for design, was doubtful about the proportions, and we spent some time peering at the model from all angles before she was satisfied.

96

Later, before we slept, she said, 'Don't leave me tomorrow morning. Cyrus will be coming later to discuss the building and I'd like you to be there. We'd better explain that you're giving me lessons, but he won't gossip anyway. I've known him all my life.'

So we slept late, and when Cyrus was announced we were sitting very decorously in the garden, with book scrolls all round us. I had met Cyrus before, because he had built a number of Cicero's villas and rest-houses. (There was scarcely a point on the road between Rome and Pompeii without some dwelling of Cicero's within a few miles. He liked to travel slowly, and in comfort.)

Cyrus was a man of fifty-five, staid and impressive, and obviously Clodia's devoted slave. He first went into the pavilion to see the mosaic and I waited eagerly to see his reaction. There was no doubt about it. He came into the garden talking animatedly to Clodia, and begging her to say where she had found it. But she said it was her secret, and he wasn't to tell anybody that he had even seen the mosaic. He patted her shoulder affectionately and swore he would observe her secret, and then inspected the place we had chosen. He gave his approval, and set his clerks to plotting the watercourse and pegging out the site. While they were working I heard Clodia asking about the apartment block which Cyrus was designing for her brother. It was the first I'd heard of it. By a sort of unspoken agreement we had never mentioned Clodius.

It was when we were sitting in the summer-house above the river, after Cyrus and his attendants had left, that I told Clodia about my father's discovery that I was spending my nights away from home, and his remark about the 'nice quiet girl'. She was delighted. 'Nobody's ever called me that before,' she said. 'I'd like to meet your father. Why don't you ever talk about your mother?'

'But what is there to say? She's everything mothers are supposed to be, worshipping my father, me and the household gods, in that order.'

'I see,' said Clodia sarcastically, 'just doing what's natural and proper, in a men's world.'

'What else should she do?' I asked, puzzled. 'She's very strict with the slaves, runs our houses well, and spends most of her time at the loom, planning how to get me married and have grandchildren.'

'Oh, we can't have that, Marcus. Not yet.'

'That's what I think.' Something caught my eye in the river

7   97

below. It was a little raft, floating down the stream, and covered with flowers. 'What's that?'

She faced me a little too boldly. 'Oh, there's someone who floats lilies downstream every day about this time. I suppose it's for the river god.'

'Or is it Catullus?'

'Oh Marcus. we've never talked about him before. Why d'you have to do it now?'

'We've got to, some time. He thinks you're going to marry him.'

She laughed, half sadly. 'How like him!' She flashed me a warning look. 'Don't let's go on with this.'

'Clodia, we must. He really thinks you promised to marry him if Metellus died.'

'I did nothing of the kind. He twists everything I say.'

'So you did say something?'

'Marcus, I won't be bullied. I may have made some silly remark that I'd rather be married to a poet than a politician – when I was feeling bored to tears with being a Consul's wife and having to give all those dreadful receptions.'

'And, of course, you were feeling sorry for *poor* Catullus, looking *so* unhappy,' I said bitingly.

'All right, I was. And now that's enough. Unless you want a quarrel.'

'Oh my love, I don't ever want to quarrel with you, and it's not that I'm jealous,' I added, lying. 'It's just that I don't want other people to pester you with their attentions and make you unhappy.'

'He doesn't make me unhappy,' she said sullenly. 'I'm very fond of him, and he writes such beautiful poems for me – not like yours.'

'At least I don't read them aloud in every tavern in the Subura.'

'No one would listen if you did.'

We were both on our feet now. There was a long moment of silence, and suddenly she held out her hand and we fell into each other's arms, and later went in among the trees and made love, and I swore that I wouldn't mention Catullus' name again.

It was only afterwards that I realised that *she* hadn't sworn anything, and that as far as her relations with the poet were concerned I had got nowhere.

*

The following night, flushed with excitement, she pulled a scroll from the drawer in her dressing-table and handed it to me. It was a contract for the lease of one of the best flats in the house that Cyrus was building for Clodius. I stared at it in amazement. It was made out in my name, and a deposit had already been paid. 'Don't you see?' she cried impatiently. 'It's going to be almost next door to my house, so you'll be near me all the winter, and free of your family, and I'll help you pay the rent.'

That I wouldn't allow, because I knew it would be a fatal step to put myself in her debt, but the idea was very attractive and I could just afford the rent. So it was arranged.

The block was in the most luxurious part of the Palatine Hill and the flats were modern, with water supplied from a tank on the roof, small private baths and large balconies – very much gentlemen's residences and far from the smells and noise of the other parts of the city, where it was becoming impossible to sleep at night for the constant racket of wagon-wheels on the stone sets.

There were bitter arguments with my parents, but in the end my father took my side and raised my allowance. I was working hard for him in Puteoli and he was becoming dependent on my help in the counting-house in Rome. I pointed out, of course, that by living among my society friends I should pick up better cases, and so in fact it proved. For the time being I was well off.

When Clodia took up her position in society again I was often seen with her, and if people guessed that I slept with her they assumed that I was a casual lover, one of many. But for the next year, at least, they were wrong.

*

I am going ahead too fast, because it was during that same year of our meetings in the quiet garden by the Tiber that the storm-clouds were beginning to gather around Cicero's head, and what happened to him is essential to my story.

Clodius campaigned hard, using his gang of toughs skilfully, and in October was elected Tribune of the People. Cicero had returned to Rome and appeared oblivious of any danger. Tiro, the secretary, told me that his master was confident that Pompey wouldn't allow him to be persecuted, and it was clear that Clodius was at pains to lull Cicero into a feeling of security. He told his friends that it was Terentia, not Cicero, who was the originator of the quarrel, made respectful references to him in public speeches, praising him for his attitude towards oppression and the restoration of democratic rights, and spoke as if Caesar were his enemy, instead of his secret backer. But I didn't forget what Clodius had told me of his plans, and asked his sister if he had changed his mind.

She shook her pretty head, looking unusually serious. 'He hasn't confided in me, but I know how his mind works. If you feel under an obligation to Cicero – and I suppose you still are, as his former pupil – you ought to warn him to stay away from Rome when the new year begins. His best course would be to go abroad.'

'But why?'

'I don't know, but please don't get involved, Marcus. I hear a lot of gossip, now that the women can call on me socially again, and I'm worried about what my wild brother is up to.'

I attended one of Cicero's levées, which he was still holding in great style in his new house, and felt his eye light on me coldly. But his greeting was friendly, and when I asked to come at some other time, when we could speak alone, he told me to arrange an appointment with Tiro. I was no longer a welcome guest at his table.

A week later he received me in the great library designed for Crassus when the house was built, and after giving me the expected lecture on the impropriety of having opposed him over Hybrida, made kindly inquiries about my work. When an opportunity occurred I told him that Clodia, who held him in high regard, had asked me to bring him a message, which I gave.

'I'm sure,' he said, patronisingly, 'that the Lady Clodia means well. But if, as it seems you are in her confidence' – his eye settled on me accusingly – 'pray tell her that I have the assurance of Pompey, no less, that he will not allow that brother of hers to kick over the traces. In spite of appearances, my dear Marcus, there are still forces for order in Rome, and while Pompey and my friends in the Senate have a say in the matter the "Father of his Country" will not be at the mercy of a gang of hooligans.'

'And you think, Sir, that they will continue to have a say?'

For a moment I thought he was going to chide me for impertinence, but he said mildly, 'I know what you're thinking, Marcus – that Pompey is too lazy to lift a finger and the Senate is intimidated by Caesar. But I can assure you that though they may shirk their responsibilities in minor matters, when it comes to affairs of national – I repeat, national importance, my friends will let their opinions be felt in no uncertain way.'

But I knew Cicero well, and beneath all the bombast and confident manner, he was a very worried man, and he had good reason.

16

Clodius in Power

I had underestimated Clodius. It was partly his effeminate features – Cicero always referred to him as 'that little beauty' – the petulant mouth under the thin patrician nose and that sniggering, high-pitched laugh. His speeches, to a trained orator, lacked all cohesion and style, and were nothing but the outpouring of whatever came into his head. I had listened to some of his orations with amusement, and failed to be warned by the way the crowd reacted. There was no doubt that he could move them. I had decided that however ingenious his plans to become a great popular leader, he was too scatter-brained to go far.

After his posting to Sicily as quaestor, while I was in Africa, Clodius had divorced his first wife and re-married. His bride was Fulvia – not Cicero's former spy but a woman from a rich patrician family, ambitious and forceful, and her active support and great wealth helped him. He had started to speculate in property – that block of flats on the Palatine was an example – and was beginning to make money of his own. (Later he extended this business with a protection racket, using his gangs to intimidate tenants, and made himself a very rich man.) I never knew whether it was under pressure from Fulvia or Caesar, or some unsuspected strength of his own mind that made him, after his election to the tribuneship, leave the baths early to get back to his desk, but he certainly worked hard in preparing his programme of legislation.

The first law he introduced, in January 696,* consolidated his popularity with the plebeians, and the Senate, in spite of the enormous cost to the Treasury, was too weak to prevent it being passed. At this time, as he had told me earlier, there were over three hundred thousand applicants for the cheap corn ration of seventy pounds a month. As the poor and unemployed

* 58 BC

live on wheat porridge and bread the concession that had allowed them to buy the ration at less than half the controlled price was an essential part of the policy of keeping them quiet. Clodius simply went one step further. His bill abolished the charge altogether, and allowed the men on the dole to get their corn free. The cost to the Treasury, in the first year, was nearly as great as the whole of the credit balance left over from Pompey's conquests in Asia. In subsequent years the burden of the free corn ration became intolerable.

Then, exactly as Clodius had told me he would, he repealed the law which forbade political associations and unofficial gatherings, and immediately began to organise openly clubs of his own followers.

Finally – and this was the only one of his acts that appealed to the equestrian class as well as to the plebs – he repealed the laws which had allowed patrician magistrates to hold up any piece of legislation by declaring that the omens were unfavourable.

When this first dollop of legislation had been digested, in February, he introduced another bill, with a special gilding to please the Consuls. They would be offered the provinces each wanted for the following year, but on two conditions; the first was that Cato, who had been a thorn in the flesh of the unofficial triumvirs, should be sent with an army to annexe Cyprus, which would keep him fully occupied and out of Rome for a couple of years; the second, that anyone who had put Roman citizens to death without proper trial should be denied fire and water. This meant, in effect, a sentence of death or exile.

It was well thought out. The Consuls, Piso and Gabinius, would do anything to get the bill passed, for selfish reasons. The people were still shouting in the streets for their benefactor Clodius, who had given them free corn; when a tribune, no friend of Clodius, tried to interpose his veto he was thrust off the stand before he could speak.

Everyone knew that the second of the two conditions was aimed specifically at Cicero, and at last the Senate rallied to his support. But they were powerless to prevent a Tribune's bill from becoming law, and all they could do was protest, and when this was of no avail, the whole Senate went into public mourning. Gabinius promptly issued an edict which forced them to dress normally.

Cicero was caught completely unawares. He still believed, pathetically, in Pompey, who turned his back. The rest of his

friends did their best, and when █
to the people by going from █
mourning robe and with his hair █
of us accompanied him. But █
Clodius' gangs were, all too well. █
and Cicero began to speak he was █
enough to make an impression. St█
and from different parts of the cro█
and heckle him.

He appealed to the Consuls in vain. █
petitioner on Pompey, who left by the ba█
the other hand, showed his generosity by off█
on his staff in Gaul but – still unable to believ█
pening to him – he refused it.

All this saddened and angered me, and altho█
begged me to stay at home I went with Cicero everyw█
thus, for the first time, made the acquaintance of Milo, █
has a role to play in my story.

We were returning from a meeting that had been broken up
in the usual way, and most of Cicero's supporters had gone
home. We came into a street where there was a throng of people
round a fish-barrow, and Cicero saw it as an opportunity not to
be missed. He began to speak to the crowd, and was making
some headway when two men appeared on the balcony of a
tenement building that overlooked the scene and emptied slop-
pails, stinking of urine, on the faces below. They were jeering
and shouting at Cicero. Then something remarkable occurred.

A great bearded face emerged behind the two gangsters and
enormous hands gripped their necks and banged their heads
together, after which they were picked up and tossed over the
railing, to fall on the people in the street. There was a delighted
shout from the crowd, 'It's Milo! Milo the boxer. Come down,
Milo, let's have you!'

He was six and a half feet tall and broad in proportion. The
railing only came up to his thighs. 'Listen, you sons of whores,'
he roared. 'If anyone speaks until Cicero has finished I'll come
down, all right, I promise you. I'll come down and make him
swallow his own bollocks, d'you hear? Then he can talk as
funny as he likes.' He took a knife a foot long from under his
toga. 'I've brought my little stylus.'

There was a roar of laughter, and then silence. 'Go on,
Consul,' shouted Milo. 'Let them hear the best orator in Rome.'

Cicero was startled, but any encouragement was enough to
get him going. 'Thank you, my friend,' he said. 'What I wish

when I condemned Lentulus to
a tyrant. I did it to save Rome,
hplace of free people . . . ' and
ce, if a bit long, but the sight of
ony with arms folded, glowering
keep the crowd respectful.

ished I tugged at his robe. 'Let's
rgently. 'I saw a group of Clodius'
orcements. There are too few of us
ne.'

he asked me, as we hurried away.
ilo.'

used to be an amateur gladiator? I remember
d at the arena loved him. But what made him – ?
ve under Pompey?'

voice came from behind us. Milo was like a bear on
trail, very light-footed in spite of his bulk, and we hadn't
heard him following. 'I served under General Pompey in Asia,
Consul,' and I heard him mutter in his beard. 'He was a man
then, not a mouse,' but Cicero missed that remark.

He turned to Milo. 'I hope you will come back with us and
share a cup of wine.'

'I will be glad to.'

I was always thankful when we returned to the house without
incident, and this time Cicero invited me in, with Milo. He
threw off his mourning robe and let his slaves dress him in a
fresh tunic. Then he joined us in the exhedra and wine was
brought.

Cicero thanked Milo for his intervention, and the big man
drained a goblet of wine at one draught, wiped his bearded lips
with the back of his hand, and said simply, 'It was an honour,
Consul.' When they first met he always called him by that title,
although it was four years since Cicero had held the Consulship.

'I must thank Pompey,' said Cicero, tentatively, 'for sending
me such a valuable supporter.'

'He wouldn't understand what you were talking about,' said
Milo bluntly. He waited while his cup was refilled and took
another gargantuan swallow. 'I haven't spoken to Pompey since
he took that daughter of Caesar's to wife. She's all he thinks
about these days; he's got no time for men.'

'Well,' continued Cicero, puzzled, 'I'm very glad that you
happened to be in that house.'

'Oh, it wasn't that. I only got back to Rome yesterday from
my house in Lanuvium, and when I heard that those yobboes of

Clodius were drowning the voice that spoke against Verres and Catiline I thought I'd go along and see for myself. I followed you, and saw those two curs slinking up the stairs.'

Cicero's chest swelled visibly. 'So you have read my orations?'

Milo put down his wine carefully on a stool and stood up, adjusting his toga over his upper arm. Then his rumbling voice began:

'Romans: your country and the lives of every one of you, your property, your fortunes, your wives and children, this centre of your illustrious government, this most fortunate of cities. . . . ' It was the beginning of Cicero's third speech against Catiline. When he had finished the opening passage he stopped and wiped his eyes, which to my astonishment were full of tears.

'Wonderful words!' he said, with a catch in his voice. 'Balls of Bacchus! The whole bleeding speech is beautiful.'

I kept a straight face, but the sound of his deep gravelly voice ploughing without pause or change of expression through that delicate artifact of balanced rhythms and phrases was almost irresistibly funny. But Cicero didn't think so; he was thinking only of the occasion when he had uttered those words, at the height of his power. Greatly moved, he rose and put his fine long hand on the big man's shoulder. 'That was well done,' he said. 'You have a gift for which great orators may well envy you, the gift of sincerity.'

Milo smiled blissfully. 'That's what I'm going to be, Consul, an orator.'

It took a great deal to rob Cicero of his tongue, but all he could do was sink back in his chair, marvelling.

'Oh yes,' continued Milo, 'that's what I decided to do when I left the arena.'

No one had paid the slightest attention to me so far, but I couldn't contain my curiosity. 'Why *did* you give up your career, Milo, if I may ask? Everyone was puzzled, I remember, because you were beating the professionals at their own game, and the fees paid to you by the aediles were the talk of Rome.'

He looked at me sternly. 'It was no career for an aristocrat.'

We were speechless again, and he went on, 'My foster-father died five years ago, when I was still fighting in the arena. As everyone knows he was a knight and well respected in Lanuvium, and I knew he'd adopted me when I was a little nipper. But before he died he told me my real father was a patrician, who'd had me on the wrong side of the blanket by a girl from Gaul. A lot of the Gauls are big, and that's why I am.'

'And you don't know – ' began Cicero, fascinated.

'I don't know who it was, except that he was my father's patron when he was younger. But he was an aristocrat, all right. My foster-father – may he rest in peace! I gave him little during his life – wouldn't lie to me on his deathbed.'

'Indeed no,' cried Cicero, 'and I'm sure you're right in choosing our profession. But it requires a long course of study, you know.'

'That was the difficulty,' explained Milo. 'At my age I couldn't get myself attached to one of the well-known orators, as your pupil here young Caelius did. So when I went to join Pompey in Asia I took the scrolls with me. Mostly yours, Consul, but some of the speeches of Antonius and Hortensius too. And I learnt them.'

'By heart?'

'Most of them. Yours certainly. I've got a good memory.'

'Do you want to plead in court?' asked Cicero, still mystified.

'Oh no, I wouldn't know enough about all the tricky little points of law. It's only the legislature I'm interested in. When I stand for tribune next year I want to be able to tell the people what their rights are, and make them fight for 'em.' He finished his wine and leaned forward earnestly. 'Look at what you've said and written, Consul, about our traditions and the whole framework of law that protects the people from misgovernment. All your counsel and wisdom during the past ten years is forgotten, and what's happening now? I'll tell you. The abnegation,' he pronounced carefully, 'of all democratic principles.'

Cicero stood up. He was more genuinely moved than I had ever seen him. 'If I am still a free man and in Rome,' he declared with a noble gesture of his arm, 'you may count on all my help in your campaign,' and was instantly engulfed in a crushing embrace.

Luckily, I realised, as I made my way out, no one had thought of asking me to be Milo's tutor.

17

Exile

I was spending the night with Clodia, and when I had bathed and we were sitting at dinner, alone, I told her the story of Milo's appearance on the scene and the conversation in Cicero's house. I gave imitations of Milo declaiming the Third Catilinarian and Cicero's reactions, and she laughed till the tears came. This was another way I'd found to make her want me as a companion as well as a lover. I could always make her laugh.

'When I left them,' I concluded, 'Milo was going to stay for dinner, and he was offering to train a gang of his ex-gladiator friends to provide a guard. When he said they'd be armed Cicero was horrified. "But it's illegal," he protested. Milo reassured him. "They don't need to *show* their weapons. Keep 'em hidden and if someone starts acting against the democratic rights of the citizen this is what they'd do. Now, suppose I want to stop you, Consul, from throwing a stone, say. Right? I stand close against you, d'you see, like this. And when you start shouting and picking up the stone I *turn away*, as if I was frightened, but as I do it – pang!" I didn't see the movement, it was so quick, but there were six inches of his great dagger sticking out from under his shoulder. You should have seen Cicero jump! And Milo says, "Of course, I was careful, so's not to hurt you. But if I'd still been standing close, as I said, you'd be bleeding like a stuck pig and no one could guess it was me. I learned that trick in the gladiator school."

' "But I couldn't sponsor the shedding of blood, my friend," says Cicero, very worried. And Milo, "It's not bloodshed, Consul. Just what I'd call a deterrent. What's the difference between a little prick in the guts and a stone thrown at your head? I'll tell you. The stone's more dangerous, so it's more anti-democratic." And the extraordinary thing is that Cicero told him it was good logic.'

Clodia was silent for a moment. Then she said, 'You must stop them, Marcus.'

I pulled the fold of my toga from my shoulder and showed her a blue-black bruise the size of an egg. 'If that stone had hit my head, where it was intended, you wouldn't want me in your bed tonight.'

She made a great fuss of it, crying with fright and kissing the bruise, and of course begging me again to stay indoors. 'Why can't you let Cicero fight his own battles now? You've made your gesture and shown that you're on his side. Now it's enough.'

'You haven't had to submit, as I have, to a hail of refuse and stones every day. Now I want to see what happens when Cicero lets Milo loose on that gang. It'll be worth watching, I tell you.'

She pulled me down beside her on the couch. 'Listen. That horrible wife of Clodius, Fulvia, told Portia, who's a friend of mine, that the whole idea is to frighten Cicero so that he'll leave Rome. Then they'll hold the *threat* of a charge under this new act over his head, and not make any further move. If only Cicero will go away for a time Clodius will have got what he wants – the humiliation of Cicero in the sight of everybody, and he'll turn his attention to other things. But once you start trying to fight it out in the streets Clodius will react as he's always done when he's crossed – and I can tell you, he's dangerous.'

'Well, it's no good my trying to give him further advice. If I suggest he runs away to Anzio what d'you think he'll say? He'll give me his speech about men who tamely submit to tyranny.'

'Which is exactly what he'll have to do, in the end. Oh Marcus, let's forget about them. Let's tell the girls to fetch your lute. Then, if you'll play, I'll sing.'

*

A few days later Cicero appeared on his round with a close bodyguard of strong men, with Milo at their head. The crowd was over-awed and gave Cicero a hearing, and when one or two stones were thrown the throwers had to run for their lives. The following day a large body of Clodius' toughs tried to break through the crowd and drive the orator from the cart on which he was standing. They had cudgels in their hands and one of Milo's men was isolated and badly beaten up before the other gladiators could get to him. But they had steel in their hands by then, and when the affray was over three men lay dead.

Next day Clodius gave notice of a bill charging Cicero with sentencing Lentulus and the other conspirators to death without trial.

By this time I felt I'd done enough. Cicero had accepted my presence among his supporters very much as a matter of course, and he still had plenty of his Senator friends to accompany him when he made his final gesture. They were no longer allowed to wear mourning for him, but the procession of Senators who went with him to the Capitol was dignified; he had come to deposit the sacred statue of Minerva, which had stood in his house, and he conducted the ceremony of dedication and left the statue with the inscription, 'To Minerva, Guardian of Rome'. On the same night he left Rome secretly, and Terentia went into sanctuary in the House of the Vestals.

In a rage, Clodius rushed his bill through the Assembly, with a rider condemning Cicero to exile and denying him the right to fire and water in Italy or within five hundred miles of its shores. Cicero took the Appian Way, hoping at first to take refuge in Sicily, and Milo accompanied him with his new bodyguard. By the time the slow cortège had reached the Alban Hills a band of Clodius' armed men, on horseback, had caught up. But Clodius had reckoned without Milo, and his men were routed with many casualties.

Cicero's troubles were far from over, however. The Governor of Sicily refused him leave to land, and he had to cross Italy, staying secretly with friends who were prepared to brave the 'fire and water' ban, and finally embarked at Brindisi for Durazzo.

Caesar and Crassus only wanted Cicero out of the way, but Clodius had wanted him dead, and when his attempt to assassinate him on the road failed he went mad with frustration. He knew very well that his bill, which contained a self-perpetuating clause, was unconstitutional, and that when his year as Tribune was over the question of repeal was bound to come up. So he took his revenge on Cicero's property, and himself led one of his gangs to the house on the Palatine, which was first looted and then set on fire. The wooden columns and beams and ten thousand scrolls, so dear to Cicero's heart, made a fine blaze, and later Clodius erected a Temple of Liberty on the site, so that it was consecrated and could not be used for a building again. He also destroyed Cicero's villas at Tusculum and Formiae.

When Pompey – Pompey the Great, as a grateful people had named him – at last protested, the gangs prevented him from taking his place in the Senate. For the rest of that year Clodius was the gangster king of Rome.

Part Three

March 58 BC – June 56 BC

18

Baiae

While Cicero was living in exile with Plancius, the Acting Governor of Thessalonika, writing miserable letters to his friends, and Clodius was rampaging around Rome, organising and training his 'clubs' and threatening to burn down Pompey's house if he didn't keep quiet, I was happy. It was the first time since her husband's death that Clodia could spend the whole summer in Baiae, and we were together.

She had decided it was to be the gayest season the resort had ever seen, and so it was. The villas were full of rich and well-born people who had left Rome to get away from the trouble in the streets. The future was uncertain and they had brought gold with them. All they needed was ideas on how to spend it.

My own money was running out, and I'd had to agree to take over all our business in Puteoli and make an extended trip to Utica to drum up more trade, but there was time left over to help Clodia to organise entertainments. We built a wooden theatre in the park adjoining Clodia's villa and brought over companies of actors from Naples and Pompeii to perform the comedies of Plautus and Terence. This inspired us to act ourselves, and we put on the *Medea*, in Greek, of course, and with a number of gags that turned it into an uproarious farce. (Medea had to kill her sons half a dozen times; as soon as one was supposed to be dead he got up and began to recite a poem.)

By the middle of the season, in spite of the heat, we were writing our own farces, the bawdier the better. Both actors and audience were a witty, licentious lot, and our home-made plays, full of barbed allusions to the politicians of the time and their known or suspected vices, were a great success.

We staged our own Olympic Games, with special races for men with one leg and women seven months gone in pregnancy. There was a conventional pentathlon, and Clodia wagered a large sum on me and lost it. (What did she expect? Living with her was incompatible with a Spartan course of training!) We stayed for a while in Pompeii, a cheerful little town, and Clodia and I rode out one day at first light, up through the vineyards on the slopes of the extinct volcano to find the place in the crater where Spartacus had made his last stronghold. We were still very much in love, and went everywhere together. She appeared to have forgotten Catullus, who had gone to Verona in the spring, to stay with his family.

For a reason which I will explain later, mention must be made of one in particular of our festivities, the battle of boats. It lasted all day, and took place on the lagoon behind Baiae. There were two sides, 'Pompey's Fleet' and 'The Pirates', and the crews were armed with long bamboo canes with sponge mops on their ends. As Clodia insisted that I should be captain of her boat we had a mock ceremony in which I was declared an aristocrat by adoption and presented with a pair of red shoes as proof. This entitled me to form part of Pompey's fleet, which was crewed exclusively by patricians.

We went to Puteoli for the grape festival, when the fountains in the Forum spouted red wine, and there was a wild revel afterwards. We all got drunk and chased each other round the streets, to be picked up at dawn by our slaves, who were equally drunk, and bundled into the boats which pursued a zig-zag course across the bay to Baiae.

There was dancing on the wooden stage after the plays were over, lit only by the stars and a few torches; picnics in the hills and midnight bathing parties; games and races on the sand. By the end of the summer appetites were becoming jaded and any new idea was welcome, so King Ptolemy found us easy stooges for his plot.

He was the exiled King of Egypt, who had taken a house at Baiae for the season and was attended by several hundred slaves, dancing girls, pimps and guards. A fat little man of about fifty-five, he was experienced in debauchery and strategic murder, and his country was well rid of him. But Clodia found him amusingly outrageous, and his entertainments were certainly rather special.

One of Ptolemy's ideas was to have repercussions for me later. The Ambassador of Queen Berenice, Ptolemy's daughter who now occupied his throne in Alexandria, was returning from Egypt and due to land at Puteoli the following day, on his way to Rome. What could be more diverting, suggested Ptolemy, than to arrange for the party to have a surprise welcome? We asked him what he had in mind.

'The Chief Magistrates of Puteoli are planning an official reception in the Forum,' he said with his oily smile, 'and only one of them, the Praetor Galba, will meet the ship when it docks and escort Dio and his retinue through the streets to where the City Fathers and the other dignitaries await them. Now I have persuaded some friends' – he rubbed his forefinger and thumb together – 'to prevent the Praetor and his lictors from getting to the quay in time, and meanwhile I will take the magistrate's place with a guard formed by some of our young friends here, dressed as lictors.' He gave a cackle of laughter. 'I just want to see Dio's face when he sees his rightful King waiting to greet him, and I'll wager a hundred gold pieces he won't even land.' Everyone thought it was an excellent joke, and several of my friends volunteered. Like a fool, I joined them.

As the Egyptian ship approached the quay, with the rowers backing their oars, Dio was standing on the prow, a solid, serious-looking man, clad in a tunic of gold cloth, with a slave holding a parasol over his head. Behind him was a group of men, some by their bearing obviously soldiers, although they showed no arms.

There were six of us dressed as lictors in red cloaks, and we marched up, clearing a way through the crowd for Ptolemy, in all his oriental magnificence. When Dio saw the hated face of his former master he only hesitated a moment, then stepped ashore and looked around, with his retinue forming up behind him. 'I see no person of authority here,' he said loudly, in Greek.

Ptolemy hissed with rage, and signalled to someone in the crowd. There was a sudden rush of men with knives in their hands, and Dio's guard whipped out their daggers and made a ring round him. At the same time I heard furious shouts behind us, 'Way for the magistrate, citizens! Get back!' The praetor and his lictors were to have been stopped by a hired mob blocking the street down which they were approaching the quay, but they must have fought their way through and were almost on our heels. If they caught us in our red cloaks we should be in bad trouble.

8

There was only one thing to be done. Ptolemy had tricked us, and that was the end of the charade. I snatched off my cloak and ran, with my friends following my example. We all got away except young Asicius, who was still struggling with the clasp of his cloak when the lictors caught him. The rest of us found refuge in one of my father's warehouses.

There was nothing to see from where we were hiding, but apparently the real lictors did their job well. They broke into the gang of toughs attacking Dio's guard, and brought the Egyptians away, with the assassins harrying them ineffectually as they moved down the quay. But when they came to the street that leads to the centre of the town they met the same mob who had blocked their way before, and were heavily outnumbered. All hell broke loose.

In Puteoli, as in every city, there are always unemployed men about who will make the most of a street-fight. The struggle became general, shops were looted and stalls overthrown. Reinforcements arrived from the Forum and in the end Dio's party were rescued almost intact. But not quite. Dio lay where he had fallen, with a seaman's knife in his back.

Ptolemy had disappeared as soon at the lictors came up, and my friends and I remained in hiding until nightfall, when we found the boatman and were rowed back to Baiae, all very sober. There was an inquiry, and Asicius was released on bail, since when he was arrested he was nowhere near Dio, then still alive. Moreover, Asicius' father was a person of influence in Puteoli, so the young man was fined for obstructing a lictor in the execution of his duty and no mention was made of his red cloak. However, he hadn't heard the last of that escapade. Nor had I.

*

A week later I had to leave for Utica on business, and when I returned after three weeks I found Clodia preparing to travel back to Rome, accompanied by her sparrow, Pius.

This useless little bird was a new arrival at the villa, and Clodia explained that while I was away she had consoled herself with his company and had trained him to sit on her finger and talk to her. His full name, she said, was Appius Claudius Passer.

Pius was certainly very tame, but I pointed out that she had failed to make him either continent or free of vermin, and threatened to let him fly out of the door unless she transferred

114

her attentions to me. She said Pius and I must learn not to be jealous of each other.

As if my only rival were a sparrow!

19

The End of Clodius' Year

When we arrived in Rome, with Clodia's friend Pius in his gold-wire cage, I was glad to be back in my comfortable flat on the Palatine. No Roman is happy away from Rome for long, as Cicero showed in every letter. Although the streets were smellier than ever for lack of rain, and there was always a chance of being roughed up by the gangs, on the Palatine Hill it was quieter and a good deal more safe than in the other parts of the City, since Clodius would not allow his gangs to commit mayhem in the neighbourhood where he lived. I was among my books again, with plenty of work to do but time for leisure and long nights with Clodia.

The baths were alive with gossip. Caesar was returning from Gaul for the winter. Pompey's prisoner Tigranes, King of Armenia, had been set free by agents of Clodius after a battle on the Appian Way in which a knight named Papirius had been killed, some said with Clodius' own sword. Tigranes was now living in Clodius' house and accompanied him in public, a walking testimony to Pompey's weakness and indecision.

There were many stories of the rapacity of Clodius' gangs, who now carried arms beneath their clothing. Tenants who refused to pay an increase in rent were repeatedly beaten up until they gave in. Clodius himself had invented a new technique for persecuting Pompey. When Pompey came to speak on some public platform Clodius would stand in a prominent place, so that his men in the crowd could see him, and shout, 'Who's the General who fornicates but won't fight?' or 'Who is it who scratches his head with his left hand?' – some of the questions were sheer nonsense – and each time he would signal by flicking the fold of his toga, and from all parts of the crowd men would shout 'Pompey!'

Pompey had always believed, in spite of appearances, that the people still loved him, and these persistent public manifestations of antipathy worried him to such an extent that he simply never appeared unless obliged to do so. Clodius had made barracking into a science.

Dolabella and young Curio and Calvus were still meeting together, and when I joined them one evening they were discussing a poem by Catullus about a sparrow, in a book that had just been published. Someone handed me a copy, and I stared blindly at the words, hoping they would not tell me what I feared to know. But they did.

> 'Sparrow, my Lesbia's darling pet,
> Her plaything whom she loves to let
> Perch in her bosom and then tease
> With tantalising fingertips. . . .'

'It's charming,' I said nonchalantly, but I was thinking furiously. He must have been with Clodia when I was away in Utica. He'd probably brought the damned bird with him as a present – all he could afford, I muttered to myself spitefully. That was how he had entered her villa – and her bed – and she must have sent him away when I was due to return. The rest of the poem showed that he was unhappy, which at least was reassuring.

Of course she'd had other, casual lovers, during that riotous summer, just as we all had, but surely none of them was serious. It was Catullus I feared; I had seen her face when she read his poems. He was a threat to our private world which was so sweet.

I said nothing to Clodia about Catullus. When the wretched sparrow died – from indigestion, probably, considering some of the things she fed him – she wept, and I comforted her with a little black boy, five years old, whom I'd bought at a sale. But of course, only a few weeks afterwards Catullus, who seemed to be keeping out of my way, was reciting a new poem to his friends in the taverns. It's well known, one of those which have made him famous – 'On the Death of Lesbia's Sparrow'. All the virtues of the little bird are mentioned but not his chief vice, which was to vent himself on my clean togas. The blackamoor I gave her was at least house-trained.

When Catullus and I met, as happened inevitably on occasion, we scarcely spoke to each other. He had never forgotten that first summer in Rome, when he'd thought Clodia was chastely waiting for him, and I had taken his place. Now that the position was in a sense reversed I comforted myself with the thought that next year he was to go to Bythinia as attendant on the Governor, and would be out of circulation for a time. Poor Catullus! He told us all that he was going to make his fortune, but came back as broke as ever. The Governor had kept all the sources of loot to himself. Catullus never had any business sense.

*

Milo had reappeared. He would never say where he had been since Cicero's exile, but I think he was taking lessons in oratory somewhere in the South, where Greek is spoken. He certainly spoke the language more comprehensively afterwards.

There was no doubt now that Pompey was supporting him with funds, for Milo had a large group of ex-gladiators who kept Clodius' men away from the election meetings without much difficulty. He was already beginning his campaign for election as tribune.

On the platform his technique was remarkable. He started off on each occasion with a number of racy stories, delivered in the coarsest of gutter terms, but funny. Then he'd stand straight, like a small boy reciting Homer, and repeat his prepared harangue, laced with noble thoughts and quotations from the classics, and all in a loud voice that brooked no interruption. In any case, the crowd loved him, not least because when Clodius' toughs once attacked him on the way to the Forum they were repulsed with heavy loss of life. (No one blinked, now, when men went about the streets with swords in their hands.) The Romans were becoming tired of Clodius already, and at the polls they elected Milo Tribune of the People by a large margin.

The feeling for Cicero had revived, and people were clamouring for his return, but on the only occasion when an attempt was made in the Assembly to pass a bill demanding his recall, the magistrates were chased off the Rostra.

Yet there were hopeful signs. One of the Consuls-elect was Lentulus Spinther, a man devoted to Cicero, and the other was Clodia's brother-in-law Metellus Nepos. It was he who had vetoed Cicero's end-of-term speech as Consul, but he was Pompey's man, and his patron was now very anxious to get Cicero's help. But he had to await the end of Clodius' tribunate.

So when the year 697* began Lentulus introduced in the Senate a bill to repeal the act of Clodius which had outlawed Cicero, and Pompey supported him. The whole Senate followed, with the single exception of Clodius, and the bill was

* 57 BC

117

accepted by the Assembly before the end of January, in spite of armed intimidation by Clodius. Then Caesar, in Rome while his troops hibernated in Gaul, interposed his veto by means of one of Milo's fellow tribunes, who was in Caesar's pay. Throughout the spring and summer Caesar maintained his opposition to Cicero's return, and only relented in August after Cicero's brother Quintus had given his personal assurance that the exile would behave and not interfere with Caesar's plans.

None of this would have been possible if Milo, as soon as he was elected and even before taking up office, had not set himself the task of clearing Clodius' gangs from the streets. There were pitched battles in the Forum, and the cleaners had to use sponges to mop up the blood. Milo's concept of a tribune's role was nothing if not forceful.

20

Storm Clouds

Cicero had landed at Brindisi, and Milo was there to greet him and give him protection on his long journey up the Appian Way to Rome. There was scarcely need for protection; the people were delighted to see him again. It was clear that outside Rome Cicero remained the popular hero he had always been. Everyone thought, like the great man himself, that his reappearance on the political scene would solve everything.

Clodia and I were sitting in the little temple in her garden on the Tiber. There had been an epidemic of marsh-fever in Baiae, and she had come to Rome to avoid it. The city was stiflingly hot, but here by the river the heat was at least bearable. I wore only a loin-cloth, because we had been swimming, and she a silk tunic with nothing underneath.

She sat looking down at the water rippling over the mosaic, very thoughtful, lazily moving her feather fan to and fro to cool her face. I watched her with a sad ache in my heart, because we had quarrelled again. I forget what it was about; all I remember is the dangerous feeling of hurt pride and frustration which remained when she had out-smarted me.

She said, 'The whole feud will start up again. As soon as Cicero gets back into his seat in the Senate he'll begin insulting

Clodius, who'll try to answer back, make a mess of it, and tell his boys to throw stones at Cicero in the street. It's too childish.'

'I'm not going to do anything about it. I've stuck my neck out for Cicero quite enough already.'

'D'you think it's possible that sixteen months of exile will have taught him anything?'

'It's doubtful. What makes you so interested?'

'Caesar wrote me a letter.'

'From Gaul?'

'Yes, he sent it by special messenger. He wants me to make Clodius calm down, so that he won't drive Cicero into doing something stupid.'

'Why are you acting as an agent for Caesar?'

'He knows that politics interest me. I admire him.' She looked up, challengingly. 'He's the only man in political affairs who really knows where he's going.'

'And how to get round the women. What else has he asked you to do?'

'Find out what the women think of Cicero's return – and Pompey.'

'Don't play his game, Clodia. You're only letting yourself be exploited because you're bored when I'm not with you.'

'I suppose so.' She smiled and said teasingly, 'What a good thing I'm not bored when you are with me.'

I kissed her soft cheek. 'I'd throw myself in the Tiber.'

'You can swim like a fish. You'll always survive, Marcus. I wonder whether I should – if you went away for ever. Perhaps I'd go on the streets; I'm all for variety.' She changed the subject. 'I'm worried about my little brother.'

'Your little brother! The King of the Subura. D'you realise that he's becoming the best-hated man in Rome?'

'Yes, I do. If Cicero takes his revenge Clodius will be exiled, too, and it'll break his heart.' She put her hand on my arm. 'I've never spoken to you about him before, but I want to explain something. Everyone whispers about him and me, but it's quite true – at least, it was when we were young.'

'You don't have to explain,' I said stiffly.

'Try to understand. He was a desperately unhappy boy. There was a brute of a Greek tutor, with old-fashioned ideas of education, and he used to flog Clodius every day, with my father's full approval. So at night, when he couldn't sleep for crying, I made him come into my bed, and that's how it started.'

I was silent. She took my arm. 'What did it matter? He was a boy, and I a girl, and fond of him.'

'Sorry for him, too,' I said sarcastically, 'as you are for Catullus.'

'Catullus is in Bythinia, so you needn't be jealous. I've told you it's an ugly thing.' She looked at me appealingly. 'Marcus, there was nothing ugly about Clodius and me – nothing at all. It's all over now, but I don't see there was anything wrong.'

'Conventionally, it's known as incest, and there's a law against it.'

'There's a law against adultery, but that didn't stop you from making love to me when my husband was away.'

I couldn't stop myself. All this talk about Clodius and Catullus was the last straw. I said slowly, meaning to hurt, 'It wasn't very difficult, was it? Either for me or any of the others.'

She hit me across the face and ran out of the temple. I watched her bare feet flying across the lawn. That precious hedge of pretence around our love had disappeared, and afterwards, however hard we tried, we could never make it grow again.

*

Cicero was given a tremendous welcome in Rome, although he still needed Milo's gladiators to protect him from Clodius. For a time he was fully occupied. His first task was to repay his obligation to Pompey by introducing a bill to give the General control over the world supplies of corn. Then there was the question of getting permission for the site of his house on the Palatine to be de-consecrated and the Temple of Liberty erected by Clodius demolished. The Consuls voted him two million sesterces compensation for the destruction of his home and three-quarters of a million for the villas at Tusculum and Formiae, both abandoned since Clodius had set them on fire. Although Cicero complained that it wasn't enough and borrowed heavily from his clients, the work of reconstruction was put in hand. Meanwhile, since he needed more clients to borrow money from, it was essential to re-build his law practice as well, and one of the cases he accepted within a month of his return was the defence of Asicius, accused of the murder of Dio, the Egyptian envoy.

Ptolemy was in Rome, still exiled but now hoping to regain his throne through the influence of Pompey. But since his reputation was very bad, for Dio was not the only man he'd had murdered, he needed a scapegoat. The evidence produced by his agents was mostly invented, of course, but the fact remained that Asicius had been arrested wearing a lictor's cloak. Cicero, who still had his excellent service of secret agents, discovered that I had been involved, and summoned me to explain.

There was nothing for it but to tell the truth, and I told him that Ptolemy had tricked us into acting as a cover for his hired assassins.

'I am tempted,' said Cicero coldly, 'to call you as a witness and make you repeat the whole disreputable story, but it won't be necessary. However, I shall want you and one or two others to appear in court and swear that at the time of Asicius' arrest Dio was still alive and unhurt. I shall hinge the defence on that alibi. But to be on the safe side I may have to mention the attempted deception. Let me have the names of the other four men, besides yourself, who wore lictors' cloaks.'

'No,' I said, summoning up my courage, 'I can't do that. We should be incriminating ourselves. However, if you will assure me that no mention is made of the fact that we were wearing those clothes, I will persuade my friends to swear the same testimony. We shall say that we were present on the quay, as bystanders, when Asicius was arrested, and saw armed men rush out from the crowd and attack the Egyptians.'

'Very well.' He looked at me in surprise. 'For someone who has just admitted taking part in an incredibly foolish escapade, you seem very sure of yourself, Marcus. You realise that you may be called by the other side?'

'If so we'll merely make the same statements. We were only seen by the crowd for a moment when wearing the cloaks, and no accusation was made against us at the time. It will be easy to suggest that witnesses confused us with the real lictors. Two of the men who will support me are patricians and the other is the son of a Consular.' I paused and added, 'I think you'll find that the prosecution will make no mention at all of the impersonation of the lictors.'

'Indeed? You seem to have it all worked out.'

I was proved right. The evidence produced by the prosecution was taken at the preliminary hearing, and nothing was deposed about young men dressed as lictors. Ptolemy was afraid that if that subject were raised there would be far too many patricians to swear it was he himself who had suggested the imposture, and that was the last thing he wanted to come out in the middle of his delicate negotiations with Pompey.

The main testimony came from two of the lictors, who had been bribed to swear that they had seen Asicius with a knife in his hand. Our evidence, which we upheld under cross-examination, was convincing, and Cicero's speech, full of veiled but damaging references to Ptolemy's record, carried the day.

*

So ended the year of Cicero's return to his beloved Rome. The year that followed was tragic, for Rome, for Cicero and for me.

For Rome, because it marked the effective end of the Republic, hastened by the action of the man who loved it almost more than his life. Cicero was quite incapable of keeping his brother's promise, and his own head down. Intoxicated by the adulation of the crowds and of his friends in the Senate, and still believing – against all experience – that Pompey would not betray his trust, he attacked bills sponsored by Caesar, who promptly called Crassus and Pompey to meet him at Lucca.

The three Generals swore friendship in the interests of their own advancement and the Triumvirate became no longer a loose and unofficial association, but a grim reality, backed by overwhelming force. Caesar had already begun looting Gaul, and the trains of booty were a common sight in Rome. Over two hundred Senators were drawn to Lucca like wasps to a honey-pot, and came away rich, but liegemen to Caesar.

After that, no bill not approved by the Triumvirs had any chance of survival; the magistrates were intimidated and tribunes bribed or beaten up. Even Cicero had to pronounce eulogies of Caesar on demand. I cannot blame him; another term of exile would have been too much to bear, and although he has his own special kind of courage he is not a man like Cato, who will commit suicide rather than give in.

So it was an unhappy year for Cicero, except for his new friendship with Milo, who was constantly in the company of his idol. To see them together was like watching a Caucasian bear taking a greyhound for a ramble. It was an odd relationship, but not as odd as it appeared, owing to a curious trait in Cicero's character.

For one who is physically a timorous man he has a strange love of violence, as long as it does not involve him personally, and is always talking of those grand old Romans who murdered for the sake of the City, or their own honour. Cicero admired in Milo the man's complete disregard for personal danger, and his willingness to shed blood on the slightest provocation. But quite apart from this, they seemed to enjoy each other's company and were always laughing at their private jokes. Milo once told me that Cicero's smutty stories were the funniest in Rome and that, for me, was yet another unsuspected facet of my former master's scintillating personality.

Milo was no longer tribune, but still paid by Pompey, and he was wise enough to see that in present circumstances it was useless to provoke the Triumvirs. He set himself two tasks: to build up a strong following among the people and to eliminate Clodius and his gangs once and for all. Caesar was no longer Clodius' paymaster and he was dependent on his own resources. But Fulvia's wealth, his own property interests and the protection rackets gave him the power to counter Milo's attacks, and the gang-battles became ever bloodier. The two men also began to charge each other with various crimes, such as violence, but nothing came of these accusations. Milo could always count on both Pompey and Cicero to defend him in court and Clodius neatly turned the tables by managing to get himself elected curile aedile. This position gave him immunity from most charges and also the opportunity of regaining his lost popularity by staging expensive games.

During this unhappy year my own misadventures began in the spring.

21

The End of an Affair

In March and April, with Clodia away in Baiae, I was very very busy. My practice was growing fast and I had cases to plead which would enable me, like Cicero, to ask my clients for loans – if possible permanent ones. I doubt whether Cicero ever repaid more than a fraction of the vast sums he borrowed from men whose lives or reputations he had saved. In any case, he always expected them to leave him the money in their wills.

One day I saw a great bearded face on the benches reserved for advocates. It was Milo, listening to my invective with attention, and taking copious notes. Afterwards he came round to my apartment with other friends to congratulate me on winning the case.

'You beat the hell out of that bleeding witness,' he said approvingly. 'He looked as if he'd like to murder you. Just tip me the word, young Marcus, if you have any trouble, and I'll settle his hash for him.'

'That's kind of you, Milo. But what are you doing in Rome? I heard you were at Lanuvium.'

'I'll tell you when the others have gone,' he said in a penetrating whisper. They took the hint and left soon afterwards. No one wanted to get on the wrong side of Milo, these days.

We sat down, and I had his goblet filled. He knocked the wine back hastily and leaned forward. 'I'm not telling other people about this, so keep your mouth shut, will you, son? Old Chick-pea and I have a plan, and we may want your help later this year.' (Chick-pea was a pun on Cicero's name, and Milo always called him that, even to his face.)

'Tell me.'

'It's like this. Old Chick-pea is going to have another crack at Caesar, and make Pompey back him up.' (As I've already written, Cicero did so, and merely precipitated the formal announcement of the Triumvirate, with all that followed.)

'Pompey won't support Cicero. He'll leave him standing, just as he's done before.'

'I think so, too, though old Chick-pea won't believe me. So I've persuaded him to have what we called in the army a fall-back position, and that's me.'

'You?'

'Yes, that's what I've come to Rome about. I'm going to stand for election as praetor next year.' His face split in an enormous grin. 'And Pompey's going to back me. He thinks I'm still his stooge.'

'But what's it got to do with Cicero?' I asked, puzzled.

'Why, in a couple of years' time, after my term as praetor, I'll stand for Consul, and then old Chick-pea and I are in business.'

Milo for Consul! At any other time in our history it would have been the greatest joke, but now anything was possible.

'Excellent!' I said, tactfully. 'You're just the type of leader we need. You want me to speak for you?'

'Yes, son. I was listening to you today, and you're good. Not as good as old Chick-pea, of course, but very handy with the vituperation. I want someone like you to make the other fellows sweat.'

'I see. When are the elections, in October?'

'Yes. Try and keep yourself free about then, will you?' He hesitated, which was unusual for Milo, and laughed awkwardly. 'If you can tear yourself away from that "Juno of the Palatine", as Cicero calls her.' He squared his broad shoulders. 'Don't get too involved with her, Marcus. She'll do you dirt.'

'That's my problem,' I told him, coldly.

'I know, son, but that's all I say – don't get too involved.'

'I think I know Clodia, Milo.'

'You don't. She'll let you down, just as that brother of hers let down his own family, making himself a pleb and dragging their name through the mud. He's a traitor to his blood, and so is she.'

'I won't take that, even from you, Milo.'

'Son, you'll have to, sometime. I know more than you'd think. Like that fellow Cotta she's got down in Baiae with her now.'

My heart jerked. 'Who's Cotta?'

'One of my boys, he used to be. He's a handsome lad, and she fancies him.'

'How d'you know this?' I snapped at him, contemptuously.

'Because he's boasted about it to one of my guards. He's had her here in Rome, too, Marcus, and she's taken him to Baiae because you're only going there later.' He saw my face and looked really distressed. 'Don't take it like that, son. She's not worth it.'

But she was worth everything to me, and I had to find out if it was true.

*

Clodia knew that there were cases to occupy me until the end of April, but I arranged a settlement out of court and left a week earlier. I travelled on horseback, with four armed slaves, in case we met bandits in the hills. We took the Appian Way and spent the first night in Milo's house at Lanuvium, beyond Lake Albano in the Alban Hills.

He made me welcome, and although I think he guessed what I was at, never mentioned Clodia, but sent me off with fresh horses at dawn. We rode down through the hills and continued on the long straight road, interminably, until we made nightfall at Formiae. The following day we rode without stopping, for I was becoming feverish with impatience, and arrived in Puteoli after dark, covered with dust.

My father's house is on the edge of the town and our way led through the market square. I had forgotten there was a local feast on that day, and we had to push our weary horses through the crowded, torch-lit streets to the open space, where we could hear music and the clatter of castanets. The warm night air was full of the scent of burning pine-knots, and the smell of the incense they had used in the ceremonies lingered heavily.

As we entered the square there was a sudden swirl of excitement and a rush of sweating people to see what was happening in one corner, where a space had been cleared for dancers. There were only two of them, so it was obviously a spectacle worth watching, and I rode nearer, curious to see what everyone was cheering so enthusiastically.

The woman was Clodia, disguised in a wig of dark hair, falling over her shoulders like a prostitute, and wearing bright colours and jewelled bracelets up to her elbows. The man was young and lithe, dressed in a gold tunic which showed off his shining brown arms and legs. He was stamping and posturing very gracefully, I'll admit.

Clodia danced like a lecherous nymph, just as I had seen her dance by moonlight, for me, in the garden by the Tiber. She was using the same exaggerated lascivious gestures which had amused me so much, swaying her hips and rolling her eyes mockingly as she goaded the man on. It was a courtship dance, and the crowd loved it.

When the click of her castanets came to an end, and she sank into Cotta's arms, I cried over the heads of the people, 'A cheer for the Lady Clodia!'

There was a shocked silence, and then a man, not recognising me, shouted angrily, 'Be careful what you say, you fool! That's not the Lady Clodia. I've seen her; she's a blonde.'

Pressing my heels into my horse's flanks I pushed the crowd aside. Cotta ran forward, but he was unarmed, of course, and I kicked at his head with my riding boot and when he fell passed him and reached Clodia. She was standing quite straight, with her hands at her sides, looking up at me with her great eyes and unafraid. I bent down quickly, took hold of the wig and yanked it off her head. 'You're right,' I shouted. 'She *is* a blonde.'

I tossed the wig into the crowd and heard a roar of laughter, but already I was turning the horse and urging him forward, through the hands that tried to seize his bridle, through the people running up, out at last and on to the dark road that led up into the hills and the cool fresh air, under the stars.

The wretched horse foundered before we came to the first inn, and I remained sitting by him in the dark until they brought another from a farm near-by. There was much to think about, much to remember, but one thing was clear. Two nights later, when I arrived at Milo's house and he came out on to the porch to greet me, with a cup of wine in his hand, I said, 'You were right, Milo. She's just a whore.'

*

A week afterwards I received a message by one of Clodia's maids. There were two tablets laced together and sealed with her ring, and I took them into my study, telling the girl to wait.

I recognised the proud twirls in the handwriting; at least, I thought, she hadn't dictated it to her secretary. The message was short. 'I have come to Rome for you, my love. Don't scold or argue, just come to me in the garden, this afternoon.'

I told myself it was no good, but went, and there she was, in a silver tunic and stole, sitting in the temple by our mosaic. For a moment I couldn't speak, and stood looking down at the defenceless little hands folded in her lap. I sat down slowly, away from her body.

'It was unforgivable,' she said. 'What you did. But I love you too much, I find. I've never said this to any other man.'

'What can I believe now? You had tears in your eyes when you left here for Baiae – tears for me, I thought. What a fool! I suppose you had Cotta in your baggage.'

She laughed, not looking at me. 'Poor Cotta! You gave him an awful black eye, you brute, and he's so vain about his appearance.'

'I'll give him four inches of steel if I find him with you again.' (So there I was, hinting that we could go on as before; already my iron resolve was breaking into pieces.)

'You won't,' she said quietly. 'I'll see to that. He might kill you. He was a retiarius, you know, before Milo bought him out of the gladiator school.'

'A retiarius? Did he bring his net and trident with him, when you took him to Baiae?'

'Only his trident. We went fishing with it,' she explained, as if it were important, 'and he caught a bass. Keep out of his way, Marcus. He's very quick and strong, and you wouldn't have a chance. What does he matter, between you and me?'

My look of righteous indignation was lost. Her head was bent, and I could only see the little fine hairs on her neck, where the heavier strands were combed upwards.

'You humiliated me beyond belief,' she said, and shuddered. 'Everyone was laughing, and they tossed that stupid wig around and an old hag put it on and said she was Clodia.' She looked up at me, wide-eyed. 'I told Cotta to go after you and kill you – but then called him back, and said I didn't want to see him again.'

'I see. So it was all Cotta's fault. *He* made you dress like a whore and dance with him in the streets?'

'Don't make me angry, Marcus. It was my idea, of course,

127

and it was fun, until you spoiled it. When you're not there, why shouldn't I enjoy myself? I don't ask what you do.'

'I'm a man.'

Surprisingly, it was that remark that triggered off her anger. 'What difference does that make?' she cried. 'You're out of date. Haven't you noticed that women are beginning to get what they want?'

'That's nonsense,' I retorted irritably, always the lawyer. 'Our whole society is based on the premise that men, not women, have the rights. We indulge you too much, that's the trouble.'

'Your archaic laws! When I was born my father was disappointed, because he'd wanted another son, and his first thought was to have me exposed outside the gates and eaten by the dogs. Do you imagine I can ever forget that, or run that risk with a child of my own? I wouldn't for Metellus and I wouldn't even for you, while that barbarous law still stands. I've given more of me to you than to any other man, and that's enough.'

'It's not enough for me, Clodia. I won't have other men playing with your body, not any more.'

'Why not? It's yours whenever you want it. What the others do doesn't count. It isn't just our bodies, Marcus. Oh my love, it's not just that. It's our minds and ideas, and the life we live together. No one else has that.'

'All I ask is that you don't –'

She stamped her foot. 'I won't have you making conditions. We go on as we were.'

'No.' I saw her look at me in astonishment, and made myself go on, 'I've seen you acting like a whore, and that's what you'll always be to me, from now on.'

She jumped to her feet in a rage, her face flushed and eyes smouldering. 'Do you expect me to plead with you, a tradesman's son?'

I looked down at the mosaic; I could never forget what that gesture had cost me. 'A tradesman's son gave you that.'

She was beside herself. 'I knew it! You've always thought you bought me with that thing. Well, you can have it back. Now!' She ran out of the temple and across the lawn, and I slumped on the bench, staring at the hunting scene under the rippling water.

In a moment she was back with her litter-bearers, all eight of them, coming forward in a confused rush. Foolishly I ran out to meet them, not wanting a brawl on ground that was still hallowed for me, whatever I might have been saying.

They stopped when they saw the stylus in my hand, but Clodia was goading them on, and they surrounded me. I charged at the ones in front and stabbed left and right with the point, hearing shouts of pain. Then someone kicked the back of my knees and I went down with a sweating mass of men on top of me. One of them brought a rope.

They had me trussed and thrown on the bench in the temple before Clodia came up, with a mason's hammer in her hand. I thought it was for me, and closed my eyes. I don't think I cried out: I was past caring.

I heard the first crack of the hammer and felt water splashing on my face, and then I saw what she was doing. One of the slaves tried to take the heavy hammer out of her hand, but she thrust him back and brought it down again on the tesserae, which still glowed and sparkled as they flew around the temple. It needed little force to make them start out of the ivory boxes that held them in, but she went on, panting and sobbing with anger, until the whole mosaic had dissolved into myriads of tiny cubes of glass and gold and lapis lazuli, and the green and brown porphyry which had given such a mellow background to the scene of the lion and his hunters. At last she stopped, and told the men to put all the tesserae into a manure sack and deliver it, and me, to my door. I could see her through the doorway as she went towards the pavilion, her hair all dishevelled and falling over her shaking shoulders.

*

They were bearing me, still bound, in the closed litter, but I knew we should pass along the river bank and shouted out that if they'd stop I would pay them a hundred sesterces. They halted, and someone opened the curtains and asked me, furtively, what I wanted. It was a place where the Tiber runs fast and deep, close under the bank, and I told the slave to empty the sack into the river. I knew the mud would quickly swallow the tesserae, and no one would ever again see the relics of my love for Clodia.

I remember thinking – it is extraordinary how the mind will turn away from disaster and fasten on something else – that fortunately, the descendant of the shophet had come over in one of our ships the year before, and I had shown him the mosaic in its setting. The old man had wept with happiness to see how beautiful it was.

9   129

22

Clodia's Revenge

I worked hard to forget her. There was another trip to Utica, which proved quite profitable, and I went several times to Puteoli, without making any inquiries about Clodia. There was no need. Even in Rome everyone knew of the wild parties she was giving in Baiae, and the names of the young men reputed to be her lovers.

There was plenty of legal work to occupy my mind, and one case in which I stood to gain nothing but fame if I won. Earlier that year I had prosecuted an aristocrat named Calpurnius Bestia for flagrant bribery in his election campaign, but with Cicero to defend him he had been acquitted. I now had new evidence, and to Cicero's outspoken annoyance I proposed to bring the action again, with every hope of obtaining a conviction. A date for the trial was fixed for the autumn, and Cicero insisted on defending Bestia for the second time, although I had warned him of the strength of the evidence I had assembled. He said he would not desert his client, but I had no doubt that he could foresee a repetition of the Hybrida affair, and his manner towards me became markedly cool.

After work, I played hard, too. My friends Dolabella and Curio were always ready for a rowdy night, and sometimes we had Catullus with us. The first time we met after my break with Clodia he made me want to kill him on the spot.

'Unhappy Caelius!' he greeted me, one afternoon in the library at the Senian Baths. 'You and I are now caught in the same net.' He patted my arm. 'I've forgiven you, my dear fellow, for your betrayal of our friendship.'

I shook off his hand. 'What was one lover,' I asked savagely, 'among so many?'

'But you were her special favourite, after me. She was always saying how witty and amusing you were.'

'How did she find the time,' I queried, crudely, 'between all those thousands of kisses?' The thought that she could have discussed me at all with another man was nauseating.

'Don't make fun of me, Caelius. It's too tragic. This woman, this golden girl we both loved so much, whose gifts we so admired, has become a common whore who stands at street corners, picking casual lovers as they pass.'

I gritted my teeth. 'Talk sense, Catullus,' I cried angrily. 'She's still rich. She can afford to indulge her lusts in the greatest comfort; she doesn't have to look for lovers on the street.'

He stared at me with his languishing, poet's eyes, astonished. 'My poor fellow, then you haven't heard? I'm afraid this will be a shock to you, but I assure you it's true. It's what everybody is saying.'

'What is this truth in everyone's mouth?'

'Her behaviour in Puteoli. She dresses like a prostitute, with a dark wig, and goes out into the streets. . . . ' I turned away from him. Any story from the provinces becomes doubly inflated when it reaches the eager gossips in the Vicus Tuscus and the Forum. I might have guessed that the events of that night would be twisted out of all recognition. Catullus not only believed the story literally – and why should I tell him the truth? – but had the impertinence to write a poem on the subject and dedicate it to me. I could never understand how the Claudians let him get away with his life after it was published. It was a crudely explicit poem, even for Catullus. For him, the lower Clodia sank the more he could indulge his romantic melancholy.

I had a letter from Clodia, begging me to see her. It must have hurt her pride grievously to write to me, but I sent it back. When she'd smashed the mosaic, my love for her had died, I thought.

There was a pretty girl from a patrician family who took a considerable fancy to me. She had been widowed, at nineteen, and was eager to make the most of her liberty and have fun. So I became her lover, and made sure that Clodia knew. There was no difficulty, for my charming, vapid, empty-headed Fabia loved going to the games and Clodia, when she returned to Rome, was always there with one man or another. Fabia was aware of my long association with Clodia and one day, while we were watching the races, Clodia passed, head held high, with a great oaf of a gladiator following. Fabia made a very spiteful remark, quite loud enough to be heard, and Clodia turned white. I gripped my mistress's arm so hard that she cried out, and dragged her away.

It was then, I think, Clodia decided that if I wouldn't have her I shouldn't have anyone else either. At least, that's my explanation of what happened a week afterwards.

*

I was at home, working on my briefs, when an officer of the permanent criminal court arrived and handed me a summons to appear before the quaestor to answer charges of murder, adultery, bribery of jurors and several other crimes. At first I was too astonished to take the summons seriously, although I felt the touch of the chill wind of fear.

The quaestor was known to me, and seemed friendly when I came into his office, overlooking the Forum. He made me sit down, returned to his desk and picked up a scroll.

'This is the statement of charges against you,' he began formally, 'signed by Sempronius Atratinus. Have you any comment to make on that name?'

'Indeed I have. He is the son of Calpurnius Bestia, whom I shall be prosecuting for fraudulent electioneering in the autumn. I suggest that knowing himself to be guilty of that crime Bestia is using this trick to intimidate me or get me out of the way. I should add that with the new evidence in my possession there is no doubt that he will be found guilty.'

'I see.' He nodded to his scribe, who began to write in shorthand. 'I'm afraid, Caelius, that I shall have to go through the formal interrogation, as you know. Is your name Marcus, son of Marcus, grandson of Marcus, Caelius Rufus?'

'It is.'

'Are you a Knight, First Class, through your father's property qualification?'

'Yes.'

'Are you an orator and advocate by profession?'

'Yes.'

'Age twenty-six?'

'Yes.'

He went through the other details – military service, address and so on, and then came to the meat of the matter. Had I assassinated Dio, Ambassador of Queen Berenice of Alexandria, on such-and-such a date? Had I attempted to murder by administering poison the Lady Clodia, daughter of Appius Claudius, widow of Quintus Metellus Celer, Consular? Had I committed adultery with the said Lady Clodia? Had I stolen the sum of two hundred pieces of gold from the said lady? Had I distributed bribes to jurors during the trial of Calpurnius Bestia? Had I instigated a riot against the Alexandrians in Naples? Had I misappropriated property, to wit, a villa and five acres of land at Palla? Had I at any time assaulted women in the streets after dark?

I denied all the charges, but pointed out that the accusation of adultery was invalid, since I was not married and the charge of adultery in such cases could only be applied to a wife. I asked if he hadn't made a slip.

He showed me the statement. 'It's adultery, all right, and I agree that it's nonsense. They mean seduction, I suppose, but –' he suppressed a smile – 'perhaps they didn't think that in this case seduction was the right word to use.' He resumed his official gravity. 'As regards the other charges, I'm recording that you deny them all?'

'Yes. With the comment that in the absence of full details of time and place I cannot prepare categorical refutations.'

'I'll make a note of that, but it'll all come out in the preliminary hearing.' He relaxed, and sent the scribe away to make out the statement for me to sign, with a copy for my retention. The quaestor wasn't a bad fellow, and from the equestrian order, like myself.

'May I ask you,' I said, 'as a colleague, if you know who is behind this ridiculous set of charges?'

'I'm afraid you may not. I'm sorry, but all I can properly say is that however ridiculous the accusations may appear you'll find they will be pressed home. You're in a tough spot, Caelius.'

So it was no mere threatening gesture on the part of Bestia. I persisted. 'Atratinus will prosecute, presumably?'

'Yes.'

'Who else?'

'When he came here with the statement, Herrenius was with him.' The advocate, I remembered, who had handled Metellus' estate for Clodia.

'Any other counsel?' I asked, fearing the worst.

He glanced at the door, and lowered his voice. 'I think Clodius may also speak.'

That was enough to make it clear to me that Atratinus was acting as a front for the Claudians. Clodia had got her family to take the field against me. It was a sobering thought.

*

I am not a man to let idle fears disturb my sleep but that night, lying on my couch in the flat on the Palatine, I was awake for hours, frightened.

Let no one who has not faced a murder charge call me a coward. Quite apart from the charges against me, which taken literally were serious enough, there is always the risk in our courts that the prosecution will bring up other accusations of which the prisoner knows nothing, in order to prejudice the jury. This was where I was most vulnerable, for I had made many enemies with my bitter attacks in court, and character smears often have more effect on jurors than the best-reasoned logic. Besides, if the Claudians used their wealth and influence they could produce any number of false witnesses; worse, if Clodius employed his toughs to intimidate my supporters and suborn the jury, what chance had I to escape death, or intolerable exile?

My first idea, naturally, was to conduct my own defence, but although I had no doubts about the power of my oratory, there is a sort of convention in Rome that a prisoner must *look* like a prisoner, that is, unhappy, down-at-heels and humble. Now it's quite impossible to act that part one moment and the next, take the stand as a suave, polished defence advocate, thundering invective at the other side. So I needed a counsel to speak for me, and ideally one of unchallenged integrity, who could raise the whole case above the sordid level of accusation and rebuttal to an emotive plane. In fact, Cicero.

Cicero! He had still not wholly forgiven me for prosecuting Hybrida, and now he knew that I was reopening the case against Bestia, his client. And it was Bestia's son who was accusing me! How could he possibly oppose him in court? It would be against all legal convention.

As I lay sweating in the dark I could imagine Cicero's gentle voice, with a fine hint of sarcasm, protesting that surely Marcus Caelius, the brilliant advocate, needed no other talent in his defence! After all, I had to admit that in his place I might have said the same.

The following day I went home. My mother fussed over me, weeping copiously, and my father shook his grey head in anguish. But he was a practical man. 'Who is that fellow who accompanied you here?' he demanded.

'An officer of the court. He has to go with me everywhere.'

'If you stay with us, will you promise not to attempt to leave Rome?'

'Of course. It's no use trying to run away.'

'Good. I'll see if the praetor will accept my bond for your behaviour.'

This was allowed, for my father was very well respected, and he then wrote to Petreius, with whom I had served at the Battle of Pistoia, and Pompeius, now living in retirement in the country. He urged them both to make sworn statements as testimony to my character, and further arranged for a delegation from our home town, Interamna, to be brought to Rome at his expense for the trial. In the meantime he went to see Cicero.

He returned looking grave, and I feared the worst, but he said Cicero had greeted him as an old friend and promised to give me advice. However, he had looked doubtful when my father asked him to conduct my defence, pointing out that Bestia was his client. He would see me three days later.

My spirits were rising a little, and I went to the baths in the afternoons and took exercise. It is wonderful how the mind is restored by a long swim, followed by vigorous massage, and it was when I was being pummelled one afternoon that I suddenly realised something that should have struck me at once. Cicero might see in my case a chance of making yet another attack on Clodius. He would have to solve the question of opposing Bestia's son in court, but he might still do it, if he thought the opportunity worth while. The last thing I must do, of course, was to suggest any such thing. If Cicero agreed to defend me, it must appear to be without an ulterior motive.

His house on the Palatine was still being rebuilt and he had rented – or more likely borrowed from one of his clients – another large house nearby. I humbly took my place on the edge of the pool in the atreum and waited with the other petitioners until I was called into the library. It was a good opportunity to go over the charges in my mind.

The assassination of Dio. I was innocent, of course, but vulnerable. However, my evidence at Asicius' trial had not been impugned and it was Cicero himself who had defended Asicius, and won.

The attempt to poison Clodia. Not me; not Clodia.

Adultery with Clodia. The charge was wrong, as I'd pointed out to the quaestor, but would they alter it to 'seduction' before they came to court – and risk the ridicule of all Rome? On the other hand, if the jurors were effectively bribed the prosecution could impose anything on the court, and get away with it.

Distributing bribes to the jurors during the Bestia trial. No comment. But they had voted for Bestia, anyway.

Stealing gold from Clodia. This was a tricky one. Let me first make it clear that I never accepted her money for myself. But during that hectic season of entertainments at Baiae, when I was doing much of the organisation, I was constantly in need of funds for hiring actors, musicians, boats and so on, and I soon used up what I could draw from the bank in Puteoli. So I'd had to ask Clodia for help. She simply told her steward to give me a bag of gold, and more when I needed it. I kept no account of what was spent – there was no time – but none of it went into my pocket. However, who could prove this?

Instigating the riot against the Alexandrians at Naples. I hadn't been near Naples when it happened. They must have confused that riot – more of Ptolemy's work – with the one at Puteoli.

The property at Palla. It had been given me by a client in settlement of his 'obligation', and it still brought in a small income. But my defence of this count was an awkward one, since as I have said we advocates are not supposed to take fees.

Assaulting women after dark. What could that be? No dates or details were given. Six years before, when all Rome was seized with euphoria after the defeat of Catiline, I and some of my companions used to swagger around in the dark streets, accosting any women who were foolish enough to go un-escorted. Most of them were very willing to be 'assaulted'. Clodius had been one of us. I was twenty.

Tiro came out of the library and called me. He is an old friend, and gave me a wink and a smile, so I began to hope. However, I knew I must play my part as a humble petitioner. Cicero would expect no less.

*

Cicero is unpredictable. He is both wise and foolish; cunning and naïve; a complete egoist, who can be extraordinarily kind and generous; devoted to his children, but more likely to say 'How my Tulliola loves me!' than 'How I love Tulliola!'

He was writing at the desk when I was announced, and in a corner of the big room Milo was sitting in an armchair, reading. Cicero put down his stylus and looked up with a smile of pleasure on his noble, strong-featured face. He crossed the room and embraced me. I let my feelings show, and for once they were genuine. Milo came up and thumped my back, growling in a friendly way.

'Dry your tears, Marcus,' said Cicero. 'You didn't think I would refuse to help my favourite pupil, surely? We'll fight them together.'

I confess I was weeping now, in sheer relief. But I spoke the piece I had prepared, humbly, expressing regret for the occasions when his advice had not been taken, begging his forgive-ness, pleading my youth and the temptations of the society which had lured me from the path of duty into the quagmire that now, alas, threatened to engulf me. If this time, I said, I could escape my just deserts, I was resolved to reform my way of life, repay my debts to my father and other creditors and devote my poor services to the State. The well-balanced phrases, interspersed with an occasional sob in punctuation, came out well, I thought. Milo was quite moved, and muttered filthy curses on the Claudians.

Cicero smiled. 'Well done,' he said. 'You haven't forgotten all I taught you. One criticism. As always, you are in too much of a hurry to reach the end and hear the applause. That tone of sombre despair in your final passage was excellent, but you should have been speaking *slower*, not faster. And another point – you threw away that line about repaying your debts. It sounded as if you were lumping together your father and your other creditors. What a waste! Never forget, Marcus, that the jurors and the crowd in the court are all fathers. You should have handled that reference to your father on its own. Like this.'

He is of course a superb actor, with an actor's memory. In an instant he was sitting in Milo's chair and looking up at me with mournful eyes, repeating, word for word, the speech I had just uttered, except for the piece about my father, which he embellished admirably.

I burst out laughing, and Milo gave a great guffaw and dug me in the ribs. 'He's a one, the old Chick-pea. He'll do you proud, son. He'll show that bunch of pimps where they get off.' He went to collect his book, and said with unexpected delicacy, 'I'd better leave you two together.'

When he had gone Cicero made me sit down and went back to his desk. 'It was a good speech, Marcus, nevertheless. I suggest you repeat it to General Crassus, with the alterations which will occur to you.'

I stared at him dumbfounded. 'Crassus?' I stammered.

'Yes. I've persuaded him to lead in your defence. After all, you were his pupil, too, and he's very willing to help you.'

'But Crassus and Clodius – ' It was unbelievable. Only a year or two previously Crassus had been Clodius' paymaster.

'They're no longer the friends they were. As one of the so-called Triumvirs,' Cicero added bitterly, 'Crassus has no need for that man's questionable talents.'

My heart gave a great leap. If Crassus spoke for me, those who sought to defame me would risk his displeasure. And he was a skilled orator. But Cicero – ?

'I,' said Cicero, 'will speak last, and sum up the defence case.'

I was overjoyed. Cicero and Crassus both on my side! I had an inspiration. 'It will be like Horatius,' I prompted, giving Cicero the idea.

He took it up at once. 'So it will,' he cried, his eyes glinting. 'The three of us will stand on the bridge shoulder to shoulder and withstand the host of the Claudians.' He even took a turn about the room with a military gait – then swung round on me suspiciously, and I scarcely had time to wipe the irreverent grin from my face. He went to the desk and picked up the stylus and a stack of freshly-waxed tablets.

'Now we'll talk about the case. First, the moulding of public opinion before the trial. Have you any suggestions?'

I told him about the delegation from Interamna, who would arrive in Rome before the trial and make propaganda for me, dressed in mourning robes; also what my father had written to Petreius and Pompeius. He nodded, and looked at me quizzically.

'At the baths yesterday I heard a story about Clodia which had everybody laughing. Something about Catullus dropping a copper coin into a vase she is said to keep for lovers' offerings, so they're calling her Halfpenny Helen. Was that your idea, Marcus?'

'Yes,' I admitted, more than a little ashamed. It was a cruel joke, for there was no vase, but it had come to me in the middle of a cruel, sleepless night.

'Excellent. My agents will see that the anecdote has wings.' He saw me looking at him uncertainly, and misjudged the reason. 'You are recalling that I, too, once had an association with the lady, although' – he put on a severe expression – 'on a somewhat higher plane. I will own to you, Marcus, that I was much tempted, not only because, then at least, she was a woman of great distinction of mind who only needed a guiding hand, but because the possibility of having a son by her attracted me greatly.'

I managed to keep my face straight. The thought of what Clodia would do with a guiding hand was irresistibly funny, and so was the picture of her in bed with Cicero. But he went on, wistfully, 'A son who would bear in his veins the blood of Appius Claudius the Blind and Claudia the Vestal, as well as my own – oh yes, Marcus, that would have been an occasion to sacrifice to the gods.'

He still worshipped the patricians for what they had been, not what they had become. It was no use telling him Clodia's attitude to the role of brood-mare, nor that she had several, and fascinating, ways of avoiding pregnancy.

'She is corrupt, Cicero, in mind and body.' I spoke with conviction. There is nothing like fear for spawning hatred.

138

'Hm.' He looked as if he were going to ask me something, but changed his mind. 'Do you wish to be called as a witness on your own behalf?'

'Yes, Sir.'

'You may do so, provided you speak exactly on the lines I shall suggest. Is that understood?'

I didn't like the idea, but had no option; I would have demanded the same complete subservience if I'd been in his shoes. An advocate of Cicero's calibre makes his plans like a general before a battle, and the first requirement is the total obedience of those who fight for him. 'Yes, Master,' I said humbly. This pleased him.

'Good. Now stand up and let me have a look at you. . . . Oh no, this won't do at all. Between now and the trial you will not appear at any of the fashionable baths and will leave your hair untrimmed and uncurled. Wear an old toga in the streets, *with a ragged hem*, and don't be seen in taverns. Two days before you appear in court you will stop shaving. Use no scent and be moderate in your drinking. I will explain why. I wish you to stand before the jurors looking *young, woebegone* and above all *clean-living*. These three aspects of your appearance are all equally important. Signs of tears, perhaps – a little onion juice at the last moment will take care of that. Is all this clear?'

'Indeed, yes, Sir. I cannot thank you enough.' My spirits were rising. If he was determined to win my case – and he had evidently put thought into it already – then, whatever his motives, I should have ample revenge for the tortures I had been suffering. But then I remembered all the power and influence of the Claudians, and my thoughts were sombre.

'Now let's see when we can talk at greater length.' He picked up the long tablet on which Tiro kept his appointments. 'I shall be free two days hence after dinner. Take my advice and eat lightly beforehand, or take an emetic. I shall need you with all your excellent wits about you. I want to know everything you can recall of the incidents about which you are being charged, and every last detail of your sordid affair with the Lady Clodia. How you first met her, when and how intercourse first took place, the lady's habits, any – er – sexual eccentricities, her entertainments, the quarrels you had with her and what led to the final break, the men who were your chief rivals, including Clodius – anything at all about her relations with Clodius. So be abstemious, I repeat.'

'I shall be fasting, Master.'

'Not if I know you, Marcus,' he said with an affectionate smile, 'and remember, I do.'

He could still, I thought resentfully, as I pushed my way through the crowd of litigants in the atreum, make me feel like a boy of sixteen, entering his chambers for the first time.

*

The trial was to begin two days before the start of the Games, and it seemed likely that influence had been brought to bear on the magistrates to choose that date, so that on the third day, when the defence counsel were to speak, the court would be half-empty. At least, that is what Cicero suspected, but he needn't have worried. No one who could attend was going to miss the chance of hearing both Crassus and Cicero confront the hated Claudians.

23

The Trial

My trial took place in the permanent court reserved for capital and other serious offences, with a praetor as President. I was brought in a closed litter, under guard, from my father's house, and made my entrance as Cicero had prescribed, head bowed, unshaven, with the onion tears rolling down my cheeks, and wearing the execrable toga whose hem my mother had so industriously unstitched and frayed that it looked like a dish-rag. I felt utterly ridiculous, but at least I had persuaded Cicero, at the last moment, not to have my hair ironed straight, pleading that the romantic confusion in which it tumbled over my shoulders might be an advantage.

On the first day, according to statutory procedure, much time was taken up in objections by counsel on both sides to members of the three groups of jurors – Senators, knights and paymaster-tribunes. The panel was reduced from the full number of eighty-one to about fifty, but this is quite normal.

Then came the reading of the sworn evidence of witnesses for the prosecution – those on the other side are only introduced by defence counsel in the course of the trial – and I was dismayed at the amount of false testimony arrayed against me.

There were freedmen who testified that they had seen me with a dagger in my hand near Dio; others who swore I had led the riot at Naples; bath attendants who said they had seen a friend of mine with a box of poison, about to hand it to one of Clodia's slaves; maids who swore they had seen me in bed with Clodia while Metellus was still alive. It was a long series of lies, but dangerous lies, and it was obvious that the jury was impressed.

I spent that night in the charge of an officer of the court, who treated me as if I were already condemned, and I couldn't blame him. My sleep was scanty, haunted by dreams of that horrible pit in which Catiline's supporters had been strangled.

On the following day the prosecution counsel made their case, and although I was subjected to the foulest abuse I began to see a glimmer of light.

The chief prosecutor was Atratinus, a young man of seventeen whom I knew well from my persistent attacks on his father Bestia. He spoke quite well, for a junior counsel, but when he produced his witnesses they had been badly briefed, and the defence juniors made the most of it. Then came Herrenius, and the informal charges followed thick and fast – my profligate way of life, my debts, my allegiance to Catiline (yes, that too!), my presumption in frequenting the society of aristocrats, my visits to Baiae posing as a patrician (that, of course, was my wearing of red shoes for the water-battle). He did his best to make me sound thoroughly disreputable. Didn't he realise that to Cicero all this would be meat and drink?

I thought I knew what had happened. I have described Clodia – gay, thoughtful, tender, lustful; Clodia the student of politics; Clodia the lover of poetry – but you have also seen her in a blind rage, that day in the garden when she smashed the mosaic. As I sat listening to the long story of my iniquities I could imagine her, small and imperious, wearing that burnt-orange gown with the silk threads, her fair hair dressed in curls around her ears, looking up into the staid, strong face of Lucius Herrenius, and stamping her foot. In that mood she simply didn't conceive that she could be refused anything. I knew that mood, as well as I knew the little foot I had loved to hold in my hand.

Clodia never did anything by halves. Once she had decided that my punishment for slighting her should not be death by poison or an assassin's dagger, but humiliation and exile, or at least the ruin of my legal career, she would have gone around searching for stones to throw at me. What is more, she would insist that *all* the stones should be thrown, for good measure — and she would have rushed the lawyers into it.

I could understand Atratinus, whom she would have enslaved at first meeting, and Clodius, who loved her, letting unwanted material be thrust into their briefs, and I supposed Herrenius must have given in against his will. For careful, selective character-smearing is one thing — we all use it — but a list of petty, unsupported charges as long as my arm is suicidal, and Herrenius must have known it. He was playing directly into Cicero's hands; the serious accusations would be lost in the flood of ridicule he would pour over the minor ones. It is always fortunate for the defence advocate that the president of the court has no power to guide the jurors, and point out gaps and inconsistencies in the speeches of counsel; they are left with the defence advocate's words still ringing in their ears. But of course our jurors, being Romans, are all amateur lawyers, and think they can assess the rights and wrongs for themselves. There is no greater mistake.

When my former friend Clodius came to the stand he revealed himself in his true colours. The crowd packing the galleries could scarcely have recognised the man who as people's tribune had so often roused them to enthusiasm with his clever, bawdy speeches, spiked with the slang of the streets, and his protestations that he had become a plebeian solely to serve them, the people of Rome. He spoke now as a patrician, haughtily furious that a man of a lower order had presumed to offend a member of his family. He accused me of assaulting a Senator (who had not appeared to give evidence); of reckless spending, in that I was paying thirty thousand sesterces in rent for a flat on the Palatine (it was the flat in his own block, and the rent was only ten thousand — I had receipts from his agent to prove it); of living apart from my father, as if that showed I was up to no good, and so on, finishing with the statement that I had besmirched the honour of his sister. The rabble in the gallery began to cheer mockingly at every new accusation, and Clodius flushed with rage. He wasn't used to hearing catcalls from a crowd, but his gangs couldn't prevent it here.

Finally, after that reference to my corruption of Clodia's morals, which brought forth such a gale of laughter that the praetor threatened to clear the court, Clodius repeated Herrenius' complaint that I had frequented the revels at Baiae — a resort, he explained, which was reserved for patricians. This — in front of a jury mainly composed of the lower orders! Those stiff-necked aristocrats never learn.

I felt, when he sat down, that we should win. Clodia, I thought with relish, would find that she couldn't so easily smash the career of Marcus Caelius.

On the last day Crassus opened the defence. I've said he was a good orator, but I could have used a more generous term. When he died in Parthia last year Rome lost a man of many abilities. His speech on my behalf was a model of good oratory and impeccable taste. He did not abuse his position as one of the three most powerful men in the world but confined his plea, as he and Cicero had arranged, to clear rebuttal of the main charges. He used no invective, but exposed the weaknesses of the prosecution's case courteously, with overwhelming logic. His witnesses had been well-prepared and withstood cross-examination, and he finished elegantly, speaking of my character and talents. I don't express gratitude easily, but I could have kissed his feet.

Crassus called me to the stand as witness on my own behalf, and I made the speech that had been rehearsed many times under Cicero's rigorous eye.

I denied everything, except to admit some youthful indiscretions, humbly apologised for the mischance that had caused certain great ones to select me as a target for their abuse, and threw myself on the court's mercy. I reminded the jurors that I was at the beginning of a career which perhaps already showed some promise, and concluded, looking around in bewilderment, that there must be some strange conspiracy behind these unbelievable charges. As I sat down there was a little clatter of applause from the jurors' tablets.

Everyone was now waiting to hear Cicero, and the aisles were jammed with people standing. The Romans love oratory, and he has never failed them. The air of the court was stifling and unbearably hot, but when Cicero appeared on the stand he was as cool and urbane as if conducting a family sacrifice. My pulse quickened. If he wished, I knew that he could ride this case home at a canter, but he had no intention of hurrying over his revenge. He had told me nothing of his line of defence, but I expected a frontal attack on the Claudians, and on Clodius in particular. It never even occurred to me that he would concentrate his whole attack on a woman.

He stood for a moment looking down at the jurors, with a serene smile on his face, and began to speak quietly, reasonably, in that resonant voice which could be heard in the farthest corner of the gallery. He commiserated with the court for having been convened, against his express wishes, on a public

143

holiday, when everyone should have been out in the open air, enjoying the Games. And all, said Cicero, blandly ignoring the capital charges, for a case in which no real crime, no outrage, no act of violence was being judged. (He could make such statements, blatantly false, with an air of such simple honesty that you could actually see jurors nodding their heads in agreement.)

All these ridiculous accusations, he explained, had been made against a talented, energetic, popular young man by a family which bore him a grudge, and the whole action, he added sadly, with a pause for dramatic effect, was financed by a whore.

It was the first crack of the whip, and the crowd stirred. Anyone who could call a member of the aristocracy a whore had their full attention. Cicero hadn't mentioned Clodia's name, but kept his hearers in suspense while he went on, gently, paying a compliment to young Atratinus for his eloquence, pointing out my father sitting unhappily in his mourning robes, with my mother beside him in floods of tears. He reproved Clodius for implying that it was somehow shameful to be a mere knight's son, when all in the court could see how dignified and worthy a Roman knight could be.

He admitted that for a short time I had been a supporter of Catiline but – his eye lingered mockingly on some of the Senators in the court – so had many other highly respectable citizens, and he could assure the jury that at the time when he, Cicero, had crushed the conspiracy and saved the City from massacre and fire, I had been constantly at his side.

He spoke for two hours, glancing occasionally at the water-clock dripping away on its pedestal, and at the time I write the speech is in every schoolboy's satchel. He began by demolishing the formal charges, including some which had already been covered by Crassus.

The murder of Dio? But everyone knew it was King Ptolemy himself who was guilty, and in any case Asicius, the only man who had been suspected of involvement in the murder, had been tried and acquitted. If anyone should be accused, it was the King. (This, of course, was no defence at all, but I swear it sounded convincing, as Cicero put it.)

The alleged theft of gold? But the prosecution had been forced to admit, under cross-examination, that it was no theft. The lady had given Caelius gold for some purpose. Caelius had said that it was for certain games, but the prosecution, without a shred of evidence, claimed that it was to bribe the slaves of Lucceius to murder Dio, who was a guest in his house. The evidence of Lucceius had shown that this was utterly impossible, and he was known to be a man of the highest honour. Which could be believed, the word of Lucceius – or the ravings of a foul tempered nymphomaniac?

The poison attempt? He made great play with that trumped-up charge. The prosecution had said I had procured some poison, and tried it out with immediate success on one of my own slaves – 'Surely a waste of a valuable asset for a young man of moderate means!' – I had then arranged that my friend Licinius should meet one of Clodia's slaves in the Senian Baths and hand it over. Herrenius had explained that Clodia, being informed of this, had sent some young men to lie in wait in the baths and pounce on Licinius with the poison box in his hand. But the trick hadn't worked, since Licinius had seen the ambush in time and escaped with the box of poison. So where was the evidence? The slave had been freed, and could not therefore be induced to give reliable evidence by torture, as the law required. Even the alleged young men who had lain in ambush could not be produced, which was a pity, said Cicero. He would have liked to learn how they had succeeded, in their street clothes, in getting into the baths at all. Perhaps, he added slyly, the lady had won the friendship of the bath attendants – with her customary halfpenny deal. The jurors exploded into laughter.

As he rebutted one charge after another I began to see the pattern of his attack. He always returned to one central theme, that it was Clodia herself who was behind all the accusations, and her credibility he had to demolish. I was beginning, unaccountably, to feel uneasy. As the fine lash of his scorn began to bite, my own flesh was smarting.

Everything I had told him about Clodia, on that night when Cicero had questioned me so inexorably and when, frightened and angry, I had held nothing back, was now twisted into a thong to lash her with. Clodius he left alone except for some sarcastic side-swipes that had the court sniggering with glee. 'I would,' said Cicero, 'be making my attack in much stronger terms if I did not feel inhibited by the fact that this woman's husband – I beg your pardon, I mean brother; I always make that mistake – is my personal enemy.' And later he said that Clodius 'must have had nightmares as a little boy' (Damnation! I could still hear her voice as she told me about him), 'since he had to go into his sister's bed for comfort'. It was funny, of course, but when he came back, time after time, to Clodia, I winced.

Would he never let up? He was raising her ancestors now, as

I'd known he would somewhere in his speech, and picturing Appius the Blind, who died three hundred years ago, asking Clodia whether she thought he'd built his great aqueduct so that she could wash herself after her filthy fornications.

I dug my finger-nails into the palms of my hands, remembering a May morning when she had pulled me out of bed to swim in the Tiber, and we had run across the lawn, making tracks in the dew, naked as the day we were born. Later, she'd made me lift her up on to a pedestal, so that she could pose as a naiad. The gardeners stood by, gaping, until she told them she was a goddess, and they fell on their knees.

'This woman,' he was saying, as he stood standing like the statue of a virtuous Roman of the past, his lip curling with scorn, 'has become so depraved that she does not even wait for nightfall and the privacy of the bedchamber to satisfy her inordinate lusts. She delights in shocking decent people by indulging her exotic and lecherous whims in the full light of day.' Why had she chosen that notorious garden by the river? But of course, so that she could pick her lovers of a moment from among the fine young men swimming in the Tiber!

Well, Clodia was honest, you could give her that, and there was a grain of truth in all Cicero said – the truth I thought with, a groan, which I had given him. But the picture he painted of Clodia was wholly false. I had wanted her chastened, of course, but not stripped naked and dragged through the gutter in front of the jeering crowd. My thoughts tried desperately to escape from what Cicero was saying.

There was a time, in that same garden, when I came on her sitting in a bower of vines above the water. She was looking across the Tiber, watching the bright sails of the barges, and had the scroll of Catullus' latest poems in her lap. She glanced at me with tears in her eyes, and said, 'I hurt him so much, Marcus, and he feels it's more than he can bear.' And being younger then, and sometimes foolish, I said that such emotions were not for her and me. We lived for our senses, and so would Catullus, if he hadn't been born a fool. She flew into a temper and thrust the scroll into my hands. 'Read it,' she cried furiously. 'Read it aloud, if you can.' So I did, or began to read the first poem, but she snatched it away and cried, 'You're declaiming it, you backstreet orator! It's not for a claque of scruffy electors, it's written for me.' She began to speak the lines with all the passion of the wretched Catullus. The rhythms flowed like

146

music, and I listened in silence, entranced, watching her vivid face; and very jealous of the man who had written those words.

The great actor was still saying his piece, smoothly, with measured emphasis, 'It is not only this woman's general behaviour but her dress, her companions, her avid glances and shocking language, her beach-parties and water-parties and dinner-parties, her shameless habit of embracing her lovers in public – all these proclaim the fact that she is not only a whore, but a vulgar and depraved whore.' He turned to Herrenius with an air of appealing to him, as a reasonable man. 'Surely, Lucius Herrenius, you would agree; if a young man is found in *that* woman's company it is not a question of adultery but lust, not outrage to chastity but mere satisfaction of appetite.' As he spoke his arm swung up, pointing.

Clodia was standing beneath an archway. Her maids shrank back at Cicero's gesture, and she was alone and defenceless as he went on. Two of the Claudians were thrusting their way through the crowd, trying to get her away. It was typical of her fierce courage that she had come to the court to face the attack. She still held her proud head high, but she was deathly pale, and there were lines I had never seen in the face I had loved so much. All my relief at escape from a sentence of exile or death had vanished, and my heart was sick. I could not understand why, except that perhaps she had become part of me, for ever.

I stood up blindly and began to stumble away, turning for a last look of abhorrence at Cicero. But I caught his astonished glance, and remembered where I was. I went back to my chair. I was still the prisoner at the bar of justice, and had to sit it out. They told me afterwards that the expression on my face made an excellent impression on the jurors.

*

They acquitted me, of course. The Claudians shouted themselves hoarse with fury, and I guessed that Clodius' gangs would be on the streets, out for my blood. The court granted Cicero's request for an armed escort to his house, and I went with him.

He was full of his triumph, boasting of his cleverness and gloating at the thought of the rage of the Claudians. Clodia's feelings were never once mentioned, because he had simply not taken them into account. After all, she was only a woman.

It was torture for me, but I stuck it out when we arrived at Cicero's house, and he called his slaves to shave and bathe me and provide a clean toga. He was genuinely shocked to find that I could scarcely speak to him, but put it down to relief. I hated him for what he had done, yet knew that my obligation was great, and would have to be repaid. Avoiding his eyes, I said I was too shaken to make proper expression of the gratitude he so richly deserved, and he looked most concerned and was still fussing over me when friends began to arrive, eager to congratulate him and drink his wine. I excused myself early, saying I owed it to my parents to be united with them in this hour of triumph, and asked to be allowed to call on Cicero the following day. Then I went out into the dark streets, alone.

I had only my stylus, but if Clodius' gangs had found me I don't think I would have run away.

*

It was a month afterwards that a messenger from Cicero brought me a publisher's copy of his speech, very pretty, rolled up in a red leather case with my name on it in gold. He had sealed it himself, for I recognised the impression of the ring he always wore on his thumb.

I stood for a long time after the man had gone, looking down at the scroll, unopened. Then I threw it on the fire and went out to a brothel.

Part Four

September 56 BC – September 52 BC

24

Roman Politics

After the trial I had to re-think my plans for the future. First of all, I was now committed to both Cicero and Crassus, and this meant following them around for a decent period, supporting their public speeches and singing their praises at every opportunity. If I didn't discharge my 'obligations' in the traditional way I should lose face.

Secondly, I had become something of a popular hero when the story of the trial became known, a deserving young man whom two great leaders had defended against the spite and oppression of the Claudians. So this was as favourable a time as any to stand election for entry into the public service. I had just reached the minimum age for the post of quaestor, and the elections were approaching. Once I was quaestor the way into the Senate and a broad purple stripe on my toga lay ahead, for what that was worth.

Thirdly, my life was in danger, and so was Cicero's. The more closely I stayed by his side, the more I could make use of the protection which his rank and prestige would afford. I didn't relish the idea. It would take a long time to forget what he had done to Clodia.

Cicero was delighted with my decision. He felt that I was bound to him from then on, and the sooner he could get my support in the Senate the better. Both he and Crassus sponsored my application, and even Pompey put in a good word. In the autumn Milo and I were elected praetor and quaestor respectively. My parents were very proud and gave a grand party for me, and Fabia came on the arm of her brother, who was a friend of mine. She looked very young and radiantly pretty.

There was nothing very deep in our affair. When I was awaiting trial she had sent messages but kept away from me, afraid I suppose that close association with a criminal might harm her chances of marrying again. But Caelius the hero of the moment, Caelius on the first rung of the official ladder that led both to the Senate and – who could tell? – to the Consulship, was another matter. She was an ardent lover and a gay companion, but when she later talked of marriage I found excuses. Even these days, in my view, marriage can be a burden on a man.

Clodia was never seen in public that autumn and winter, and perhaps it is true, as some people said, that her elder brother Appius, the head of the family, was so enraged after Cicero's attack on her morals that he shut her up in one of his villas, under guard. He was Governor of Sardinia at the time and aiming at the Consulship, and had no intention of letting his family ruin his chances. For the same reason he put Clodius under a measure of restraint, but only after two attempts to assassinate me had failed.

The first was shortly after my trial. I had gone back to live in my flat, with a couple of strong slaves to protect me, and when I ventured forth one morning to attend Cicero's levée there were two ruffians waiting at the turn of the stairs. I recognised one of Clodius' gangsters, and retired hastily. My flat door was near the top of the staircase, and when I came out again, with a sword in my hand, my two slaves were following me, with pails of boiling water concealed behind their backs. I called to the thugs to get out, but they began to run up the steps, so I stepped aside and let the slaves hurl the water at their faces. The last thing I wanted was to have blood on my hands, and the water was enough. We disarmed them while they were still shouting with pain and half-blind, and tied them up. Some of my fellow-tenants had come out on to the landing when they heard the noise, and I said the men were thieves, and showed their swords. Everyone said it was a scandal to have thieves walking into an apartment block at eight in the morning, and on the Palatine, at that. The owner ought to do something about it, they said. (The owner, of course, was Clodius!)

I had a closer look at the two men. They were strong, filthy hooligans, freed slaves probably, and their faces and hands were in a bad way from the scalding. I said I would have salve brought at once if they would tell me who had sent them, but they shook their heads, and it was sheer good fortune that at

150

this moment one of Milo's guards came up the stairs to say that he was waiting for me below.

'Tell Milo what's happened,' I said, 'and ask him what I'd better do.'

While he was gone I told the onlookers that Milo would help us, and had the men taken into my flat, where the slaves laid them out on the floor and stood over them, with meat axes in their hands.

Milo arrived quickly, having run up three flights of stairs without any sign of being out of breath. When the toughs saw him they quailed, but still refused to answer until he told them what he'd do if they didn't. Nobody likes being castrated, and he had stripped off their loin-cloths and was prodding impatiently at the parts in question with his sword, so they talked. Cloelius, a Senator who was one of Clodius' lieutenants, had told them to murder me on my way to the levée and report to him for payment at a certain tavern, at ten o'clock. Milo smiled.

Now that the action was over I admit I was badly scared, and Milo didn't make me feel any better. He thumped me on the back. 'You'll get used to it, son,' he said kindly. 'This is just the beginning.'

'We'd better take them to the aedile and lay a charge.'

He shook his head. 'You'd get nowhere. Clodius would deny everything and let them rot. Leave it to me, young Marcus. I'll make sure these two won't trouble you again, and arrange a little surprise for Cloelius.' He looked at me with approval. 'That was a smart bit of work, son. I didn't know you had it in you. Come on now. We'll get some of my men to look after this offal.'

I never saw the two hooligans again. Cloelius was attacked on his way to the tavern and beaten up. The next time I saw Milo he handed me a leather purse containing two hundred sesterces. 'I reckon that's yours, Marcus. They're a mean lot, aren't they? Only a hundred each for knocking *you* off!'

After that incident Milo gave me a guard of gladiators, who sat in the entrance porch of the block, playing dice and making remarks about the women passing in and out. The other tenants were glad of their presence and put up with a lot of bawdy comment on their womenfolk.

It was early in October, when Milo and I were both canvassing hard, that the second attempt was made, and this was more serious. Cicero had spoken for us, standing on a platform in the Subura, and it was when we were leaving that we saw a large group of men filling the street in front of us. Cloelius was among them, and he pointed with his sword and shouted my name. The toughs hurled insults at me and began to advance. The crowd of Cicero's supporters melted away and we were left alone, with four of Milo's huge Spanish gladiators to defend us.

Milo took charge. 'It's no good running,' he said. 'Old Chick-pea wouldn't make it. Get into that porch.'

It belonged to the house of a merchant, who had already barred the door, but it was more difficult to attack us there because the porch had steps. The gladiators whipped off their togas and wrapped them round their left arms, and Milo and I did the same. Cicero's horror when he saw the sword I always wore strapped to my side in those days was laughable. He, of course, would never dream of going armed in the streets; it was not only illegal but undignified.

The gang came at us in a rush, with Cloelius behind, urging them on; but Milo and his men were first-class swordsmen, and I could at least defend myself, having learnt something of the art on the Campus Martius. Milo was leaping forward, thrusting, and back again, so quickly that the man in front of him was hit before he knew what was happening. I had glimpses of the gladiators fighting like wild-cats on both sides of me, toppling their opponents over on to their companions pressing in from behind.

I raised my protected left arm to ward off a slash and thrust my sword under it. The man staggered back, clutching his stomach, and behind him was Cloelius, coming at me. He was much better at this game than I, and parried my lunges easily with his sword. Then he thrust at me, like lightning, and his point was at my ribs before the weapon was knocked clean out of his hand by a blow from Milo. Cloelius turned to run, and by this time the gang had had enough, and followed him.

The Spanish gladiators hooted with laughter and uttered strange war-cries, racing after them and neatly picking off the stragglers. Milo roared at them to come back and they returned, only stopping to clean their swords on the clothing of the men who lay on the ground. There were twelve of them by now, three dying or dead.

The point of Cloelius' sword must have been into me by the time Milo knocked it away, for there was a great rent in my tunic and blood was spreading fast. I had felt nothing, but now I sat down on the steps, feeling sorry for myself.

'Jove's thunder!' cried Milo. 'They got Caelius. Hold on, son.' He ripped off my tunic and exposed a deep slash across my ribs. 'No harm there. Put his toga on for him, Verco.' I stood up and let the man hustle me into my robe. Then I turned to look at Cicero.

He was white as a sheet, leaning against one of the pillars of the porch, but his eyes were blazing. 'See,' he declaimed, 'how the right hand of virtue drives out evil!'

'There'll be a lot more bleeding evil to drive out in a moment,' said Milo, with his gruff laugh, 'unless we hop it. We've got to *move*, Chick-pea.'

Cicero cried. 'Look at Marcus. Get help for him, Milo.'

'He's only scratched.'

I was annoyed. The blood was pouring down my leg. But I helped Milo to get Cicero away. The gladiators, unusually cheerful and animated, came chattering in their outlandish tongue behind us.

*

Cloelius had disappeared when the summons was issued for his arrest, and after a discussion with the praetor in charge of cases of violence Cicero withdrew his accusation. He couldn't admit that his own guard had been carrying weapons, and his explanation that one of his attendants had fortunately been carrying a bundle of swords to the armourer for sharpening was not well received. But his speech in the House was terrific, and both Clodius and his brother Appius were shouted down when they tried to speak.

It was at this point that Appius must have forced Clodius to leave Rome, for he, too, disappeared, and it was some time later that stories were heard of what he was at in Etruria.

Clodius was quite independent now of any support from Caesar and Crassus, and operating on his own as a brigand – there is no other word – in the Tuscan hills. His gangs terrorised the countryside, drove wealthy farmers off their lands, and cut down great areas of oak trees to provide timber for housing. He began to build houses everywhere within reach of the bigger towns and sold them to the new-rich who were anxious to live in the country and try their hands at farming. Being isolated, such families were perfect subjects for Clodius' protection racket, which went into action as soon as they had settled in. He also operated in the Alban Hills south of Rome, where there was a great demand for summer villas, and built for himself a sort of fortress-cum-gentleman's residence at Alba, on the Appian Way. It was designed by Cyrus, and quite unlike anything that had been constructed before.

The luxurious living-quarters were built over a grid of arches enclosing enough rooms and dormitories, according to Cicero's estimate, to house a thousand men, so that if necessary Clodius could withstand a siege. From this stronghold he could sally forth, rampage around the countryside collecting his protection money from terrified householders and retire to enjoy himself in comfort. The dowry he had obtained with Fulvia was being multiplied many times. He aimed to build up his fortune until he could return to politics with a politician's most persuasive arguments, in our democratic era, bulging money-bags and bands of experienced men trained in the techniques of gangster rule.

*

These years that immediately followed my trial are not of importance to my story, since as I have explained Clodius was temporarily missing from Roman politics, and so was Cicero, who spent much of the time writing books at one or other of his many villas.

Pompey and Crassus had their term as Co-Consuls, and the year after, Pompey gave himself the Governorships of Spain and Libya, but ruled them both by proxy. He and Julia were happy together, and now that he had obtained all the power he felt was his due he had no wish to exercise it, but lived in partial retirement. Crassus, who was richer than ever, now owned large parts of Rome, including most of the Palatine Hill, where his fellow-millionaires had their houses. He had acquired much of this property by an ingenious scheme of his own.

We have no municipal fire-brigade in Rome, but Crassus had his own force, with three fire-engines, and had trained the crews to use them quickly and effectively. Most Roman houses are built of wood, and if fire takes hold nothing can be done to save the premises unless action is taken at once. Thus, as soon as one of Crassus' neighbours discovered that his house was on fire he sent for the fire-brigade, and the bargaining started. It often happened that the owner held out against the exhorbitant terms demanded by Crassus' agent until it was too late, and the whole house was destroyed. The agent then offered spot cash for what was left, including the site.

Now came the second operation in Crassus' plan. He had bought no less than five hundred Greek and Asian slaves with architectural experience, and could repair or re-erect a house quicker and cheaper than any competitor. But apart from the role of Phoenix, Crassus' team had another use. Modern houses, especially those built in a hurry by Clodius, frequently fall down, because they are constructed with supports made of a mixture of lime mortar and pebbles, as a substitute for wood. Again, Crassus' agent would be on the spot before the dust had settled, making an offer for the site and the heap of rubble, and the frantic owner would often be glad to accept.

It's perhaps significant to record that in all his life Crassus only built one house for himself – the one to be sold to Cicero, which Clodius burned down. If you build for yourself, said Crassus, you need no enemies. The house is enough.

However, Crassus' appetite for gold brought his downfall. Still unsatisfied, he chose for himself the province of Syria, hoping to carry war beyond its frontiers and sack the Parthian cities in Mesopotamia; but even his subtle brain was no match for the treachery of the wily Parthians.

My father died, and I sorrowed for him. The business passed into my hands, but not openly, for I was standing for election to the Senate at the time and Senators are not allowed to engage in trade. I moved into the family house, chiefly to keep my mother company in her grief, but kept on the flat for occasional use. I had been maintaining an expensive way of life, and what with that and the generous gifts my father had made me during his lifetime the inheritance was smaller than I had hoped, and I had to build up the business as best I could. Prices were still rising, and what would have been a handsome fortune ten years ago was now just enough to provide a modest income for my household. I needed more, and the list of loans from my grateful clients increased.

Fabia and I had parted, when I still refused to marry her, and a succession of other girls followed, all pretty and gay, and all rather expensive.

I was made a Senator, and my mother wove with her own hands a very fine toga with the broad purple stripe. Milo married a fortune. Catullus died. Clodia was nothing to me now except an occasional dull ache in my heart.

Caesar had his term in Gaul extended and was given more legions. He crossed the Rhine and the Channel and found the opposition tougher than he had expected. (He is still there, as I write, building bigger and better armies and greater stores of treasure, waiting for the moment when he can return to Rome, and dictate all our destinies.)

Now I must relate what has been happening during the past eighteen months, those last chapters in the story of the feud between Cicero and Clodius.

25

Milo for Consul

Milo had been a good praetor, and in the Senate had made his common sense and the vigour of his invective felt. He was now Dictator, as it is called locally, of his native town of Lanuvium, about twenty-five miles from Rome in the Alban Hills. In Lanuvium the dictator is just the head man in the little town, a combination of chief priest and mayor. Milo's fortunes had been vastly improved by his marriage to Fausta, daughter of the great Sulla. She was the richest heiress in Rome, and that is saying much. They had a splendid house on the Palatine, several villas in the country and a sort of palace at Lanuvium, and they enjoyed living in all of them.

They were well matched, too. She is a woman of staggering proportions, but handsome in a monolithic way and devoted to her husband, who treats her with a mixture of old-fashioned courtesy and rough handling, which she obviously likes.

'What a woman, Marcus!' he would say affectionately, slapping her monumental buttocks. 'There's nothing like a well-bred mare to give a man a smooth ride.' (He was proud of her patrician ancestors.) And she would catch him a buffet that would have felled a lesser man, and tell him not to give Marcus ideas. They always made me welcome, and tried to marry me off, without success.

Milo's popularity was at its height, not least among the bankers and tax-farmers of the equestrian order, who gave him credit for having chased Clodius out of Rome. His position and influence grew, and I began to realise that he was a man of considerable ambition on his own account, and by no means merely the willing tool of Cicero. Several rich men died and left him properties. He sold off three of these and in honour of his dead benefactors staged funeral games, the most lavish Rome had seen since Pompey's Triumph. This had to be done unofficially, because Milo was not the curule aedile, and Cicero thought the whole thing a great waste of money. It always annoyed him to see people spending money which they might have left for him in their wills.

Milo for once paid no attention to Cicero. 'It's this way, young Marcus,' he explained. 'I'm going to stand for Consul, right? Early in the New Year I'll be starting my campaign. Now old Pompey has smelt a rat, and I've got a suspicion he's not going to back me up. Since Julia died he's been getting restive and beginning to take an interest in politics again.' The death of Pompey's beloved wife a few months before had left Pompey frantic with grief, but free to confront her father, Julius Caesar, in the final struggle for power.

'So what I need is overwhelming support from the people,' continued Milo. 'Now what do the poor sods want? I'll tell you, games. It's the only amusement they have, and that's what counts. I don't hold with these fellows who give every Roman citizen twenty sesterces. It sets them back twenty million, and what do they get for it? Sweet nothing. The chap in the street has to give half to his wife for the kids and he goes on a blind and drinks or gambles away the rest. It's all gone in a couple of days, and nothing to remember. What I'll do is give them five hundred pairs of gladiators. That's going to take up quite a number of days, and all good fun. What's more important to me, they'll go on talking about it for years.'

'But it'll cost the earth!' Even Julius Caesar's famous games twelve years before had only staged three hundred fights.

'I want to equal Pompey, and I've got no fighting bloody elephants. So it's a case of sheer numbers and good quality. I can pick 'em. I know all the gladiator schools and they'll give me good men at cut prices. Anyway, Fausta always likes a bit of bloodshed and she's paying for most of it. It'll nearly clean us out, but you'll see the results. I'll be Consul before the year's out, and then I can start to get it back.' He paused for a moment, scratching his hairy chest. 'There's another reason. A man like me *ought* to make a good show. We aristocrats have our obligations.'

Milo's reasoning was sounder than Cicero's. The Romans are fickle in their loyalties, which follow the man of the moment. After Catiline, it was Cicero; after his spectacular Triumph, Pompey was the most popular man in Rome until Clodius began to insult and harass him publicly, when obviously Clodius must be the leader worthy of support. Now it was Milo. The games were a tremendous success. The acres of blood-stained sand, changed every day, the triumphant shouts of the victors, the dying screams of the vanquished, the processions, the dancing in the evenings, were all provided by Milo, out of his own pocket, with no contribution from the State. He was doing it just to please the people; in fact, he told them so. Who could doubt that he was the right man to be Consul?

157

Pompey, for a start. Milo was quite right in mistrusting the General's attitude to his tactics. Pompey had helped Milo, who after all had been his henchman and his protector in the street fighting, to gain the praetorship, but was by no means willing to see him made Consul. He could foresee that Milo as Consul, with Cicero to support him, might prove a dangerous combination. In fact, he saw through Cicero's game, and to counter it took a step which was the last thing anyone expected, and which plunged Rome into chaos for seven months.

*

It was in July of that year* when we held a sort of council of war in Cicero's house. All Rome was talking of the bad news from Syria. Crassus' army had been defeated by the Parthians in Mesopotamia, with twenty thousand men killed and ten thousand taken prisoner. Some said Crassus had been captured alive, and that the Parthians had poured molten gold down his throat; others, that he had been killed fighting. But whatever had happened to him, he was dead, and the Triumvirate was at an end. It was now Pompey and Caesar.

Cicero said, 'Pompey will be more than ever afraid of Caesar, and try to cut short his command before he gets any stronger. So he'll want his own men as Consuls, and that means he'll oppose you, Milo.'

'I know he will, the double-crossing bastard! But he won't find it easy.'

'It'll be easier if he gets the help of the man he's already approached,' said Cicero.

'Who's that?' I asked idly. It was a hot afternoon and we were sitting beside the pool in the atreum. Cicero thought my attention was wandering. 'I am speaking of Clodius,' he said sharply.

'Clodius!' exclaimed Milo. 'Blood of Bacchus! The man who tried to kill Pompey at least twice? And would have, if I hadn't been there. It's nonsense, Chick-pea.'

'I'm afraid it's quite true,' said Cicero. 'One of my agents is with Clodius now, in Etruria. I've just had a report from him, to say that Metellus Scipio came to Clodius' house in Perugia with a message from Pompey. The agent is a trusted slave – one of Clodius' scribes.'

'And the message?'

'That the scribe couldn't say, but after Metellus had gone he was summoned by Clodius and told to get together all his notes

* 53 BC

158

for campaign speeches, since Clodius would be returning to Rome at once to stand for election as praetor. He boasted that Pompey would support him.'

I said, 'It's almost unbelievable. Is there any confirmation at this end? You know what a liar Clodius is.'

'There is confirmation,' said Cicero, 'of a kind. Pompey's been seeing a great deal recently of Metellus Scipio – and his daughter Cornelia.'

'The old fornicator!' exploded Milo. 'At it again, with Julia scarcely cold in her tomb.' He looked puzzled. 'But what's so important about that?'

'It means,' I explained, 'that Pompey's seeking an alliance with the Caecilii Metelli, who are cousins of the Claudians. He'll want to see Metellus elected Consul, so you'll have a tough fight on your hands, Milo.'

'You think Pompey would bring back that little pervert Clodius to run wild in the streets again? He'd be mad if he did.'

'Clodius is coming back to Rome, if what Cicero's agent says is true, in any case, for the praetorian election. You don't think he'll come without his gang?'

Milo picked up his wine-cup and drained it. 'Then I'll just have to go to Etruria and smoke them out first. I want a nice quiet election, so's I can deliver my speeches properly.'

'Milo, you wouldn't have a chance,' said Cicero, very seriously. 'All the roads to Etruria are picketed by Clodius' men; I know that for a fact.'

'All right, then. We'll fight it out in Rome, as soon as he arrives.' He pondered. 'If I could provoke a row – have a free-for-all in the street, say – I'd kill Clodius with my own hands.'

'I know you would,' said Cicero warmly, 'and it would be a patriotic deed, but it would end your election prospects – and all the plans we've worked out.'

'That's true,' said Milo regretfully. 'We'll just have to bring up that violence charge again, and this time make it stick.'

*

In fact, just the opposite happened. Clodius entered Rome, apparently on his best behaviour, and took his seat in the Senate. When the business on the agenda was concluded he stood up and laid a formal charge against Milo for insolvency, unbefitting a member of the House. Plautius Hypsaeus and Metellus Scipio, Milo's opponents in the Consular election, supported him strongly.

Luckily, Milo kept his temper and made a dignified speech,

and Cicero spoke on his behalf. So did I, defending Milo as the man who had restored order to the City, and attacking Clodius with every weapon in my armoury. Pompey was neither for nor against, but recommended that while a slur on the reputation of one of the candidates for the Consulship remained uninvestigated, the election should be postponed. This, of course, was the object of the manoeuvre.

Later, Pompey adopted other delaying tactics. He repeatedly blocked the appointment of the Interrex, or regent, who would rule between the end of term of the current Consuls and the accession of the next pair. The elections continued to hang fire.

While all this was going on, Cicero was happy. With Pompey's support he had been selected to take Crassus' place in the College of Augurs, an almost entirely honorific position but one normally reserved for patricians, and therefore holding great snob-value.

I was fighting for my election as Tribune of the People, and both Cicero and Milo gave me their support. When I was elected Fausta gave a dinner for me, and some good advice.

'Watch your step with your co-tribunes, Marcus,' she said. 'Young Pompeius Rufus is up to no good.'

'He seems anxious not to make friends,' I said thoughtfully. 'I said I'd serve under his father in Utica, and he laughed scornfully and said it wasn't his father.'

'No more it was,' said Fausta. 'He's the son of a man of the same name who was killed young, although,' she added, 'knowing my sister Cornelia as I do I doubt whether anyone could say for certain who her son's father was.'

'So Pompeius is your nephew?' I asked, puzzled. The intricacies of the Sullan and Cornelian families were always difficult to unravel.

'He is, and I've known him since he was little. He was a fancy-boy of Clodius, and they're still as thick as thieves. So watch him.'

It was good advice. It soon became evident that both Pompeius Rufus and his friend Plancus, another of the nine tribunes who were duly elected with me for the coming year, were backing Metellus Scipio and Hypsaeus and doing their best to obstruct Milo.

Just when we thought Pompey couldn't drag his feet any longer, and that the consular elections would have to take place, Clodius' gangs, far more formidable than we had ever known them before, began to cause riots in the streets, systematically and intensively, and when the year came to an end there were still no Consuls elected, and therefore no magistrates. The whole of the judicial procedure had been completely disrupted.

On January 17th, Clodius let it be known, there would be a great mass meeting between the Rostra and the Comitium at which he would present his friends Metellus Scipio and Hypsaeus to the people as candidates for election. The meeting took place; the candidates spoke, demanding that the Interrex, Lepidus, should declare the elections open; the tribunes Pompeius and Plancus also made speeches. There were some unpleasant remarks aimed at me, sitting alone on the tribunes' bench which in theory rendered me inviolate, and Plancus shouted that the enemies of the people would have short lives. Clodius' men were active in the crowd, but he himself was nowhere to be seen. It struck me as odd, for this demonstration was just the sort of occasion for him to exploit, and he it was, after all, who had arranged the meeting.

I learned that he had left that morning for Aricia, where the Appian Way passes through the Alban Hills.

26

'Clodius is Dead!'

I have explained how it was that on the following day, January 18th, we had no State magistracies at all, and such authority as still existed was in the hands of Lepidus the Interrex, and the Tribunes of the People – myself, Pompeius, Plancus and seven others. Strictly speaking, we had no executive power, and our main task was to hear complaints against oppression. The door of our court in the Forum was open day and night for citizens to come for advice and help. We took our duty in shifts.

I was in court until five o'clock and as I was leaving, weary after a long day, I heard an uproar outside and one of our messengers came running in, spluttering with excitement.

'What's the matter, man?' I asked impatiently.

'Clodius is dead, Tribune!'

I ran out into the dusk of the Forum and saw a litter being carried past, followed by a crowd of people. Elbowing my way through the crush I stopped the litter-bearers. 'I am Caelius,

Tribune of the People,' I said. 'Whose men are you?'

It had been a dry, sunny day, and the men were covered with the dust of the road. The leader turned to me and wiped the sweat from his face. 'We belong to Tedius Sextus, Sir. He found the body of Clodius on the Appian Way, twelve miles from here, and told us to take it to the Lady Fulvia.'

'But where is your master?' None of Clodius' attendants was around and I could see no sign of Tedius.

'He went home, Sir, after he had given up his litter for Lord Clodius. He's gone to our villa at Alba.'

'Let me see the body.'

They opened the curtains, and the crowd strained forward to peer at the body of the man who had been my friend and my bitterest enemy. His toga was caked with dust and blood, but his fair head, thrown back on the cushions, was unmarked. The expression on that familiar face, with its patrician nose and small, petulant mouth, was something I cannot forget. He had died in pain.

'It *is* Clodius,' I said to the crowd, and turned to the bearers. 'Carry him to the Lady Fulvia, and then go home, all of you.' I raised my voice. 'Whoever did this deed, citizens, will be punished. Now show your respect for the dead and leave the widow with her grief. If you want to accompany the body to her house I will lead you. But come quietly, showing your sorrow.'

A man in a butcher's apron cried, 'The Tribune was Clodius' enemy!' and there was an ugly murmur from the crowd.

'Yes,' I shouted, 'he tried to kill me. But I didn't kill *him*. You know a tribune cannot leave the City, and some of you must have seen me in court all day.'

'That's right,' came from a woman near me. 'I saw him.'

'Then who did it?' cried the butcher. 'We'll find who it was and hang him, won't we, brothers?' There was an enthusiastic response from the mob. Clodius had lost the popularity he had once enjoyed, but his death seemed to be restoring it. I called to my guard to stand around the litter.

'You can find that out tomorrow,' I said. 'For the moment, we will go to the Lord Clodius' house, and let there be no shouting.'

Rather to my surprise they came with us quietly as we walked up the slope to the Palatine and into the street in which Clodius had bought a new house for himself a few months before. The door was closed, and there were no torches on the steps of the porch. The leader of the bearers banged on the oak panelling, and an old servant appeared.

I didn't wait to see Fulvia's grief. However much I and many others had disliked Clodius, and with good reason, she had loved him well enough. So when the door finally closed and the crowd remained waiting outside, eager to hear sounds of distress, I walked down the street to my apartment block, and relaxed thankfully in a hot bath. But not before I had sent a messenger with all speed to Cicero.

The slave returned while I was drinking my first cup of wine before dinner. Cicero, he said, asked me to call on him at dawn, without fail. Rather a peremptory message, I thought, to someone who had just given him the best news he'd had in his life. But I could imagine Cicero receiving my note – the shout of joy, followed by an immediate assumption of his commander-in-chief role, striding up and down, rapping out commands right and left. I smiled, and settled down to eat oysters, little realising that to Cicero my news had been no news at all.

*

In the grey light of dawn, at about half-past seven, I was on my way to see Cicero, and had to pass by Clodius' house. The street was blocked by the crowd, and above their heads I could see my fellow-tribunes Plancus and Pompeius in the porch trying to calm Fulvia, who was beside herself with grief and rage. Behind them emerged an open litter bearing Clodius' body, completely naked except for his patrician's red shoes with their ivory crescents. It was a disgraceful exhibition, but I could see why Fulvia had exposed the slight body. There must have been twelve stab-wounds, and they were clearly visible.

She turned to the crowd, her hair falling over her shoulders and her face ravaged. 'Take my lord's body to Cicero,' she shrieked. 'Let the murderer see what his butchers have done.'

There was a roar of excitement in the street. Pompeius spoke to her urgently, and although she at first shook her head, in the end she turned away, and went slowly into the house. Pompeius came forward and spoke to the crowd.

'The Lady Fulvia agrees,' he shouted, 'that we take the body to the Rostra, where you may all hear how this dreadful deed was committed, and the name of the murderer.' He and Plancus walked down the steps, with the litter-bearers following, and the crowd gave them room.

While the people pressed after them down the slope leading

to the Forum I stepped back into a doorway. There was nothing I could do. Just as I was leaving, the door above opened again and Cloelius, the dead man's lieutenant, came out, carrying a bundle of scrolls under his arm. He ran down the steps and was hurrying into a side-street when I caught up with him. There was no one about.

'What are you doing, Sextus Cloelius?' I asked. 'Robbing the dead?'

He started violently, and glared at me. 'What's that to do with you, Caelius? Keep away from me.' His eyes darted to right and left, but he was alone. His guards must have followed the litter.

'I'm a Tribune, and the people have a right to know if you're suppressing evidence. What are these scrolls?'

He tried to get at a weapon beneath his toga, but the scrolls were in his way and two of them fell to the ground. As he bent down hastily to retrieve them I knocked him sprawling, picked up the scrolls and ran. By the time he had collected the rest, scattered all over the street, I was well away, and slowed to a more dignified gait as I approached Cicero's house.

When I was shown into the library he was looking oddly shaken and ill at ease, and he greeted me with a cry of relief.

'The gods be thanked!' he exclaimed, jumping from his chair. 'I thought they must have got you in the street.'

'Why me? My alibi is unbreakable; I was in court all yesterday. But what happened? Do you know?'

'Of course I know,' he cried irritably. 'My agents have been bringing in reports all night.' He sat down and signed to me to do the same, as he went on more calmly, 'You know Milo had to go to Lanuvium yesterday? He was to induct a new priest there this morning.'

I nodded. 'I saw him before he left.'

'As I understand it,' said Cicero carefully, 'Clodius must have laid an ambush for him on the Appian Way.'

'So that's why he missed the meeting two days ago. Is Milo safe?'

'There was a fight, and Clodius was killed.'

'But Milo?'

'He was unhurt, and went on to Lanuvium. He'll be back tonight.'

'We must warn him, then. He'll be attacked by the mob. Plancus and Pompeius are stirring them up at this moment. They've got Clodius' naked body on the Rostra, and are showing the wounds to the crowd.'

He gave a cry of alarm. 'I thought the body was still in his house. How did this happen?'

I told him, including the accusation Fulvia had made, mentioning Cicero's name as the murderer.

He said in a strained voice, 'But how can she think I had anything to do with it? I was here – '

'Of course you were here, and everyone knows it. It's Milo who's in danger. Cicero, I still don't understand. Clodius' body is stuck full of wounds. If it was Milo – '

'It wasn't Milo!' he shouted. 'It was his slaves. Milo was nowhere near when he died.' He seized my arm. 'You must help, Marcus. It's our last chance to get Milo elected Consul.'

'He'll never make it now.' I looked at him thoughtfully. 'How many of Milo's men are dead?'

His glance shifted. 'Only one or two.'

'If I'm to help you,' I said slowly, 'I've got to know the truth. You're covering up for Milo. If Clodius had laid an ambush for Milo his thugs would have killed half his retinue, and Milo, too. *What happened?*'

'It's better for you not to know.'

'Nonsense!' I cried. 'I can't work in the dark. As Tribune I can give Milo a lot of help, but I will not do so unless you confide in me.'

'All right, if you insist. It was an accident.'

I stared at him. 'Remember I've seen Clodius' body,' I told him coldly.

He was on his feet, pacing up and down. 'It came about through an accident, Marcus. I ask you to believe that. Milo and Fausta were in their coach, surrounded by guards as usual, and behind them came a retinue of about three hundred, what with serving-men and maids, and all the entertainers and musicians Milo was taking with him for the ceremony. There were cooks and pages, grooms and kennel-boys – you know how Milo likes to do things in style, as he'd call it. He wanted to make a great show, after the religious part of the proceedings was over, with a feast for the city fathers, and so on. It was at Bovillae, twelve miles out on the Appian Way, that he met Clodius, who was on horseback, with a few friends and some armed slaves, coming back towards Rome. Now this is the important thing, Marcus,' he sat down and leaned towards me earnestly. 'They had passed each other, and when Clodius was a quarter of a mile further on, alongside the end of Milo's baggage train – it happened.'

'What happened?'

'Don't try to bully me, Marcus, I beg of you. Clodius was shouting insults at Milo's slaves and they replied. He tried to ride one of them down, but Birria got in his way, and they fought.'

'Birria?' He was the head of Milo's guard, an ex-gladiator and formerly one of the best swordsmen in Rome. 'What on earth was Birria doing in the baggage train, and not guarding his master?'

He snapped at me. 'How should I know? He was there, and he cut Clodius down and left him lying in the road. Clodius' slaves carried him into the inn at Bovillae.'

'So he wasn't dead then?'

'Birria may have thought so, but he was still alive. Some of Milo's slaves, who hated Clodius, saw their chance and ran to the inn, killed the innkeeper and threw Clodius out on to the Way. Then they killed him, too. They'll have to be crucified, of course, if they're found.'

I shook my head. 'I don't believe that, and neither do you. It wasn't Milo's slaves who did it; they're unarmed. I tell you, I saw the body. They were sword wounds. You're still covering up. It was Milo's guard who killed Clodius, wasn't it?'

'I suppose so.'

'Then Milo told them to.'

'No, Marcus, you mustn't say that.'

'I'm not talking to a court of law; I hope I'm speaking to a friend who can trust me.' I was exasperated. He was still trying to fence with me, and in the most muddle-headed way, quite unlike Cicero. 'Listen,' I said. 'You told me the guard was around the coach, a quarter of a mile ahead. If they killed Clodius it was because someone told Milo he was still alive, and being tended at the inn, so he sent armed men to finish him off. That is what occurred, isn't it?'

He refused to meet my eyes. 'It was a humane act, Marcus. The man couldn't have recovered.'

'I see. So on Milo's orders one of his gladiators performed this act of mercy – not once but a dozen times!' I was really angry now. 'Don't you see it's those dozen wounds that make nonsense of your story of an accident? Milo will need every bit of help we can give him, but I can't understand why you tried to put *me* off with that – '

That roused him at last. 'Be quiet, Marcus! I will explain. The facts are simple – '

166

'It sounds like it!'

'The facts are simple. Clodius is dead. There was a *chance* encounter on the Appian Way and although it was Clodius who started the quarrel it was on Milo's orders that he was put to death. But that is what we dare not admit, or Milo will be charged with murder and his name struck from the list of Consular candidates. So our first story is that it was all an accident, and that some of Milo's slaves acted in anger and self-defence. Milo will be tempted to brave it out, but we mustn't let him. If a formal charge is brought against him we change our ground, and say it was a plot by Clodius that failed. We need time to build up feelings against Clodius. There's bound to be a reaction in his favour at the news of his death.'

'There is already. It was evident last night. With Plancus and Pompeius in full spate it's getting worse.'

'That's what I'm afraid of,' he said eagerly. 'There must be no excuse for wholesale rioting, for that would give Pompey the excuse he needs to bring troops into the City, stop the elections altogether and set himself up as Dictator. I'll send agents to the Forum at once to see what line the two tribunes are taking.'

'It wouldn't stop them talking. No. I'll go myself and speak from the Rostra. That might help to keep tempers down.' It wasn't something I looked forward to, with the crowd in the mood I had just seen, but Cicero was delighted. He told me to go there at once, and lent me his guard.

'Wait a moment,' I said, 'I've got something to show you.' I told him of my encounter with Cloelius, and opened the scrolls. 'See what Clodius was going to introduce in the House.' The first was a draft law decreeing the mass liberation of slaves; the second, restoration of the right of free association, the same law that Clodius had passed when he was Tribune, and which Crassus had later repealed.

Cicero read them through with delight, rubbing his hands. 'Well done, Marcus. This is just what I wanted. Proof that Clodius was planning to kill Milo.'

'Proof of *what*?'

'Did you know that only last week he told Favonius that within four days Milo would be dead? He knew he couldn't pass any legislation as radical as this through the Assembly if Milo was alive, and Consul. Clodius was planning to make himself Dictator.'

As I went out through the atreum and into the street a thought struck me. Cicero had shown no sign of relief that his

167

enemy was dead. There were far greater issues preying on his mind, and I was still not sure that I understood them all.

*

The crowd was in an ugly temper when I managed to force my way on to the Rostra, behind the bow-shaped balustrade with the ships' prows which commemorated a long-forgotten naval victory. Level with the rail was a bier, supported on barrels, and on it lay Clodius' slight body, still uncovered. I had to speak to the crowd across it, and it was just as well, everything considered, that there was a cold north breeze.

Pompeius had finished a long tirade, accusing Milo of every crime under the sun and finally, of having lain in wait for Clodius and slaughtered him with his own hand.

I called for justice, saying that when a man was done to death it was for the law to judge who was guilty and give him the punishment he deserved. They all knew Clodius, I shouted, and they all knew Milo. If Milo was guilty he would be punished; if not, no one must dare to raise a hand against him. So far, I said, there was no scrap of evidence that he had even known Clodius had been killed until after his death. At this moment, I told the crowd, Milo was officiating as Head Priest at a solemn ceremony in Lanuvium, but as soon as he could leave he would return to Rome to offer himself to the people and prove his innocence of this hideous crime. The crowd was listening now.

'Believe me, citizens,' I cried, 'I have not come here to rant and rage and utter false accusations against anyone, before I know all the facts. I have come to tell you what we know at present – all we know, so that you may be properly informed, as is your due. I've no doubt that your sense of fair play and justice, for which the people of Rome are renowned throughout all the world, will counsel you to wait for Milo's return before being led into any hasty action.' Astonishingly, there was quiet, and I looked out over the body of Clodius at the faces of all the riff-raff of the city, and continued, 'There was no ambush. There was no carefully calculated plot by either side. Milo was in his coach. You all saw him leave yesterday morning with the Lady Fausta, after making a dignified speech in the Senate. You saw the splendid retinue that accompanied him, and you saw that they were cooks and dancing girls and maids, all required for the entertainment which, in Milo's generous way, he planned to give tonight to the citizens of his home town. That entertainment will not take place, for as soon as the solemn rites are concluded, as I have told you, he will hasten back to Rome.

But my point, citizens, is this: did Milo look like a man going out to ambush his enemy? Perhaps Clodius intended some such thing; it would be only what we might expect of him, but I won't suggest it because I may not speak ill of the dead. What I do know – and I ask every honest man among you to believe me – is that Milo and Fausta had passed Clodius, and were a long way further along the road, when the squabble broke out. In fact it was Clodius, citizens, who provoked the attack by threatening a defenceless baggage-slave with his sword.' Plancus was trying to push me aside, but the crowd roared at him to let me finish.

'When the other slaves,' I continued, 'saw this act of gross oppression, with Clodius trying to kill an unarmed, simple man like yourselves, they dragged him off his tall horse and killed him. That is a bad thing, my friends, and the men will be punished, but who can blame your champion Milo, who gave you the most lavish games you have ever seen and to whom you owe protection from the murderous and rapacious gangs of Clodius – who can blame Milo, I ask, if *his slaves* let their righteous anger overcome their good sense? Milo knew nothing of their action until afterwards. Wait until tonight, when Milo himself will speak to you.'

That was as far as I got, for my time was up, and Plancus waiting to speak. He looked at me with rage in his eyes. 'You've committed yourself now, Caelius,' he muttered. 'When Milo's head falls, yours will be on the next spike.'

'Let's hear what you have to say, Plancus,' I replied. 'If you deliberately stir them up to rioting I'll have you charged with violence before the day's out.' He hesitated, then pushed me away and took the stand. I had my tribune's bench brought to the foot of the Rostra and sat there, inviolate, while the speeches dragged on.

Plancus accused Milo of the murder, of course, but was careful not to incite the crowd to take justice into their own hands. He was followed by Hypsaeus, who was in the middle of his speech, and not making much headway, when Cloelius arrived, at the head of a group of ruffians carrying swords. He told Hypsaeus to give him place. The Consular candidate, not unnaturally, refused, and was simply pushed off the Rostra. My bench was overturned and I had to escape into the crowd.

Cloelius stood behind Clodius' body and shouted, 'Enough with speeches! Take Clodius to the Senate House.' The mob roared with delight; at last there was going to be action. Way was made for Cloelius' thugs, who picked up the body like a broken puppet and raised it on their shoulders. The crowd followed them across to the Curia building, which is consecrated for the use of the Senate. I was drawn along with them, and saw the naked body thrown down in the porch while the toughs smashed the doors and pushed inside the hall. They began to pick up desks and benches and pile them together in the middle of the floor. Record scrolls were snatched from the filing racks and scattered, unrolling as they fell. Then fire was brought from the lamps burning in the nearby Basilica of Porcia. The crowd was silent now, avid for excitement.

I thrust my way through the crush of shabby, stinking bodies and reached the Tribunes' Court, where Plancus and Pompeius were standing in the doorway, looking apprehensive. 'You started this,' I shouted. 'You'd better stop it.'

'Talk sense, Caelius,' said Plancus. 'It's nothing to do with us. You saw what Sextus Cloelius did. How can we stop it? We've sent a message to the Interrex, but by the time his guard arrives the Curia will be in ashes.'

'Caelius is right,' said Pompeius, grudgingly. 'We tribunes are on the spot and have got to do something.' He turned to me. 'What bright ideas have *you* got?'

'What happened to Crassus' fire-brigade?'

'Lucullus owns it now,' cried Plancus, 'It's still in the arcades under the Palatine. I'll show you.'

By this time some of the other tribunes had come into the court and we all left in a body, and found the place under the arches where the fire engines and horses were kept. Only half the resident team were to be seen and they protested that they couldn't act without instructions from Lucullus' agent, but we pushed them aside and commandeered all three engines, put the horses into their traces and checked that the barrels were full. Then Pompeius, another tribune and I mounted the lead-horses and drove down into the Forum.

The Senate House was well ablaze, and the wooden columns of the Basilica of Porcia already smouldering. We urged the horses into the crowd, who resisted at first, not wanting their fun to be spoilt, but when they saw the great bronze levers of the engines they fell back, realising that this, also, was something worth watching.

I had seen the things in action before. Each engine had two wooden cylinders, with plungers operated by a transverse lever, worked by three men at each end. As the plungers were forced down water was pumped out of the barrels through a leather hose, and the harder the lever was worked the greater the force

170

of the jet. We soon had volunteers taking turns at the pumps, and I and the other tribunes directed the hoses and beat at the flames with folded togas. Cloelius tried to interfere, but I soused him with my hose, and the crowd shouted with laughter. His toughs were pushed out of the way by sheer weight of numbers. I stopped for a moment, wiping the sweat from my eyes, to look at the extent of the fire. The oak benches and desks were burning slowly, but the record racks were roaring sheets of flame and the pine rafters were ablaze. Clodius' body, charred but unburnt, still lay on top of the pile of furniture.

The crowd was delighted with the fire-engines, and there was a general sigh of frustration when the water ran out. Before we could get the fresh barrels in place the roof crashed in, sending showers of sparks in all directions. What remained of the fire was put out soon afterwards.

Our tribunes' benches were brought and placed in front of the ruined building, and we took turns throughout the rest of the night, keeping looters away. It was impossible to see if there was anything left to loot, but the men of the Subura always try to make something out of a disaster. The crowds began to drift away, and I saw nothing more of Cloelius nor, for that matter, of any men from the Interrex's guard. The messenger had evidently been stopped from warning him.

It was much later, when I was sitting alone on my bench, my face blackened by smoke, and weary beyond belief, that I saw a litter being carried across the square, with torch-bearers and a group of women in black attending it. I thought it must be Fulvia or her mother. Then I heard my name called.

'Marcus.'

I staggered to my feet. It was Clodia. She waved an imperious hand and her maids fell back. There was a thick veil over her face.

'Is he still there, inside?' Her voice had not changed.

'I suppose so. He must be under all that debris. Go home, Clodia. You can't do anything.' I hesitated. 'I did my best to stop them.'

'So I heard. Now help me to find him.'

'It's impossible. You shouldn't see him, anyway.'

'Who else should see him?' she cried bitterly. 'Fulvia let him be stripped naked and taken through the streets. I must look after his body.' She came forward. I seized her arm, soft and yielding under the heavy silk.

'It's no good,' I said thickly. 'Look!' I took one of the torches and we went through the porch, which was still standing.

Holding her arm I let the light shine on the heap of smoking beams and rafters, covered with a mass of shattered roof-tiles. No one had thought that there could be anything left of Clodius, and we had made no attempt to find his body. But in the flickering light of the torch I saw his hand, beneath a beam which lay across an unburnt desk. Clodia saw it, too.

'Oh help me, Marcus,' she cried, weeping. 'We can't leave him for the dogs to find. The men will hold the torches.' They came up, trembling, and stood round in a ring with the crackling pine-knots held high.

We got him out. There was a space beneath the beam, and his body was only held by a charred rafter pinning down his legs. I levered it up with a door-post, and Clodia dragged the body clear. It wasn't a sight for anyone to see, and my stomach turned. The hair was burnt off, the face black and swollen horribly, limbs crushed and charred. But Clodia showed the extraordinary strength of spirit which I remembered far too well. When I had carried the corpse outside and lowered it carefully on to the floor of the porch, she knelt down beside it and gently straightened the twisted limbs. Then she stood up and took off her long black veil and spread it over him. I could see her face for the first time.

The lines were still there, deeper now, and her eyes were swollen with weeping when she turned to look at me. But she was still the woman I had loved, and I took her in my arms and comforted her. For a long time she clung to me, then shook her head and freed herself.

'That was kind of you, Marcus. No one else would help me, not even the family.'

The bearers brought up the litter, and we raised Clodius' body and placed it inside. One of her women took a veil and spread it over Clodia's fair hair. She held it up for a moment, looking at me, then let it fall, concealing her face.

Plancus had arrived to relieve me, and I caught his astonished glance. I walked with Clodia across the empty Forum and up the hill towards her house, neither of us speaking. Then I left her and went home to fall into my bed and sleep, still hearing the voice I had loved.

27

Milo's Contio

I awoke to find Milo at the side of my couch. He said, 'You need a bath, young Marcus. I never saw such a sight.'

'When did you get back?' I was sitting on the edge of the bed, stripping off my clothes. A slave brought in some wine and we drank. Milo was looking quite imperturbable, dressed in his Senator's toga, his beard newly curled.

'Only an hour ago. I stopped off at Pompey's villa and got him out of bed to hear my confession.'

'Your *what*?'

'I told him Clodius had been killed, and I was responsible.'

I stared at him. 'You fool! You've put your neck in the noose.'

'No I haven't. He took it quite well. I offered to withdraw from the election, but he wouldn't let me. To tell you the truth, young Marcus,' he added complacently, 'I think he's a bit scared of me.'

'Of course he is, when you come to him in the middle of the night with a gang of toughs at your heels. Don't you realise he'll change his tune when he enters Rome and can call the praetorian guard around him?'

'He had guards enough at the villa, and I went in alone.' He pondered. 'But you may be right. He certainly told me I could continue with my campaign, so until he says anything different that's what I'm going to do. There's a lot of gold in my baggage.'

'Haven't you seen Cicero?'

'No, he's gone to the Senate. Lepidus has called an emergency meeting, and I ought to be there myself. Listen, Marcus. I want a chance to talk to the people. Will you arrange a contio for me?'

'When, today?'

'Yes. I want to reply to all the things those sons of bitches said about me yesterday, from what I hear.'

'All right.' As a Tribune I had powers to give any citizen the opportunity of addressing the crowd in the Forum. My bath had been prepared and I got into it and let the slaves remove the grime from my face and body. Milo stood by, talking.

'You see, son, what you have to do in a case like this is attack. Don't wait for the other fellow. When they see me with my lads around me, quite cheerful and anxious to please, with a few coins to spread among them, they'll think I'm not such a bad fellow after all.' He scratched his head thoughtfully. 'As a matter of fact, if anyone tries to stop me he won't get very far. I've already got Cloelius' gang on the run. They tried to make a fuss as I came through the Forum and we left a lot of them bleeding like the pigs they are. This is going to be a proper, democratic election, with no interference, and may the best men win.'

'That sounds fine, but what d'you think is happening now, in the Senate?'

'Old Chick-pea is speaking up for me, I'm sure of that.'

I wasn't. Old Chick-pea, I thought, would be shaking in his Senatorial shoes.

*

I sent out messengers from the Tribunes' Court, calling the people to hear Milo speak. By the time they had assembled and he had taken his place on the platform I'd had erected near the Rostra, we knew the decision of the Senate. In the absence of Consuls, the Interrex Lepidus and Pompey the Triumvir were given full powers to restore order, and if necessary raise levies of troops. If Milo was to obtain the overwhelming support of the people, as he had said, this was the moment to do it.

It was late afternoon by now, and the sun was gilding the roofs of the temples and throwing long shadows across the paved space between the Rostra and the Comitium, where the crowd had gathered. They looked restive, and eager for more excitement, and I begged Milo to be careful what he said, and not provoke them. They were idle words. He clapped me on the shoulder and told me he knew what they wanted.

I spoke first on his behalf, and gave the same story as the day before, making it clear that Clodius had started the brawl. I said Milo had at once confessed to Pompey that he had been obliged to defend himself, and that in the ensuing fight Clodius had been killed. Now, I concluded, Milo himself wanted to tell them in his own words the story of that tragic meeting.

Milo had badly miscalculated the state of public opinion. The crowd had taken my speech well, but they expected Milo to address them as a suppliant. They didn't like his confidant appearance and his light-hearted dismissal of Clodius' murder as an unfortunate occurrence which, nevertheless, should be welcomed by every reasonable man. If he had humbly begged for their help and told them he was in fear for his life they might have listened more willingly. But that wasn't Milo's way, and the hissing and booing grew in volume.

There must have been some of Cloelius' agents working in the throng, out of reach of Milo's gladiators. There were cries of 'Murderer!' and 'Hang Milo!' and the big man began to look disconcerted. The crowd paid little attention when he went into his Number One style, all a pious expression of his intention, when they elected him Consul, to serve the City and its gods to the best of his ability by introducing reforms, controlling corruption in high places, working for the return of the old virtues, and so on. He had prepared it all carefully and was determined that they should hear him out.

'Citizens, when yesterday I stood before the altar in my town of Lanuvium and introduced to the people a young priest who has dedicated his life' (loud interruptions) – 'who has dedicated his life to the gods, my thoughts turned' (further interruption) – 'my thoughts turned to the people of this far greater city, these good, hard-working men and women – Will someone stop that crotty little bastard's mouth! – who deserve all that the State can offer them, and my prayers – Listen to me, you sons of whores! – my prayers ascended with the smoke of the sacrifice to those immortal Beings who hold your lives, and my life, in their august hands. These worthy people, I prayed – I'm talking about you, you bunch of snapping curs! – these people who have chosen me to lead them to a fuller life, will not find Titus Annius Milo wanting.'

This was the point when he had expected an ovation, but what he got was a storm of boos and whistles, and his style changed. 'You shower of excrement!' he roared. 'Can't you recognise a good speech when you hear one? What do I pay you for? Who's going to look after you if I don't, when you're only fit to pull dung-carts and clean sewers?' Men were shouting, 'You killed Clodius!' and Milo replied. 'I've told you what happened to that rotten little pervert. He started a brawl and my men let daylight into his tripes. That's what you should have done years ago, you spittle-lickers, if you'd got any guts. But all you think of . . . ' The rest of his speech was imaginative, but crude.

At any other time he might have got away with it, but the sluggish blood of the people had been stirred by yesterday's sight of Clodius' body and the fire consuming the Senate House. For once the crowd was in a fighting mood, and Milo's insults drove them on. There was a spontaneous rush at the platform. The guard got us away just in time, forming a square, with

Milo and me in the centre. Their swords were out, and the men nearest were frantically trying to get out of the way, but the sheer pressure of people behind them was too great. Other men stumbled forward over their bodies and pushed us across the square towards the line of shops which flanks it, under the slope of the Capitoline Hill.

The shop-owners were hastily closing their shutters, but one of them, a fuller, had too many pieces of cloth spread out on his counter and was still struggling to clear it when we irrupted into his shop. The last of the gladiators turned in the doorway and faced the crowd with the points of their swords. The rest of us were crammed into the shop itself and the vat room in the rear, which stank of the urine used in the trade.

Milo was stripping off his toga. 'No good being brave now, son. Get those clothes on.' He pointed to some drab tunics which the fuller's slaves had hung on pegs, so that they could work more easily in the steamy heat. I whipped off my own toga and put on one of the dirty garments. It smelt horrible. A guard who had gone out of the back door to look for a means of escape came running in to say that men were already coming round the end of the line of shops into the lane behind.

Milo sent half his guard to stop them, and meanwhile he and I walked down the lane in the opposite direction, leaving the rest of the guard to defend the shop-front. We met several people trying to find their way to the back of the shops, and Milo pointed forward and urged them on in his execrable Greek. It seemed incredible that he wasn't recognised by his size alone, but the light was failing and one glance at his slave-clothes was enough. To a Roman a man who doesn't wear a toga is not worth looking at anyway.

The gladiators, I heard afterwards, defended themselves in the fuller's shop until dark, when the crowd went off, grumbling. We gave our own group of trouble-seekers the slip and skulked round the back-streets until we came to a tavern owned by one of Milo's supporters. An hour later we were sitting in Milo's study, freshly bathed and dressed in clean clothes, drinking wine.

'You'd better sleep here, Marcus,' said Milo. 'There was some trouble last night, but one of my Spaniards loosed off a few arrows at them and they mucked off. I think they may try it again tonight. Cicero said they had a go at the house of the Interrex as well – tried to set it on fire. We're going to be in for a lot of trouble now.'

We went out into the atreum, where braziers were burning

and there was a pleasant smell of roasting meat from the kitchens. Fausta came in – Milo had refused to see her until he was clean – and wrapped her husband in an elephantine embrace. She called for more wine, and sat drinking with us and listening to the story of the ill-omened contio.

'What's come over the people?' she said, shaking her head. 'My old bear can usually get them to listen to him.'

'It was my style,' said Milo, regretfully. 'I should have used the medium style throughout, not that high-flown stuff. Don't you agree, Marcus. It's no good appealing to their higher feelings.'

'Their higher feelings,' I said tactfully, 'are submerged at the moment. The trouble is that when you spoke to them they already knew that Pompey had been given power to levy troops. They're not as afraid of your gladiators as they were.'

'Afraid?' he said, puzzled. 'What have they got to be afraid of? Anyway, we'll stick to the story of an attack provoked by Clodius. That's one good thing, they can't see that body of his any more. It was a bad mistake to drill him full of holes.'

'You're wrong there, my love,' said Fausta. 'Clodia has his body. Her slaves told mine in the market.'

'Body of Bacchus! I thought he was cooked to a cinder. You should know, Marcus. You were there.'

'I was there,' I said flatly, and faced him. 'You're bound to hear the story sometime, so you may as well know. Clodia came in the middle of the night. I helped her to find the body and take it away.'

He jumped from his chair. 'You stupid jackanapes! She'll invite everyone to come and see it. What got into you? She's no friend of yours.'

'She won't show it to anyone, not even Fulvia. I'm sure of that.'

'How can you be sure, you fool?' he shouted. 'She does what comes into her head.'

'I tell you this, Milo.' I was on my feet, now, and very angry. 'Rather than let anyone else touch him, or even see him, she'd go naked through the streets herself.'

'That wouldn't be – All right, all right, son, don't fly off the handle. I'll only say this. If you're wrong I'll beat the hell out of you.'

'Don't speak to Marcus like that, you ignorant oaf,' shouted Fulvia, throwing a motherly arm round my shoulders. 'He's taken his life in his hands for your sake, and he's right about Clodia. I'd do the same, in her place. So belt up!'

Milo gave a great roar of laughter. 'Women!' he muttered, wiping his eyes. 'They'll be the death of me. I apologise, son. You've been a good friend to me in these days of trouble. Now what's happened to those palsied cooks of ours. I want food.'

28

Pompey in Charge

Next morning I went to Cicero's house and told him the story of the contio. We were sitting in the library and by the time I had finished he was slumped in his chair, head in his hands, groaning.

'It was bad enough,' he said, 'when he confessed to Pompey, but to throw away his one chance of speaking to the people and winning their sympathy is too much. Couldn't you have stopped him, Marcus?'

'You try and stop Milo in the middle of one of his orations! I warned him to be careful, when I saw what the crowd was like, but that's all I could do.'

'Sneaking away in slave-clothes!' he said scornfully. 'Very dignified behaviour for a couple of Senators, wasn't it?' He looked up. 'What line did he take about the murder?'

'What we agreed, that it was an accidental encounter.'

'I know I said that,' cried Cicero testily, 'but it's no good now. Metellus Scipio and the Claudians are going to charge Milo with laying an ambush, if what I hear is true. So our plea will be the contrary – Clodius attempted to ambush Milo.'

'Have we any evidence?'

'Only what he told Favonius, if they don't silence him before he can give his testimony. But if it comes to a trial I think I can make a credible case. Faustus Sulla, Fausta's brother, will join Hortensius and me as counsel. It's a pity you can't plead, while you're still tribune, but we should have enough talent without you. Of course, the last thing I want is that it should come to a trial. It would be the end of Milo's chances of getting the Consulship – and the end of all my hopes,' he added sadly, looking at me for sympathy.

I didn't give him sympathy, having no great opinion of his

famous plan. It would never have worked. 'There are riots in the streets again this morning, and Plancus, for one, is involved. If the situation gets any worse Pompey will use his special powers and make himself Dictator, as you said.'

He shook his head. 'I was wrong. It's clear to me now that as long as Caesar shows no signs of returning to Rome with an army Pompey will continue to hesitate. He might even change his mind again and support Milo, now that Clodius is dead. After all,' he added, more hopefully, 'Milo was always his man, and Clodius his enemy.'

'Perhaps,' I suggested coldly, 'Pompey suspects what you have in mind.'

He groaned again. 'That's it, of course. He's never trusted me, although the gods know I've done my best to serve his interests. If only Pompey had played his part, accepted all the advice I offered him so freely, used his prestige and his leadership in the Senate – if he'd done that, d'you think I'd be engaged now in pushing Milo forward like a battering-ram, to make an entry for my plans for better government?'

'But Cicero, Pompey knows that's what you're trying to do – and that if you succeed he'll suffer. The only way he can stop you is by eliminating Milo from the Consulship. He tried during the past half-year to put off the elections for that very reason. Now he's got a perfect excuse to eliminate Milo by letting him be tried for murder. Whether he's found guilty or not, he'll be out of the running for the Consulship, if the election takes place soon.' I looked at his downcast eyes with some affection, and went on more gently, 'My dear Master, you are running your head into a wall. Unless you can persuade Pompey, now, that you will not attempt, ever again, to oppose the *de facto* dictatorship of him and Caesar, or whichever of them succeeds the other, he will not raise a finger to save from trial the man you're trying to use as a screen. But if you do come to terms with him, he'll be glad to save Milo and accept his help, which is more formidable than ever, now that Clodius is dead. In this way you can get part of what you want for the country, at least – order in the streets and perhaps a gradual return to responsibility in the Senate. It's a compromise, I know, but the best course you can take.'

He was silent for some time. Then he shook his head and stood up. 'You're a persuasive advocate, Marcus, for a materialistic policy, but although you may well be right – and I don't blame you for your views – I will not give up yet. I am staking everything on this last throw.' He took a turn about the room. 'We *must* try to avoid a trial. I've told Milo to free the slaves who were involved in the incident.'

'It's a good thing you still have your agents working for you. Can they give evidence?'

To my surprise he became angry. 'I wish you wouldn't refer to them as my agents.' (It was the term he had always used himself, and proudly!) 'I have many friends who tell me what's going on; that's all.'

'But surely,' I said, mystified, 'the more inside information we have about what's happening in the other camp, the better. You have that slave in your pay still, I hope – the scribe who told you about Clodius' movements in Etruria? He should be very useful now.'

'Marcus,' said Cicero in an icy voice, 'I have told you I have no secret agents. Kindly remember that.'

It was not for many months that I understood what lay behind that curious remark.

*

For two months there was a constant rioting in the streets. As one Interrex succeeded another at five-day intervals, each decided that no election could be held until there was order in the City – but did nothing effective to produce order. Pompey was still in the country with his newly-recruited troops, in no hurry to bring them inside the walls. The greater the chaos, I suppose, the better his chances of being welcomed as the saviour of Rome.

Thirty days after the murder of Clodius, Metellus Scipio made a long speech in the Senate, revealing at last the story that Milo's enemies had worked out.

Milo, he said, had set out from Rome with three hundred slaves, most of them armed, to find Clodius and kill him. They met at Bovillae and in a regular battle Clodius and eleven of his men were killed. Milo had then gone on a couple of miles to Clodius' villa at Alba, where he hoped to find one of the dead man's sons. The child wasn't there, and after torturing one of the slaves to death in an attempt to find where the boy was hidden, Milo murdered the bailiff and two others before proceeding to Lanuvium to perform his functions as Head Priest. Only two of Milo's men had been slightly wounded, and they and twelve other slaves had been given their freedom.

On these grounds Scipio gave notice that he would charge Milo with the murder, and asked Pompey to allow all the slaves still employed by Milo and Fausta to be held for interrogation under torture. I countered with a similar application for the arrest of the households of Clodius, Metellus and Hypsaeus, alleging that we should thus obtain evidence of a plot to burn down the house of Lepidus. Pompey, still at his Alban villa, made no reply to either application. No charge was brought against Milo.

This happened on February 18th. The next development took place on February 25th, five weeks later (because this year an intercalary month was introduced into the calendar to bring our dates into line with the movements of the sun). Servius Sulpicius was the Interrex at the time, and he decided to appoint Pompey sole Consul, and thus end the continual postponement of elections. Pompey accepted, and entered Rome with his troops.

Cicero was in despair. Milo had again offered Pompey to withdraw from the election, and Pompey – only a week previously – had again refused. Now he had become Consul himself. What, Cicero demanded, was the great man playing at?

We learned soon enough. Pompey was playing at marriage again. He had secretly married Cornelia, Metellus Scipio's child, a very attractive and intelligent girl young enough to be Pompey's daughter. It was as Cicero and I had feared. In effect, Pompey had married the Caecilii Metelli and the Claudians as well, and Milo's chances of escaping trial faded.

Once Pompey makes up his mind he can move fast. Three days after assuming office as Consul he enacted two laws. The first was directed against breaches of the peace and specifically mentioned the burning of the Senate House, the attack on the house of Lepidus and the bloodshed on the Appian Way. The second aimed to suppress corrupt electioneering and the bribery of jurors. Both laws stipulated severe penalties. It was also laid down that in cases arising under these laws the examination of witnesses must be concluded in three days, and that the prosecuting and defence counsel should then share one day between them. I made a speech in the Senate, protesting that these decrees were aimed at Milo, but I could not get enough support for a resolution.

Milo made no pretence of disbanding his gladiators when Pompey's troops took up their positions in the City, and still went about accompanied by armed men. This led to an accusation in the Senate that he even had a weapon hidden under his toga, at which the big man stood up, threw off all his clothes and displayed himself in impressive nudity. 'That's the only weapon I've got with me,' he roared, 'and I'll challenge any

181

honourable colleague to show me a better one!' There was a wave of laughter through the House, a rare occurrence in those desperate days.

The formal accusations under the new law against Milo and one of his companions, a man named Saufeius, who had killed the inn-keeper at Bovillae, followed shortly afterwards. At the first hearing Hortensius informed the magistrate that Milo's slaves were now free men and not available to give evidence under torture. Pompey was told of this, and that the Claudians were complaining bitterly. By this time he was finding his new in-laws a little too demanding, and replied impatiently, 'Oh well, they can have Clodius' slaves to interrogate, if they must torture somebody!' (Oddly enough, this was done.)

The trial was fixed for April 4th, over three months (counting the intercalary month) after Clodius' death. Milo was charged on three counts: corrupt electioneering, wholesale bribery for political purposes, and causing the bloodshed on the Appian Way. (He was *not* specifically accused of the murder of Clodius.)

For the purpose of trying cases under the new laws Pompey had set up a special commission, headed by Domitius Ahenobarbus, and including specially selected magistrates and men eligible for the juries. Bribery of jurors was now practically impossible and even Cicero did not cavil at the choice of Ahenobarbus as Chief Commissioner. It was in his own court that Milo would appear in person; the charges of corruption were to be tried in other courts and he would be represented by proxy.

As Cicero had said, while I was Tribune I could not plead in court, but I offered to defend Saufeius, whose trial would come up after my term was ended. Milo accepted gratefully.

For a man facing such serious charges he was in remarkably good humour, pointing out that on his side were ranged the best orators in Rome, whereas the Claudians had entrusted the prosecution to two young and relatively inexperienced advocates, nephews of the dead man. But I knew the power of the Claudians, and feared for Milo.

29

The Trial of Milo

The court met on April 4th in the open Forum. Wooden stands had been erected for the Chief Commissioner and the jurors, there was an enclosure for relatives and Senators, and special benches set apart for the lawyers, tribunes and Milo. The advocates spoke from a raised platform near the judge's stand. It was a clear day and people had come in hundreds to watch from every porch and window. The centre of the court area had been packed since sunrise.

The first few days of the trial were taken up with the selection of the jury and the production of evidence for the prosecution. The bench examined three hundred and fifty ballot balls, each inscribed with the name of one of the men eligible for jury service, drawn from three orders: Senators, knights and paymaster-tribunes. Twenty-seven men were chosen from each order and their number reduced to a total of fifty-one by challenges from counsel on both sides. The final panel consisted of eighteen Senators, seventeen knights and sixteen tribunes.

When the cross-examination of the prosecution witnesses began the Claudians and their hangers-on started barracking, and the uproar increased until Marcus Marcellus, cross-examining for the defence, had to take refuge on the judge's bench. Pompey stopped the trial and re-convened it for next day.

When it reassembled Pompey himself was standing in one of the porches of the Treasury building above the Forum, whence he could overlook the whole of the court, and soldiers with drawn swords were picketed everywhere. There was no further barracking.

I went to dine with Milo that night. He was under house-arrest, and a heavy guard was stationed outside his doors. He was still cheerful, but worried about Cicero, and so was I. He could have been expected to take a closer interest in what was going on, but he had made no appearance during all four days.

'He's very unhappy about those accusations of Plancus and Pompeius,' said Milo. They had charged Cicero with being the instigator of the attack on Clodius, but had produced no evidence and the charges had not been accepted by the magistrates.

'What's worrying him?' I asked. 'They've got no further, and Plancus and Pompeius are going to be tried for the attack on the house of the Interrex, so they'll have enough on their minds for a bit. Everyone knows Cicero was in Rome for the whole of the day in question. I saw him myself in the Senate.'

Milo looked away, and said nothing. I knew there was some secret that neither he nor Cicero would reveal to me, and it was annoying. But when Milo wanted to keep his mouth shut no one could open it.

'What d'you think of their evidence so far?' he asked.

I thought for a moment. 'The most dangerous part of it is the evidence of the innkeeper's slaves at Bovillae. They all said the same things, and it's very damning for Saufeius. But that'll be *my* problem, at his trial. There's no proof that *you* told anyone to murder Clodius, and no witness so far has even testified to what happened when they dragged Clodius out on to the road. I suppose if there were witnesses when he was stabbed to death – well, they're dead, too.' I looked a question at him, but he only grunted.

'So now,' I went on, 'there's the allegation that you went into Clodius' villa at Alba and tortured and murdered people there.'

'That's all balls,' growled Milo.

'I know, and they've tied themselves into knots with their evidence. No one's going to accept the testimony of Clodius' slaves on that score, and it would have been practically impossible for you to arrive at Lanuvium when you did, if you'd spent all that time at the villa.'

'I did go there, you know.'

'I did not know,' I said angrily. 'What on earth for?'

'It's only half a mile off the Way, opposite the shrine of the Good Goddess. I took a horse and got there fast.'

'But what for?'

'Cicero had heard from one of his agents that Clodius was preparing some new laws, so as soon as I knew he was dead I did what – I mean, I thought I'd have a look for them, before the fuss started. But they weren't there. I gather from old Chick-pea that you got hold of a couple of the scrolls in Rome. That was smart, Marcus. He can make good use of them.'

'You weren't looking for Clodius' son?'

'What d'you take me for? I'm not interested in little boys,

184

you ought to know that. All I did was ask a scribe where the study was, quite politely – he wasn't hurt at all, just a little scratch. He showed us the way fast enough. I hadn't time to make a proper search.'

'So you arrived at Lanuvium on time?'

'Yes.' He frowned. 'Half the town met us as we came over the pass. They like me there all right. It's these puking alley-cats in Rome who've got no loyalty for the man who gave them those games.'

'Cloelius has the gangs working on them. You saw how they tried to get at Marcellus.'

'Yes, son. That's one thing I wanted to tell you. I'm really worried about old Chick-pea; he's losing his guts. Tell him to take a closed litter to the court tomorrow and stay hidden until it's time for him to speak. If the crowd see him in the street they'll scare him proper. Besides, there are all Pompey's troops standing around, and he can't abide the sight of bare steel.' Milo took a great draught of wine. 'He's got enough on his mind already,' he muttered.

'What d'you mean?'

'Never you mind, son.' He put down his goblet and stretched his great frame on the couch, relaxed and comfortable. 'So you think I've got a good case?'

'I didn't say that. But if Cicero pleads that in spite of your confession to Pompey – you don't make it easy for him, do you? – all that happened was done without your knowledge, you've got a case. It's impossible to prove the contrary, with the evidence produced. In fact, I'd say you were more vulnerable on the charges of bribery and corruption, in the other courts.'

'You think if Chick-pea takes that line he'll get me off?'

'He can get you off the murder charge, but you'll still be held responsible for what your men did.'

'Well, son, that's straight talking, which is what I wanted. I can't get old Chick-pea to give me any idea what he's going to say. He just grumbles that three hours isn't enough for three counsel.'

*

I won't describe the speeches of the prosecutors next day, because they followed predictable lines, smearing Milo as a common criminal, giving their story of his plot to ambush Clodius and making the most of the evidence of the slaves at the inn.

185

Milo need have had no fear that Cicero would be molested on his way to the court. The streets were full of soldiers, and they lined the entrances to the Forum. Oddly enough, as Milo had foreseen, it was this that seemed to strike terror into Cicero. When he stood on the platform he could scarcely speak. It was particularly unfortunate, because the prosecutors had taken up more than their share of time, and it had been decided that Cicero alone should speak for the defence.

When he got going, however, it was a work of art, beautiful to listen to, rich with gestures, dramatic asides and pregnant pauses, and even more remarkable for its content. For besides retailing a series of lies that left me gasping in respectful admiration he changed his defence line completely in the course of his speech. In fact he switched from one plea to another, and back again, with bewildering facility, and finished up with the most extraordinary plea of all. To a lawyer it was a strange and fascinating performance, and worth examining in as much detail as my story will allow.

After apologising for showing fear at the flashing swords he acknowledged that Pompey, in his wisdom, had provided the guards solely for the protection of Milo from the paid gangs of his enemies. This, he said, was indeed right, for he would show that it was with these same gangs that Clodius had foully plotted to murder Milo, and if in the event he was killed instead, no one could say that Milo was guilty of *murder*. It was our inalienable right to defend ourselves when attacked. Even the Twelve Tables of the law laid down that a thief who offered violence might be killed with impunity, and there were innumerable famous incidents in our history which proved that in certain circumstances it was a man's duty to take life.

Therefore, said Cicero, it was nonsense to argue, with the prosecution, that because Milo had admitted responsibility for the killing he himself was a self-confessed murderer. It might well be that even if he had killed Clodius with his own hands – which he had not – he would be fully justified. For to kill a known bandit, declared Cicero, was no sin. Otherwise, when we carried swords in passing through bandit country, what were the swords for?

In fact, he said, there was a law written nowhere but in our hearts which allowed us, when our lives were in danger from plots or violence, to kill our enemies. For when swords are drawn, laws are silent.

I stirred uncomfortably. Invoking the 'unwritten law' is hardly a legal exercise.

But Cicero went on to labour this point, citing the name of a young soldier in the days of Marius; a military tribune had tried to seduce the youngster – and got killed for his pains. Yet the general who tried the case, said Cicero, although he was a relative of the dead man, refused to allow the soldier to be convicted. How just that act of mercy had been! There were indeed many other Romans, all famous men in our history, who had killed persons for acting against their honour or the interests of Rome. No one had blamed them, so why blame Milo?

Having thus affirmed that homicide might be justifiable either in self-defence or for vaguer reasons of honour or patriotism, Cicero let these ideas simmer in the jurors' minds while he went on to explain what, in his submission, had *really* happened on the Appian Way. Clodius had needed a year as praetor to complete his plans for the disruption of the constitution, plans which included the introduction of laws which would have freed thousands of privately-owned slaves and given them full rights as Roman citizens. (The jury shuddered in horror.)

The only person who stood in Clodius' way, said Cicero, was Milo, who as Consul would soon have put a check on that evil man's plotting against the State. So Clodius had sworn to end Milo's life, and repeated the threat at mass meetings and even within the hallowed precincts of the Senate. Cicero called Favonius, who testified that on January 15th he had asked Clodius what use his gangs would be, once Milo was Consul. Clodius, averred Favonius, had replied that in four days Milo would be dead.

'How,' asked Cicero rhetorically, 'did that scheming traitor plan to end Milo's life? I will tell you. He knew that Milo would be leaving for Lanuvium on the eighteenth day of January to perform a ceremony on the following day, and although Clodius had been billed to address a meeting on the seventeenth he left secretly that same day for Aricia.

'On the eighteenth, all unaware of the ambush that lay in his path, Milo left the Senate when it broke up at ten o'clock, went home to change his clothes and put on his heavy travelling cloak, waited as usual for his wife to finish her preparations' – he paused for the sympathetic titter from the court – 'and set off in his coach, accompanied by a substantial train of very peaceful maids, serving-men, pages and entertainers, all needed for the lavish festival he proposed, generous as ever, to offer to the people of his home town after the ceremony. He had a guard – I don't deny this. He had been attacked too often by

Clodius' gangs not to take some protection with him. But, I repeat, he had no idea that there was any specific danger awaiting him.

'How could he have known that Clodius, after spending the night at Aricia, had suddenly left in the direction of Rome? Clodius travelled fast, on horseback, and made his way to his villa at Alba, where he arranged for parties of armed slaves to take up positions on high ground overlooking the road. There they lay in wait.

'When Milo's party drew level, they charged down and attacked. The coachman was killed at once, but Milo, like the hero he is, threw off the heavy cloak, took up his sword and jumped down from the coach. There on the road, jurors, he laid about him so fiercely that the attackers fell back. Clodius was too cowardly to engage Milo himself, and he had led another party of slaves against the men following the coach on foot. They resisted, and in the hope of frightening them Clodius shouted that Milo was dead. Perhaps he thought so; in any event, it was for Clodius a tragic mistake. For the slaves did not flee. Maddened with anger at the false news that their beloved master was no more, the gallant fellows rushed at Clodius and plunged their daggers into his body. Which one of you,' asked Cicero dramatically, raising his right arm, 'would not wish your own slaves to do the same, if bandits attacked you on the road?'

Fine, I thought. Back to the safe plea of self-defence, and no awkward mention of the inn at Bovillae. It was, of course, a neat device to explain the multiple wounds in Clodius' body – but Cicero must have thought the jurors had short memories. For if the attack had really taken place at Alba, why on earth had Clodius' slaves carried him to Bovillae, nearly two miles away? Why not to the villa, where there would be servants to tend to his wounds?

But Cicero wasn't interested in the truth. He was telling a story which, *taken by itself*, would sound credible and tie in with the arguments that followed. For no other reason than to make the encounter sound more dramatic, he added that it took place at five o'clock, when it was already dusk. In fact, of course, as I knew myself, it was only half-past five when Clodius' body had been carried past my court, after at least a three-hour journey by litter. There must by now have been considerable confusion in the minds of the jurors.

With one of those smooth changes of style of which he was master, Cicero now began to talk in a quieter, gentler tone, sweetly reasonable. The jurors, he said, were all men of the world, men of standing in the community, accustomed to using their own judgement. They were already asking themselves – he could see by their thoughtful faces – the question which so often pointed the way to a true verdict. The question of motive. *Cui bono*? Who stood to gain most by the other's destruction, Milo or Clodius? How right it was to think on these lines, for it was here, indeed, that the kernel of this problem lay.

'Let us leave aside,' said Cicero, 'the suggestion that the fight was sparked off accidentally. The prosecution says there was a plot, an ambush, by Milo. I agree there was an ambush, but by Clodius. So, gentlemen, you are asking yourselves which of these two men was more likely to have laid an ambush for the other. Now it goes without saying that Clodius was a reckless and inhuman scoundrel, so if I can prove that he had every reason to kill Milo you need be in no doubt that this is precisely what he planned to do.' I could see some of the jurors – those without any legal training – nodding their heads.

Cicero went on, 'If Milo had been killed Clodius would have gained in two ways. First, he believed that the electors would be foolish enough to award him the praetorship. But as I have said, what use would that honourable post be to Clodius if Milo, as Consul, could thwart his foul plans for the downfall of our constitution? Secondly, with Milo out of the way, who would have been elected Consuls? Why, two men who were known to favour Clodius' cause – one of them his cousin and the other that madman Hypsaeus who is even now awaiting trial for attempting to burn down the house of the Interrex! With them in power it would have been easy for Clodius to introduce the extremist legislation he had already drafted. Aha!' cried Cicero, pointing, 'see how the face of Sextus Cloelius changes, how he glares at me! He knows I have in my possession the drafts of two of those laws. One restores the right of free association which Clodius introduced as Tribune, and which was so wisely repealed when we saw how directly it led to the gang warfare and corruption from which we all suffered. I have already mentioned the other law, which purports to declare thousands of our slaves, yours and mine, free men – free to join political clubs, free to exercise the full rights of Roman citizens, free therefore to vote according to the dictates of their paymasters. It was no less, I repeat, than the utter disruption of our legislature, of our whole way of life, that Clodius had in mind. And, gentlemen, it was only Milo, the strong, upright man with all the traditional virtues of our ancestors, who stood in the path of that evil design.

'Now look at him, this man you are asked to judge. Milo had everything to *lose* by Clodius' death. But for that event he would by now be Consul. Moreover, jurors, do not forget that Milo owes his whole rise to fame – to Clodius! You look startled, but surely you remember that it was the ever-increasing violence of Clodius' acts that forced Milo, a quiet man then only interested in his legal career, to set up a counter-force, to oppose irresponsible violence and corruption with a strong and steely resistance – and thus save Rome from those who sought her ruin.'

Cicero paused, took a sip of water from the carafe, and passed on easily to pronounce a lie worthy of Ulysses. 'Do not imagine for a moment, therefore, that Milo had any *ill-will* against Clodius to whom, as I have said, he owes the position he occupies in Roman life today. He did not hate him. Milo's feet were on the road that would have led to the end of gangster-kingdoms and petty tyrants, and Clodius as a person was of no interest to him. Let him live, or let him die, all Milo wanted was that his power should be broken and the integrity and virtue of our way of life restored.

'And finally, while I am dealing with the question of motive, put yourselves in Milo's place on that fatal day in January. He was impatiently awaiting the election, when all his aspirations would be fulfilled and he would be awarded the highest honour which Rome can confer on her most deserving sons. Can you imagine that Milo, with that prospect in mind, would have considered for a moment presenting himself at the sacred ceremonies of the Consular election with his hands red with the blood of murder? In a man as devout and noble as Milo such behaviour is unthinkable!' I remember Milo's arrival in Rome the day after the murder, with his jingling money-bags, and suppressed a smile.

'I will now turn to the question of opportunity. There has already been evidence of Clodius' fatal boast to Favonius, when he said that in four days Milo would be dead. I told you how he discovered that Milo had to go to Lanuvium on the day in question. Clodius knew that Milo would attend the Senate and leave shortly afterwards to reach his home town by nightfall. Therefore he could be sure of the timing of his ambush.

'Now let us look at the other side. Could Milo have known that Clodius would return along the Appian Way on that very day? The prosecution had two stories to tell us. When they were trying to prove that Milo plotted the ambush, they said he had bribed a slave in Clodius' employ to tell him in advance when his master was returning to the City. Later, when the prosecution was at pains to show that Clodius could not have left Rome with the intention of waylaying Milo, they produced very credible evidence – I grant them this point – that Clodius had intended to stay several days in Aricia, and that it was only on the spur of the moment, when he heard of the death of Cyrus the Architect, that he decided to return to Rome.

'Well, now. If the story of the slave were true – and it is not – don't you see that if he had reported to Milo *in advance* his report would have been false; he would have said that Clodius was to leave for Rome in a few days' time. Thus Milo could *not* have known when to expect him.

'As for the news about Cyrus – ' Cicero paused, and cast his eye around the Forum at the soldiers with their drawn swords – 'I have something to explain to you, something that touches me personally.' He seemed less certain of himself, and I was puzzled. But he pulled himself together and proceeded, 'Two days before the killing of Clodius, he and I – strange companions! – stood at the bedside of Cyrus, who had undertaken much building work for both of us and had decided to make us his joint heirs. He was dying, and had asked us to witness his will. The following day Clodius left for the hills, expecting to stay away, according to the prosecution, for several days. On the morning after, my old friend Cyrus died, as everyone expected. If indeed it is true that on the eighteenth, the day Clodius was killed, the news of Cyrus' death reached him at Aricia, why should Clodius have found it so important that he had to leave at once for Rome? There was, as I have said, nothing unexpected in Cyrus' death. Clodius had seen him on his death-bed and had heard the physician offer no hope of recovery. This story simply doesn't make sense.

'I must now refer, gentlemen, to certain horrifying charges that have been made against *me*, the man you once chose to name the Father of his Country. The tribunes Plancus and Pompeius have maintained, without a shred of evidence, that although Milo committed the murder, as they claim he did, it was I who was the instigator. It has greatly distressed me that even a man as demented as Plancus could have expected such a story to be believed. But here you have the proof that it is nonsense. For how could I, in Rome, have known that Clodius would so unexpectedly decide to return to the City? As I have shown, the news of Cyrus' death was no reason at all for a change of plan. What happened, gentlemen, was something much more sinister. The news brought to Clodius was not of

Cyrus' death, but of Milo's approach along the Appian Way. That is the only possible explanation of his sudden departure, on horseback, without his wife or his usual retinue of little Greek boys and prostitutes, but surrounded by armed slaves.

'How is it, you may ask, that Clodius, not Milo, was killed? Jurors, the hand of Mars is impartial, and strikes even the victor in the moment of victory, and sometimes through the medium of his humblest enemy. Clodius had eaten and drunk too much, and his natural forces were spent with evil living. Perhaps he thought he had only the slaves in the baggage train to deal with, and that they would run when he told them Milo was dead. But loving Milo as they did, they slew the man they thought had killed him.

'You ask, why then did Milo emancipate them, if they had taken life? But they had saved Milo from death! How else could he reward them? Even if they had been tortured by the court examiners, what could they have said? Only that Clodius had been slain. It is not for the torturer to ask *why*. He is only concerned with eliciting facts. It is for this tribunal to say whether the killing was justified.

'Let us look at the prosecution witnesses. The only slaves who have been interrogated, by permission of General Pompey, are those forming part of Clodius' household, who now belong – to whom? To Appius Claudius, who has brought this case against Milo. The slaves were held by him all this time and brought by him to be interrogated in the courtyard of the Temple of Liberty. Imagine what happened! A slave (let's call him Rufio) is on the rack. The examiner asks, 'Now, Rufio, you must tell the truth. Did Clodius plot to kill Milo?' What does the wretched man reply? If he says yes, he knows what awaits him when he returns to Appius' house, Crucifixion, for certain. If he says no, Appius will give him his freedom, perhaps. There's a reliable kind of evidence for you!

'But what need is there for such evidence, when Milo instead of running away or showing any trace of guilt, returns to Rome as soon as the sacred rites at Lanuvium allow and goes straight to place himself in the hands of General Pompey, the man charged by the State with control over all our armed forces. This answers the many cries we have heard, "Milo will break out! Milo will start a civil war! He has incendiary arrows in his house on the Palatine, ready to burn down Rome, and stores of shields and weapons of every sort!" All these tales have no foundation whatever. Neither Pompey, whom we rightly call "The Great", nor the Republic, has anything to fear from Milo.

All his efforts have been directed towards one end, that order and peace may be restored. Give him his liberty and he will prove a wise and peace-loving statesman.'

There was more of this, and I was just thinking that Cicero was making a brilliant case of it, when he suddenly went back to the law of the wild, the unwritten law, call it what you will.

'I have proved,' he said, 'that Milo is not guilty of Clodius' death, but let me imagine the contrary. Let me picture Milo *admitting* that he killed him, and you will find, jurors, that your verdict remains unaltered. For which man would you rather have alive, Milo – or Clodius? You cannot be in doubt. With Milo, your protector, performing his duties honourably in the service of the State, you will be safe and prosper. You will be able to look forward to all the good things in life for yourselves and your children. But with Clodius, nothing – nothing would be safe. He plunged the Forum in blood, he oppressed the weak, he took away men's property by threatening death, he indulged every lecherous whim and fornicated with his own sister. He threatened the whole order of our time.'

It was rhetoric, and I hoped the jurors had forgotten the opening sentences in that passage. He was silent for a moment, taking another sip of water from the carafe on the table, and letting his eye range over the jurors' benches. Then he drew himself up in the military pose I knew so well, and I wondered apprehensively what was coming.

'Citizens, jurors, Domitius Ahenobarbus! Let me imagine Titus Annius Milo raising his blood-stained sword and crying, "I have killed Publius Clodius! With this sword, with this right hand I have rid you of the man you could not curb with the instruments of law." If Milo said this, who among you would not applaud, who would not approve his action?'

I was stunned. What possible purpose was there, in putting the idea into the jurors' minds? They would take it as an alternative defence, and there was no need for it. The plea of killing in self-defence, by other persons not under Milo's immediate control, was perfectly adequate.

'What country,' Cicero was declaiming, 'does not honour the men who destroyed her tyrants? What altars have I seen in Greece, what songs do they sing to heroes of the past! And in Rome, are there not men in our own glorious history who are no less honourable? Ahala, who slew the tyrant, and Nasica, Opimius and Marius.' Modestly, he lowered his eyes. 'I may even mention myself, for I too, citizens, slew Lentulus and his fellow-conspirators to save my country. When men commit such actions of sheer devotion to the State, why should they be condemned as criminals?'

Cicero, I thought, must be out of his mind. In effect, he was saying that Milo had killed Clodius, and *deliberately*, for patriotic ends.

I had known he would drag in religion somewhere, and I was right. Now Cicero the Augur was speaking, his arms outstretched like a priest before the altar.

'Oh Jupiter! Ancient god of the Latin League, whose sacred groves Clodius defiled, whose hills he flattened to provide space for his bandit's stronghold, how long have you waited to take your vengeance on this blasphemer! Yet how aptly you chose for his death not only the same high road, built by his great ancestor, on which he slew Papirius, but the very spot where the pious revere the Good Goddess in her shrine. You did not forget how he had dishonoured her, how he was found during her most sacred rites in the adulterous bed of the Chief Pontiff's wife!'

So *that* was why Cicero had shifted the scene of the crime a mile or so along the Appian Way – to bring it near the shrine! He was going on, to show himself a true prophet, 'I said then, after that iniquitous trial, that Clodius had been acquitted only to await a sterner sentence. Thus, indeed, it has proved, thus have the gods shown that they neither forget nor forgive. The Goddess stretched forth her hand, and Clodius is dead.

'Gentlemen, you saw Clodius burn my house, and my brother's house; you saw him eject men from their homes, devastate Etruria, bring swords into the Forum and force that gallant Tribune Marcus Caelius from the platform; you saw Clodius commit every kind of outrage – and you did nothing. Only Milo stood out against him. You hoped in your hearts that he would rid you of Clodius – and when he did you brought him to trial for murder! How ungrateful we must seem to this hero! If you see no tears in Milo's eyes – for he is not a man to weep easily – do not flatter yourselves that he is not hurt by your inhuman treatment, that he is not plumbing the depths of his soul's despair!'

Cicero made a dramatic gesture in Milo's direction, hoping that at least he would stop grinning. But Milo was enjoying every minute of the performance. 'Good old Chick-pea!' he was saying to himself. 'He's the lad to kick 'em in the slats!'

There was much more than I have written, and it may be that I have treated a great speech with little reverence. No one can condense Cicero's oratory with any justice. You have to see the gestures and the changing expressions on his actor's face, hear the noble rhythms uttered in that golden voice, to appreciate the beauty of his art and feel the emotional impact of our greatest orator. It suffices to say this: I am firmly convinced that if Milo had obeyed Cicero's instructions – as I did at my own trial – he would have been acquitted. And this in spite of the fact that Cicero had abandoned a perfectly safe line of defence for one of patriotic homicide, which is not recognised by the law.

Yet, I repeat, Milo would have left the court a free man if he had played his part. But he couldn't play a part, and Cicero ought to have known it. There sat Milo, smiling confidently at his friends, shaved, beard curled in the latest fashion and wearing a shining white toga. He was so sure that his illustrious friend would get him off the hook that he saw no reason why he should try to look like a prisoner.

The jury resented his attitude, and convicted him by thirty-eight votes to thirteen. In the other courts, where he was being tried by proxy, he was also found guilty. But later, when Pompey came to ratify the verdicts and pronounce sentence, he treated Milo leniently. His rights as a citizen were withdrawn and he was condemned to indefinite exile, but although part of his property was to be sold to liquidate outstanding debts, the rest of his fortune was left untouched. The Claudians shouted and swore, but Pompey paid no attention to them. After all, he was now rid of both Clodius and Milo, and the suppression of their gangs would follow. He had plenty of troops to enforce order.

He allowed no charge to be brought against Cicero.

*

It was during the night after the trial ended that I said goodbye to Milo. It would be some days before Pompey pronounced sentence and at that time we feared the worst and urged Milo, who still could not take in his defeat, to leave Rome. It is one of the humane customs of our courts to turn a blind eye if a man convicted of a capital offence chooses to go into exile before he is sentenced.

I had emerged from Fausta's embrace and Milo took me in his arms and gave me a rib-cracking hug. 'I've got no right to ask you for anything, young Marcus,' he said. 'You've done quite enough for me already. But I'd rather trust you than Cicero to look after my affairs, if there is anything left when Pompey's had his say. And one other thing – I'd be very happy if you can manage to get Saufeius a light sentence. He was only

doing his bleeding duty. If he hadn't I'd have skinned him alive.'
I promised to do my best.

The only charge against Saufeius was the murder of the inn-keeper, but the testimony of the slaves at the inn was united and damning. However, I cross-examined them with all the skill I could command, and put a lot of work – and vituperation – into my closing speech. My client was acquitted by one vote.

In the other trials under the new laws my fellow-tribunes, Pompeius and Plancus, and also Hypsaeus, the Consular candidate, were condemned and exiled for the disturbances they had caused. But not Metellus Scipio, who was almost equally to blame.

After all, he was Pompey's father-in-law, and Pompey was very happy with his young wife. He made Metellus his Co-Consul.

30

Milo in Marseilles

Milo's debts were enormous, and he didn't seem to have kept any accounts worth speaking of, but he had so much real estate that it was mainly a question of seeing that any properties sold fetched good prices. I took over his household slaves and found jobs for those he had freed before his trial. Cicero bought one of the country estates, promising to maintain it and let Milo have the income. From what I heard afterwards this promise was not kept.

Cicero's relations with Milo had appeared rather strained after the trial, and in the frantic rush to get Milo and Fausta on the road I had no chance to get to the bottom of the matter.

In the City there was order at last. Cicero was offered, and accepted with alacrity, the Governorship of Cilicia for next year. Some time later, after the news of my successful defence of Saufeius had reached Gaul, I received a message from Caesar that he would like to talk to me. Three weeks ago I set out for Gaul.

I had two good horses, and with a few armed slaves as guard took the Via Aurelia, which skirts the west coast. On the Mulvian Bridge I turned to look back at the City. With all its faults I had no wish to live anywhere else. My reputation was now established beyond any doubt, and I could take my pick of cases to defend or prosecute. I should have a chance of the Consulship in years to come, but was in no hurry to continue my career in State service.

It was becoming increasingly obvious to me that Pompey would fail in a final conflict with Caesar, and in any case Caesar was the lesser of two evils. At some time I should have to throw in my lot with him, and it seemed likely that he would make me some offer of a post on his staff when I came into his camp. For the moment, however, I could put the prospect out of my mind and look forward to the long ride along the coast road and over the passes into the northern provinces which I had never visited. Even that nagging ache in my heart for Clodia seemed to have gone. There had been something curiously satisfying about that last meeting over Clodius' body. She was rarely seen in public now. I turned my horse, and we passed over the Tiber and began to canter down the smooth paved road.

Milo and Fausta live in luxurious retirement in a villa on the coast near Marseilles, and here they welcomed me a few days ago. They looked sunburnt and well, and proudly showed me their vineyard and the great wine-presses the Gauls use. Both of them have adopted the local custom of drinking unmixed wine, and by the time the evening was well advanced it took three strong slaves to get Fausta to bed.

We sat on, drinking, while I gave Milo an account of my stewardship. He was very pleased, and pressed me to stay for a week, offering me a girl he said would suit any man's taste. But I refused; I still had a long way to go and Caesar would know if I dawdled on the road. I opened my satchel and found a scroll.

'What's this?' he asked when I handed it to him.

'Cicero's speech at your trial. This is the copy he's sent you, with a letter.'

Milo disappeared into his study with the scroll and joined me half an hour afterwards. I was interested to know what he'd think of the published version. Cicero was very proud of it, and had told me it should be in the library of every school of oratory. So it should, although it isn't the speech he made, but something much longer and grander, with every passage carefully polished. The crazy lines of his defence, however, are the same. When I tried, tactfully, to get an explanation he said, in his loftiest tone, that I had never fully appreciated the ancient virtues of the Romans. I replied I was more concerned with their modern vices, but failed to raise a smile.

When Milo returned he was starry-eyed, as always after reading anything written by Cicero. I asked him what he thought of it.

He held out his cup for more wine. 'It's even better than what he said. If he'd made this speech I shouldn't be eating the excellent mullet they have here. I'm getting to like this place, Marcus. Nice and clean. Friendly people. Good sport.'

I wouldn't be put off. 'So you think his defence was right?'

'Poor old Chick-pea! He tried hard, for my sake.' He paused, and muttered to himself, 'He was too bloody scared.'

'He said he was afraid of the troops in the Forum.'

'Blood of Bacchus! It wasn't that. They were there to protect him.'

'Then why was he scared?'

'He was afraid he'd follow me into the dock, and he couldn't have stood another term of exile.'

'Nonsense! I paid no attention to those accusations by Plancus. Cicero was in the clear.'

'Oh was he?' he growled.

Now, of course, I was determined to get the story out of him, and he was fretting with it like a boy with the pox, and out it came — prefaced by a solemn warning that I didn't take lightly.

'If you spill this, young Marcus, in spite of all I owe you, you'll be sorry.'

'I'll be as discreet as the tomb.'

'That's where you'll be, son, if you open your trap.' He put down his wine and gave a shout of laughter, slapping his thigh. 'It was old Chick-pea who planned the whole thing, with that clever brain of his.'

'He couldn't have. How could he be sure that Clodius would change his mind and turn back to Rome?'

'Chick-pea fixed it, I tell you. There they were, Cicero and Clodius, at Cyrus' bedside, and that's when Cicero got the idea. The following day old Cyrus slung his hook, and Chick-pea collared me when the Senate broke up — that was on the eighteenth — and in five minutes he told me what he'd arranged.' He grinned nostalgically. 'I say five minutes, but there were ten more to explain why it was the duty of every virtuous Roman to shed blood when blood would save the country. It was all a lot of history, but he nearly had me in tears. Still, I was forced to cut him short, because I wanted to get to Lanuvium before nightfall and if I did what he wanted it might take a bit longer.'

He swallowed another great draught of wine. 'You remember

Cicero had that slave, one of Clodius' scribes, who used to send him reports? Well, the scribe happened to be visiting Rome on an errand for Clodius, and first thing after Cyrus' death Cicero sent him off at a split-arse gallop, to catch Clodius in Aricia and tell him Cyrus was dead.'

'But that wouldn't have made him come back. Clodius knew Cyrus was dying before he left Rome.'

Milo smiled. 'The fellow was to say, as if he'd heard it from one of Cicero's slaves, that old Chick-pea was going to claim Cyrus' whole estate, pleading a legal irregularity.' He shook his grizzled head, admiringly. 'There's Chick-pea for you – sheer genius! He knew that message would set Clodius racing back down the Appian Way, and he'd never discover the truth because – this is the other clever bit! – he'd never reach Rome! So all I had to do was stay in the coach with Fausta, all respectable, surrounded by guards, while Birria would lurk among the baggage slaves, a quarter of a mile behind. Cicero said I mustn't get involved, because of the election.'

'And so?' I asked, drawing a deep breath.

'Birria made a balls of it. He missed his stroke. Tried to get Clodius through the heart, all clean and tidy, but you know what Clodius was like – quick as a cat. He must have turned, so the blade went in under his shoulder, just taking enough flesh to knock him off his horse. He hit his head on the road and passed out, and Birria, the fly-blown cur, seeing all the blood and Clodius on the ground, thinks he's dead. Birria,' explained Milo judicially, 'has just about as much sense as a latrine-sponge.'

'But what happened then?'

'It was when we were chatting about it later, very cheerful, with Birria leaning in at the coach window, that a slave comes tearing up on a horse and tells us the little bastard's alive, and they've carried him into the inn. I told Birria if he didn't finish the job I'd have him on the rack before the day was out, so he went off with Saufeius and hauled Clodius out of the inn. And carved him up, to make sure.'

'That was the mistake. It was all those wounds to show to the crowd that started the riot. But why didn't you tell me?' I looked at him reproachfully. 'I was on your side.'

'I know you were, lad, and you deserved better, but old Chick-pea wouldn't hear of it. He said you were a Tribune, and it'd put you in an awkward position.' I laughed until the tears came, then jumped to my feet as a thought struck me.

'So that explains his defence,' I cried. 'He wasn't only defending you, but *anyone* who had slain Clodius or had a hand in it. And of course, that's why he was so scared, because I suppose the scribe was one of the slaves they interrogated?'

'That's it. They had the poor little fellow on the rack, and he'd got as far as saying it was Cicero who'd planned the whole affair, when they shifted the lever a knotch too many, and he had a heart attack and died on them. Cicero only heard about it after the trial was over. He couldn't understand why Plancus obviously knew something, but couldn't produce any witness. Right through, he was expecting someone to rush into the court with a statement of evidence.'

'Of course,' I cried, 'that explains everything. Cicero was trying to save his own skin, the cunning old rogue!'

Milo stood up, his huge frame towering over me. 'A young fellow like you,' he said in his grating voice, prodding me with a painful finger, 'should show more respect for a man like Marcus Tullius Cicero. What he did was for the good of Rome, which is more to him than his own honour. If the Romans are too bleeding rotten to appreciate him, it's not old Chick-pea who's at fault. It's all the rest of us sods who've made Rome what it is today. All right, then, let's go to bed. And remember, young Marcus, just one word out of you and I'll string you up on your own guts. Nobody's going to put old Chick-pea in the dock. After all' – he stopped for a cavernous belch – 'he's a friend of mine.'

NOTE TO THE READER

The main characters and events in this story are historical. The extent to which Cicero was involved in certain events, such as the forged letters, his proposed use of Milo as a means of checking the power of Pompey and Caesar, and in particular his responsibility for the murder of Clodius, are fictitious, but in my view compatible with his character and motivations.

Most of the chief actors died violent deaths. The narrator, Marcus Caelius, joined Caesar in 50 BC, but was dissatisfied with the treatment he received. Two years later, when Pompey had been defeated, Caelius rebelled against Caesar and persuaded Milo to break exile and join him in starting an insurrection in northern Italy. It was a strange action for Caelius, whose political acumen was of a high order, and quite useless. Both he and Milo were captured and executed.

Clodia's fate is unknown; so far as we know she did not remarry. Fulvia, Clodius' widow, remarried twice, first Curio and then Mark Antony, and died, broken-hearted, in the middle of his affair with Cleopatra. Terentia, whom Cicero divorced when he was fifty-seven so that he could marry a rich heiress of sixteen, also found two more husbands, and finally died at the age of a hundred and three. Those Roman women had staying power.

Cicero himself, against all the sound advice which we can read in Caelius' letters to him, sided with Pompey, but survived to renew friendly relations with Caesar. After Caesar was assassinated Cicero was proscribed by the Second Triumvirate and died bravely. They cut off his head and set it up on the Rostra.

Fulvia, who had always believed that Cicero was responsible for Clodius' death, came to look. She spat at the head, then called for a needle and thrust it through the lolling tongue that had made the name of Clodius hated and despised.

Glossary

AEDILES

Officials of the Roman municipality in charge of the maintenance of streets and public buildings, the corn supply, etc. *Curule* aediles were in charge of the Games.

ASSEMBLY

The official law-making body, which also elected State officials and declared war and peace. It was formed of Roman citizens (including those from other cities which enjoyed Roman citizenship) summoned in groups according to their 'tribes'. Traditionally, the Assembly accepted the guidance of the Senate.

AUGURS

One of the four orders of priesthood. They deduced, usually from the innards of a dead bird, whether the auspices for a given event were favourable.

CHIEF PRIEST

Also known as the Pontifex Maximus. Head of the State religion. Always a patrician, q.v.

CONSULS

The two men who shared the supreme civil and military power of the Republic for one year.

CONSULARS

The ex-Consuls, who formed an inner ring within the Senate and were called to give their opinions before their colleagues. They were 'nobles', and passed on the rank to their descendants.

DENARIUS

A silver coin worth very approximately 4 NP.

GOVERNOR

Usually an ex-Consul or ex-Praetor sent to govern a province or conquered territory for a year or more. They could plunder their subjects more or less at will, but ran the risk of a trial for extortion on their return to Rome.

JURORS	Also called judges, because the President of a law court had no power to sum up or judge a case. The size of the panel varied from thirty to eighty-one.
KNIGHTS	Members of the equestrian order, who could qualify for admission by satisfying a property requirement. Among their many privileges was that of passing on the rank to their descendants. They formed the business and banking class. They wore black shoes.
LEGION	The main military unit, of 6,000 men.
NOBLES	Consulars and their descendants. The main ruling class.
PATRICIANS	Aristocrats. The very small upper, and by tradition ruling class, formed by the remnants of a few ancient families with a kind of 'royal' status, like the Claudii, Caecilii Metelli, Julii and Cornelii. They were Senators by birth and wore red shoes with a crescent buckle.
PRAETORIANS	The picked troops who formed a bodyguard for a Roman general.
PRAETORS	Eight men, ranking immediately below the Consuls, and holding office for one year. Chiefly concerned with the administration of justice.
QUAESTORS	The lowest rank in the State service. Twenty were selected to serve for one year in the capital and abroad.
SENATE	Six hundred men, including patricians, nobles and those knights who had held quaestor rank. They debated affairs of State and guided the legislative body (the Assembly). Most of the equestrian order (the knights) were debarred from election to the Senate because of their involvement in certain kinds of trade.
SESTERCE	A small silver coin worth about 1 NP, the quarter of a denarius.
TAX-FARMERS	The publicans of the New Testament. There were corporations of 'publicani', controlled by knights, who contracted with the Government to collect taxes abroad.

TRIBUNES OF THE PEOPLE	Their task was to protect the interests of the people against oppression and exploitation. They held their elected posts for one year and had considerable powers, including the right to introduce legislation and veto the actions of higher officials.
TRIUMVIRS	A junta of three generals, usurping the supreme power.
VESTAL VIRGINS	Six priestesses serving the temple of the Goddess Vesta, who symbolised the greatness and continuity of Rome.

THE UNPLEASANTNESS AT THE BELLONA CLUB

by Dorothy L. Sayers

Lord Peter Wimsey bent down over General Fentiman and drew the *Morning Post* gently away from the gnarled old hands. Then with a quick jerk, he lifted the quiet figure. It came up all of a piece, stiff as a wooden doll ...

But it was not a simple case of death from natural causes. For instance, who was the mysterious Mr. X who fled when he was wanted for questioning? And which of the General's heirs, both members of the Club, is lying?

This sinister case takes Dorothy Sayers' unique detective from London to Paris and finally back to the austere and sombre dignity of the Bellona Club itself.

THE NEW ENGLISH LIBRARY